The Sexton Blake Library

Published 2020 by Rebellion Publishing Ltd,
Riverside House, Osney Mead, Oxford, OX2 0ES, UK

ISBN: 978 1 78108 795 4

10 9 8 7 6 5 4 3 2 1

A CIP catalogue record for this book is available
from the British Library.

Designed & typeset by Rebellion Publishing Ltd

Cover art by Crush Creative

Printed in Denmark

The Sexton Blake Library

ANTHOLOGY III: SEXTON BLAKE'S ALLIES

Selected, edited and discussed by Mark Hodder and Sexton Blake

BAKER STREET, LONDON

"Brighter today!" Sexton Blake announced as I entered his consulting room. "A welcome respite from the rain! Come in, sit down. Would you care for some wine?"

Brandy, coffee, cigarettes, pipe—Blake seemed always to have an indulgence of one sort or another on the go. It hadn't occurred to me before, but this epicurean aspect of his personality, whilst never being directly alluded to in any of the stories I'd read, was evident in the majority of them.

It would have killed a normal man.

"Thank you," I said, taking up my—by now—customary position in the saddleback armchair opposite his own.

He poured a generous glass of red and handed it to me.

"Good health," he murmured.

The wine was superb but I coughed and almost spluttered it out through my nose when there came a scratching at the door and it was pushed aside by an enormous bloodhound. Remarkably, the dog, a truly magnificent beast, shouldered the portal shut before padding across the room. It sniffed my hand, slumped onto the hearth rug, and gave a prodigious yawn.

"Your mouth is hanging open," Blake observed.

I thought he was addressing the hound.

He wasn't.

I stammered, "It can't—it can't be Pedro! Surely it—it—"

"A descendent of the original," Blake said. "From a long and illustrious line, all specially bred and trained to emulate the talents of their late and lamented forebear. Surely it occurred to you that the Pedro of the later stories couldn't possibly be the same as the Pedro of the earlier?"

"I—I—yes, I suppose."

As if I hadn't considered that the Sexton Blake of the 1960s couldn't possibly be the Sexton Blake of the 1890s!

I gazed at Pedro.

Sprawled and contented, he gazed back.

Blake interrupted my inexpressible ruminations.

"What have you brought for me today?"

I turned my attention to my briefcase and withdrew from it a binder. As I passed it to him, I said, "You touched on the subject as I was departing yesterday. Your allies."

"Splendid," he said. "Happy memories."

"You told me that something called the 'Credibility Gap' gave rise to the master crooks and also to those possessing the wherewithal to oppose them. Can you explain exactly what it is?"

He tasted his wine and pulled a cigar from his pocket. A brief exchange of micro-gestures clarified that, as on previous occasions, I had no objection to him smoking but no desire to do so myself.

"A theory of mine," he said, employing a tool to snip the end from his cigar. "A state of consciousness wherein cognitive dissonance is so severe that a person experiencing it can find no means to cope with the unfamiliar and so develops what might be termed a 'blind spot' in regard to it. Denial. In conjunction with this, a converse state arises that prospers under the same conditions and which employs incredulity to further its own ends. Thus, for example, the often very eccentric master crooks who thrived in the wake of the Great War and the Scotland Yard men who could neither comprehend nor deal with them."

"And you, Mr Blake? Do you operate within this Credibility Gap?"

"Most certainly," he answered, and his tone seemed to add, 'more than you will ever know.'

"My allies and I managed to transcend the cognitive dissonance that was gripping the masses— or we at least achieved a high degree of functionality whilst under its influence."

While Blake was speaking, I was scratching my ballpoint pen across my notepad at high speed, my handwriting a tangled scrawl. I couldn't write fast enough. Where food for thought was concerned, Blake was serving me a veritable banquet!

"Losely," I murmured. "Sir Richard Losely was the first, and one of the most notable, of your supporters. He appeared in 1907."

"I had the author Cecil Hayter write up the cases in which he was involved. Losely is—was my oldest friend. We were at school and university together."

I noted that slip—is not was—and filed it away for later consideration.

"And the next to arrive on the scene," I went on, "was the Honourable John Lawless, introduced by Andrew Murray in 1914."

He put a match to his cigar and smiled. "His surname was actually Lawliss but he thought the 'e' made it more dashing than the 'i'. John was what you might call the prototype of the gentleman adventurer. I was assisted by quite a few such fellows but he was the most outstanding of them."

I put my wine glass to my lips. Incredible flavours flowed over my tongue. My god, how much must this wine cost? Exactly how rich was Sexton Blake?

He continued, "However, don't overlook the women. They were ahead of their time. Yvonne Cartier—" He stopped, and I was amazed to see him gripped by strong emotion. When he went on, his voice was slightly hoarse. "I encountered her a year before Lawless. She was a remarkably strong and resourceful woman. The author G. H. Teed wrote about her with all the sentimentality of his time but, in truth, she surpassed every expectation of the period and, in many respects, outmatched her male equivalents. There were others of her ilk, too."

"Mademoiselle Roxane," I suggested. "A very similar character."

"Forged by a very similar misfortune," he noted.

"One that, in Yvonne's case, initially made her an opponent rather than an ally. That's why I gave Lawless chronological precedence." I tapped my pen on the binder. "But if we may, we'll return to Yvonne presently."

Blake offered an insouciant wave of assent.

Pedro's tail had started to thump enthusiastically on the rug. I grinned down at the dog. "He recognises the names of friends. How, though? Surely he's too young to have met them?"

"Tone of voice," Blake said. "Tinker and I often reminisce."

I indicated that he should open the binder. "For the first story in this selection, I've chosen an ally who worked in a more official capacity than most: James 'Granite' Grant."

"The King's Spy," Blake said. He opened the cover. "He often teamed up with Mademoiselle Julie of the French Secret Service. Where either or both of them were concerned, I gave my case notes to William Walter Sayer, who wrote under the pseudonym of Pierre Quiroule." He examined the Union Jack story paper contained in the top plastic sleeve. "Hmm! This was an interesting affair!"

THE CASE OF THE SEVENTH KEY

"GRANITE GRANT WASN'T the only Secret Service agent you worked with," I said. "Anthony Skene introduced Julia Fortune. Anthony Parsons wrote of Beltom Brass and Yvonne de Braselieu. Gwyn Evans's stories often featured the newspaper man, Derek 'Splash' Page."

"Page was introduced in 1925," Blake said. "Which was actually two years after I'd met him. By 1927, he'd left the Service. He found journalism more exciting."

"More exciting than being a secret agent?"

"As a reporter, he had greater independence. I understood his need to play a free hand."

"Yet you and Tinker were agents."

"After a fashion."

"Can you expand on that?"

"It's better that I don't."

"Not fully-fledged members of the Service, then?"

"Our role was fairly unique. Let's leave it there—unless you're willing to endure a rather intensive and not altogether enjoyable vetting process."

I leaned away from him and raised a palm. "No thanks! Granite Grant has obviously led me into dangerous territory!"

"He frequently did the same to me."

Blake lifted his glass and contemplated its contents. In a reflective tone, he said, "Grant was one of the bravest men I ever met, tremendously powerful and extraordinarily focused. A force of nature. Once he set his mind to something, he was akin to a runaway locomotive. If you ever found yourself standing in his path, you'd need to get out of the way quick sharp."

"A good job you were running on the same tracks."

"I should have hated it to be otherwise!"

THE CASE OF THE SEVENTH KEY

by W.W Sayer
UNION JACK issue 1,115 (1925)

THE FIRST CHAPTER

The Caller and the Key.

THE MAN WHO entered Sexton Blake's consulting-room in Baker Street was a little below the average height, but of thick-set and sturdy appearance.

A reddish, drooping moustache concealed his mouth, and his features were somewhat flat and characterless except for a certain shrewd glint of his small, restless eyes. He was dressed inconspicuously, his clothes being a trifle threadbare, and altogether there was little about him to arouse one's interest or curiosity.

Appraising his visitor with one of his swift, searching glances Sexton Blake put him down at once as a foreigner, but was rather doubtful of his nationality. Neither could he answer the question when the newcomer spoke with just a faint, puzzling trace of accent.

"You are the Mr. Sexton Blake referred to here?" he inquired, thrusting forward a newspaper and pointing with his finger.

Blake casually noticed that his visitor's hand trembled—the only sign he gave of being mentally agitated.

Glancing at the newspaper, Blake saw that it was that morning's issue of the "Daily Mail." The article in question was concerned with the theft of a pearl necklace that had occurred at Kensington the previous night, and the paragraph to which his visitor pointed went as follows:

"Doubtless the necklace has already been disposed of to a receiver of stolen property, or a 'fence'—to employ the term used by the criminal fraternity. These men openly carry on a legitimate trade as a blind to their unlawful but more lucrative enterprise, and although their illicit business is suspected—probably most of the 'fences' in London are known to that shrewd investigator, Mr. Sexton Blake, of Baker Street—yet it is exceedingly difficult to catch them in the act of handling the stolen goods."

Having perused this brief reference to himself, Blake glanced across at his visitor.

"Yes," he admitted, "apparently I am the person referred to there, Mr—"

"Falcon—John Falcon," interpolated the other.

"Mr. Falcon," nodded Blake. "And is it concerning this stolen necklace that you have come to consult me, Mr. Falcon?"

"No, no!" replied his visitor somewhat hastily. "I know nothing about this stolen necklace; it does not concern me. But the paper says you are acquainted with men who receive stolen property. It was when I read that these men were known to you that I thought you might be able to help me."

"Help you in what way, Mr. Falcon?"

"By recovering something that I have lost, sir."

"I see," said Blake slowly. "You have lost some article that you have reason to suppose has been disposed of to a receiver of stolen property?"

"I have been robbed!" came the excited reply. "My pocket was picked less than an hour ago. I was in Mare Street at the time, having lunch. I know it must have happened then, because a moment before the things were in my pocket."

"Mare Street, Hackney," said Blake reflectively. "And what things were taken from your pocket, Mr. Falcon?"

"Several things," replied the other vaguely. "There was a key," he added with some hesitation, "which I am very eager to recover. The other things don't matter so long as that is returned to me. That key is of no value to the thief, and I am prepared to give him five pounds for its return and to ask no questions."

"Um-m!" murmured Blake. "But I am afraid the key won't help us to get on the track of the thief, Mr. Falcon. He certainly wouldn't have taken the key to a fence expecting to raise money on it."

"No, no; I'm aware of that. But there was something else—an old-fashioned pair of gold earrings each set with a single diamond weighing about two carats. They were in a washleather bag with the key."

"Ah, they certainly might help us to get on the track of

the thief. Probably those earrings are already in the hands of a fence. Was there anything else in the washleather bag?"

"Nothing else, sir."

"Then that is the extent of your loss?"

"Not quite. I had two ten-shilling notes in the same pocket. They were also stolen."

"In which pocket?" asked Blake.

"In this one," said Falcon, indicating the inner pocket of his coat.

"And you say the theft occurred in Mare Street, Hackney?"

"Yes; I was having lunch in a little eating-house at the time. It was when I came to feel for my money that I discovered my loss."

"And what was the name of this eating-house?"

"I did not notice the name. But there is a fire-station immediately opposite. It was rather dark inside, and it was crowded at the time."

"Well, I'm afraid there's little chance of recovering your earrings for you, Mr. Falcon. The stones will soon be removed and the gold melted down."

"I am not asking for the recovery of the earrings," said Falcon quickly. "It is the key that I am so anxious to get back. As I said before, I am willing to pay five pounds for its return and to ask no questions. It is the key to a certain safe, you understand? And its loss will occasion me considerable inconvenience."

"What is the key like? Describe it to me."

"A key about three inches long. But it has the figure

seven engraved on the shaft—you will know it by that."

"And the earrings, have they any further distinguishing marks?"

"They are shaped in the form of a twisted serpent."

"Yes, I will try to recover that key for you," said Blake, "although I cannot promise to be successful. Where can I communicate with you, Mr. Falcon?"

"I am leaving for France at once," replied the other. "That is my country, as you have probably already guessed. But I have no fixed address at present, as I am constantly travelling to and fro. If you should recover that key, please insert a message in the personal column of the 'Continental Daily Mail,' and I will get in touch with you immediately."

"Um-m! All this sounds a little mysterious," observed Blake, eyeing his visitor shrewdly. "I suppose you do not feel disposed to take me more fully into your confidence, Mr. Falcon?"

At this suggestion Falcon appeared to grow suddenly irritated and confused, while little beads of perspiration glistened on his forehead.

"There is no need of further confidence," he muttered half angrily. "I have asked you to undertake a simple task for me, and surely my personal affairs do not enter into the matter!"

"Well, perhaps not, Mr. Falcon. At any rate, we will not inquire into your personal affairs at the present stage. I will go along to Hackney at once and see if I can recover this key for you. If I am successful, I will communicate with you by the method you suggest."

"Thank you. Then here are the five pounds I offer for its return. What is your fee, sir, for acting for me in this matter?"

"We will leave that until the next occasion," said Blake dryly. "But supposing the thief refuses to part with your key for five pounds, what then?"

"He will jump at the offer," said Falcon confidently. "The key is of not the slightest value to him. And now I must leave, sir; I have a train to catch." The visitor said this with a note of relief, and he rose hastily from his chair, as if only too anxious to make his departure.

Then suddenly he started violently, and gave an exclamation. For the first time he had noticed Tinker sitting half concealed in the easy chair by the fire.

"I thought we were alone, sir!" he cried in excited tones, turning swiftly on Sexton Blake.

"Then obviously you were mistaken," replied Blake gravely. "However, you need have no cause for alarm. My assistant is entirely in my confidence."

Falcon glanced again at Tinker with obvious suspicion, muttered something below his breath, then gave an uneasy chuckle, and hastily made his departure.

"A queer customer, that!" remarked Blake, thoughtfully, glancing at the door as it closed on his perturbed visitor.

"He certainly was," agreed Tinker, getting up from his chair. "Almost jumped out of his skin when he spotted me."

"Got the jim-jams over something," muttered Blake, and then, with sudden decision, added: "Just follow him, Tinker, and see if you can find out more about him."

Accustomed as he was to act instantly in such a

circumstance as this, Tinker stayed not to argue the matter.

Left alone, Blake still remained glancing at the door for some moments, as if pondering something in his mind. Then he pushed back his chair and got into his hat and coat.

He was just about to leave the room when the door was flung open and Tinker entered, looking somewhat hot and bothered.

"Gave me the slip, guv'nor," he growled resentfully. "Saw a cab just starting away from the rank along the road; he must have been in that. But I couldn't get hold of another quick enough to follow."

"Nuisance!" muttered Blake. "Can't be helped, though. Something rummy about our friend Falcon. That's not his real name, of course."

"It doesn't sound French, guv'nor."

"And neither is he a Frenchman, Tinker, in spite of what he said. I was puzzled to know what his nationality was, until he gave himself away at the last moment. He's a Czech, unless I'm greatly mistaken."

"A Czech, guv'nor! What makes you think that?"

"By that startled exclamation he let out when he spotted you in the chair, Tinker."

"What was it he said? Sounded to me something like chemeesel."

"So it was, only it's spelt P-R-S-H-E-M-Y-S-L in the Czech language. And Prshemysl is the name of a town in Czecho-Slovakia. It also happens to be the name of a legendary Bohemian king. And I suppose our friend Falcon uttered it in much the same way as we might exclaim 'Great Scott!'"

"You're cute, guv'nor," muttered Tinker admiringly. "Don't suppose anyone else would have noticed a little thing like that."

"You flatter me!" observed Blake dryly. "Well here's another little thing that may interest you. The Czech word for 'falcon' is 'sokol.' And the Sokol happens to be the name of a society that exercises a very strong influence in the lives of the Czech people. It is easy to understand, therefore, why our mysterious friend Falcon should have instinctively chosen that name."

"Why, you're a walking encyclopaedia, guv'nor!" laughed Tinker. "But what do you make of his yarn?"

"Nothing much at present. But our friend Falcon has aroused my curiosity. I can't quite get to the bottom of him, that's why I did not hesitate to take on what purported to be a simple case of pick-pocketing. At any rate, I'm going along to Hackney to investigate his story. Perhaps there's nothing in it after all. We shall see."

"Then I'll come along with you, guv'nor."

"No," said Blake. "I want to know where Falcon went to when he left here. If he took a cab from the rank along the road, you shouldn't have much difficulty in getting hold of the taxi man when he returns and finding out from him where he dropped our friend Falcon."

"That should be easy, guv'nor," said Tinker. "I'll go along to the rank."

The two of them left the house together and parted outside, Tinker going off to execute his commission and Blake clambering on a bus going in the direction of Hackney.

THE SECOND CHAPTER

Kelly "Cops a Packet".

A HALF HOUR or so later Sexton Blake dismounted in Mare Street, and walked along to the fire-station. A little eating-house was immediately opposite, as Falcon had stated. So much of his story was apparently true.

Blake crossed the road and casually glanced inside. It was an evil-smelling little restaurant, of dingy and uninviting aspect. Obviously, its clients were not exactly fastidious with regard to their palates. At the present moment it was empty, save for its fat and greasy-faced proprietor, whose name, Tim Booker, was painted in faded characters above, for it was now in the middle of the afternoon.

Having made his cursory inspection, Blake turned away and walked on swiftly. A few moments later he had plunged into the network of mean streets of that insalubrious neighbourhood known as London Fields.

The writer of the paragraph in the "Mail" had not

exaggerated the case when he had stated that probably most of the "fences" in the metropolis were known to the Baker Street criminologist. Sexton Blake's knowledge of the underworld was exhaustive; he was acquainted with nearly all the secret haunts of the criminal fraternity, and, indeed, experienced little difficulty in gaining admittance to that most exclusive society when the occasion demanded it.

So now his task was a comparatively simple one. He could name half a dozen "fences" in the immediate vicinity off hand, and if any one of them had handled the property stolen from Mr. Falcon he felt that he could secure the return of the key by the use of a little judicious persuasion.

But as chance would have it, Blake was saved the trouble of making inquiries himself. For as he was directing his steps to his first place of call he happened to have an unexpected meeting with an "old lag."

Turning the corner of a certain narrow, squalid street, he almost collided with a short, ferrety-faced individual, of unshaven and seedy appearance, who was shuffling along with his hands thrust deep into his pockets and his greasy cap pulled down low over his brow.

The man shuffled out of Blake's path with a sullen growl, and would have passed on had not Blake suddenly grasped him by the shoulder.

"What, you, Kelly!" he exclaimed. "So they let you out, have they?"

Mick Kelly started violently as if he were burdened by an uneasy conscience—which probably he was—and instinctively shook himself free from Blake's grasp. But immediately he recognised the identity of his accoster a furtive grin crept into his face.

"Yus, I've just got me ticket, Mr. Blake," he sniggered. "Came out only yesterday. Had a stretch this time."

"Well, you needn't crow about it," observed Blake. "Hope you will be running straight this time, Kelly."

"Thankee kindly, Mr. Blake, but I reckon it's too late to turn over a new leaf at my time o' life," was the old lag's philosophical reply.

"I'm sorry to hear you say that, Kelly. Never too late to mend, you know. What's doing—anything?"

"Nothing in particular, Mr. Blake. Reckon I'm jest strolling round for my 'ealth, like yerself," said Mick Kelly. And he sniggered again.

"Strolling around is sometimes an unhealthy occupation," admonished Blake, preparing to depart. "But I'm afraid you are incorrigible, Kelly. Well, here's a ten-shilling note for you. Dare say the brewers will profit by it."

And, thrusting the note into old Mick's palm, he turned away.

But he had scarcely taken a couple of steps when he stopped abruptly, struck by a sudden idea.

"One moment, Kelly," he called. "Do you happen to know that little restaurant in Mare Street, opposite the fire-station?"

"Wot, ole Tim Booker's?" asked Kelly.

"Yes, that's the name. What were you doing there at lunch-time to-day, Kelly?"

Blake eyed the old man sternly as he asked the question. But Mick Kelly's face only betrayed an innocent surprise.

"Weren't in there, Mr. Blake," he declared. "Ain't set foot in old Tim Booker's since I stepped outa 'stir' yusterday. S'elp me, if that there ain't the truth!"

"Um-m. So you're not guilty this time, eh? Well, d'you want the chance of earning an honest fiver?"

Old Mick's manner immediately became suspicious.

"Honest is it, mister?" he questioned doubtfully. "Wot's the gime?"

"I was just about to pay a visit to certain friends of yours round here," explained Blake, "but probably you can save me the trouble. Listen, Kelly, a certain person, whose name we need not mention, had his pocket picked while lunching at Tim Booker's to-day. Two ten-shilling notes were stolen from him and a washleather bag, which contained a pair of old-fashioned earrings and a key. The key had the figure seven engraved on the shaft, and the earrings were of gold, shaped like twisted serpents, and each set with a single diamond weighing about two carats. Are you following me?"

"With both ears, Mr. Blake."

"Very well. Now, that key is of no value to the thief, while its loss will occasion my client considerable inconvenience. Therefore, he is very anxious to recover it. Bring that key to me, Kelly, and you will earn five pounds. I promise you no questions will be asked. Are you taking it on?"

"Sounds easy money," muttered old Kelly dubiously. "Sure there ain't no ketch in it?"

"You have my word for it, Kelly."

"Will yer gimme me a couple o' quid in advance, Mr. Blake?"

"I will. Here you are." Blake gazed at the old man sternly. "You play me false, Kelly," he said, "and I'll refuse to help you the next time you are in trouble."

"I'm playing straight, Mr. Blake," replied Mick Kelly. "Well, I'll say so-long! You'll be seeing me again shortly if I'm lucky."

Blake watched him turn the corner, then proceeded to retrace his steps, feeling satisfied at having saved himself an irksome task.

When he arrived back at Baker Street he found Tinker already awaiting him in the consulting-room.

"No luck, guv'nor!" he said. "Falcon didn't go off in that cab. It's curious he should have vanished so suddenly after leaving here."

"You got hold of the taxi man?"

"Yes; he said he dropped his fare at the Bank—a tall, clean-shaven man, wearing a silk hat. It certainly couldn't have been Falcon."

"Obviously not. Funny he should have disappeared so suddenly."

"That's what's puzzling me, guv'nor. Did you manage to find out anything?"

"I happened to meet old Mick Kelly in London Fields," explained Blake. "He came out of quod only yesterday. So I saved myself further trouble by passing the job onto him."

"The old gaolbird!" chuckled Tinker. "So he's out again! Probably it was he who picked Falcon's pocket."

"No, I don't think so, Tinker. But I bet it won't take old Mick long to discover the thief. One of his charmed circle of acquaintances, I'll be bound. Well, we shall see!"

With this reflection Blake turned his attention to other matters, and for the time being no further reference was made to the mysterious Mr. Falcon's affairs.

It was not until nearly nine o'clock that night that he was again reminded of the matter, and in a somewhat curious fashion, when Mrs. Bardell, his housekeeper, appeared at the door of the consulting-room to announce a visitor.

"A little ragamuffin girl, Mr. Blake," she explained disdainfully. "I don't like the looks of her. Shall I send her about her business?"

"Certainly, Mrs. Bardell—that is, show her up at once," replied Blake.

Mrs. Bardell departed with a sniff; and a moment later there sidled into the room a little, pinched-faced girl of some nine or ten years of age. Her clothes were in rags, her hair tousled and hanging untidily about her face; she wore no stockings, and from the pair of old shoes that clung to her feet her toes were peeping forth.

Standing there timidly, clutching a boy's cap in her dirty fingers, she gazed about her with wondering eyes, as if never before had she beheld from such close quarters the interior of a civilised habitation.

"Well, young lady, and what can I do for you?" inquired Blake in his kindly tones.

"Please, sir, dad ses as 'ow I've gotta give the message ter Mr. Blake," came the reply, as if it had been learned by heart.

"Yes, I am Mr. Blake. You have a message for me?"

For answer the little girl felt beneath her ragged garments, drew forth a dirty, crumpled piece of paper, and held it out.

With some curiosity Blake unfolded it and proceeded with some difficulty to read the following, written in an almost illegible hand:

"*Mr Blake, sir,—I copped a packet wots lade me out over that little job yer arsked me to do for yer this arternoon. If yer honour feels like coming along, Mary will show yer ware to find us.*

"*Yours respecfuly,*

"*MICK KELLY.*"

Under the signature of this strange communication was an ugly, brown smudge. To Sexton Blake's expert eyes its meaning was clear—it had been made by bloodstained fingers!

THE THIRD CHAPTER

"Mr. Falcon is a Crafty Knave!"

THE CRIMINOLOGIST GAZED at that significant brown stain, with his brows knitted, in silent perplexity. It seemed to bear a very eloquent testimony to Mick Kelly's strange message. The old lag had "copped a packet," so he said, in carrying out the little commission he had undertaken for Blake that afternoon. Queer! What precisely had happened to Mick Kelly?

"Is your father very ill, Mary?" asked Blake, glancing up at his youthful visitor.

"He ain't more abashed abaht than he's been afore," came the unemotional reply.

Blake smiled faintly, but forbore to put a further question. He handed Tinker the note without remark and rose from his chair.

"We'll go along and see your father at once, Mary," he said. "Where is he staying—somewhere near Mare Street?"

"'Tain't more than five minutes from there," replied Mary, still gazing about her with wondering eyes.

"Better get a cab, Tinker," said Blake; and, with a nod, Tinker went from the room.

Blake glanced down at the girl, and his eyes softened.

"Poor little beggar!" he muttered; and, searching in the drawers of his desk, came across a box of chocolates. "There you are, Mary," he said. "Don't eat them all at once and make yourself ill. Now we'd better be off!"

Mary gasped with delight and hugged the precious box close to her. She had another wondrous experience a moment later when she was ushered into the waiting cab.

"Seems a rummy business, guv'nor," whispered Tinker, as the vehicle sped rapidly in the direction of Hackney.

Blake nodded, but made no comment. He had lapsed into a thoughtful mood, and did not speak again until the cab reached Mare Street. There the driver slowed down and turned his head for further instructions.

"Is it far from here, Mary?" asked Blake.

"It ain't no distance now," replied Mary somewhat regretfully; for she was thoroughly enjoying her novel experience, and obviously did not wish it to come to an end.

"We'll walk the rest," said Blake, opening the door. "Don't want to attract attention by arriving in a cab."

He paid the fare, and took the little girl by the hand.

"Which way now, Mary?" he asked.

"It ain't no distance," repeated Mary, and plunged into the dimly lit environs of London Fields.

A brief five minutes' walk brought them to the house—a

dilapidated hovel tucked away in a dark, narrow alley of crumbling bricks and mortar.

Mary unlocked the front door by the simple expedient of pulling a piece of string that hung through the letter-box, and admitted her visitors to the "parlour," which was in darkness, and contained only a few sticks of furniture.

A chink of light was creeping from beneath a door on the opposite side, and, crossing to it, Mary flung it open without ceremony.

"Here's Mr. Blake come to see you, daddy," she announced, and turned her attention at once to her precious box of chocolates.

Blake stepped through the door, followed by Tinker. He found himself in a bare, cheerless compartment illuminated by a flickering candle-flame. An old deal table minus one of its legs, several broken-down chairs, and one or two other trifling articles were the only furniture it boasted of. Lying on a dirty mattress in the farther corner was old Mick Kelly. At Blake's entry he raised himself on his elbow, with a muffled groan.

"I wouldn't have fetched yer, Mr. Blake," he said apologetically, speaking with obvious difficulty, "only I couldn't come to see yer meself, as you see."

"I quite understand that, Kelly," replied Blake. "You did right to send for me." He drew up one of the chairs and sat down on it astride, resting his arms on the back and gazing down at the prostrate man.

Old Mick Kelly certainly appeared to have "copped a packet"—to use his own expressive term. His battered face bore unmistakable evidence of a recent pommelling, his lower lip was split, and there was also dried blood on his bruised hands. Only his left eye was visible; the right one had vanished beneath a bluish-black contusion. Nevertheless a ghost of a smile crept into his ill-used face as he squinted up at Blake with one game eye.

"Yus," he observed in matter of fact tones, "they didn't 'arf lay into me. But they wouldn't 'ave got away so easy if I 'adn't er slipped and twisted me blamed foot!" And old Kelly cautiously moved his right leg and gave a grunt of pain.

A shadow of interest crossed Blake's face. Several possible explanations of Mick Kelly's queer message had occurred to him while journeying from Baker Street in the cab. The old sinner might have got drunk on the money he had received, and got mixed up in a pot-house brawl, had seemed the most likely explanation. But the vague reference Kelly had just made put a more significant aspect to the problem.

"What is all the trouble about, Kelly?" he asked. "Just tell me the story."

"That there key's the cause of all the trouble, Mr. Blake," replied old Kelly, somewhat reproachfully. "Yer didn't tell me as 'ow there was likely to be some fireworks when yer asked me to take on the job."

"No, I didn't, Kelly; I certainly had no idea that there was likely to be fireworks. You didn't manage to find out who stole the key, I suppose?"

"I 'ad the key in my pocket a little more'n an hour ago, an' the wallet as well," replied Mick Kelly. "It was jest as I was abaht to make a call on yer, as I promised, that these two blokes pitched into me. I gave 'em a roughhouse all right, you bet. But they got me whacked between 'em, an' done a guy with the key and wallet. I 'adn't any stuffing in me, only to crawl back here."

"Um-m! I'm sorry you've been so badly knocked about, Kelly. When I asked you to do that job for me to-day I hadn't the slightest idea you would get into trouble over it. Who were these two men who attacked you?"

"Dunno. They didn't stop ter interdooce themselves, Mr. Blake. But I reckon I was follered to-day arter leaving you. I sorta suspicioned it at the time."

"And where did you go to after leaving me, Kelly?"

"Went along to Tim Booker's, Mr. Blake, and found out who was 'aving grub there to-day. Wasn't long in figuring out who'd dipped inter yer pal's pocket. Jim we'll call him—I ain't giving no names away. Well, I reckoned I'd find Jim at a sartin little beer 'ouse round here. He dropped in jest before eight this evenin', an' I tackled him. He was a bit shy at first, but he got friendly arter a few drinks. He 'ad the key an' the wallet on him, an' 'anded 'em over there an' then for a quid. They wasn't of no use to him, o' course. I 'ad another drink and came out, meaning to come right away to your show in Baker Street. But I 'adn't gone a dozen yards when these two guys pitched into me."

Blake had listened with close attention to this recital. He glanced significantly at Tinker as old Mick Kelly ceased speaking, and met the former's look of perplexity.

"So there was a wallet also, Kelly," he said. "What was it like?"

"An old thing made of green leather," replied Kelly. "Wasn't of any value. There was a little book inside with some writing on it, but neither Jim nor me could make nothink of it. Seemed like Chinese to me. But yer friend's name on the envelope was plain enough. The envelope was inside the wallet."

"What was the name?" asked Blake, showing nothing of the sudden eagerness he felt at this possible and unexpected clue.

"Funny name—Lipsky, that was it. But yer oughter know the name better than me, Mr. Blake, seeing as 'ow the gent's a friend o' yourn."

"Quite so, Kelly. And was Mr. Lipsky's address also written on the envelope?"

"No; only jest his name there in pencil. But the envelope had come from the Rutland Hotel, for the name was printed on the back as plain as a pikestaff."

"Um-m! And the envelope was empty?"

"Yus, there wasn't nothink in it."

"Think carefully. Did you notice anything else in that wallet?"

"There was no Bradburys, if that's wot you mean, Mr. Blake. A slip of noosepaper, that's abaht the only other thing I recollec' seeing."

"A slip of newspaper! What newspaper?"

"A bit o' the 'Daily Mail'—the 'Mail' was just showing at the top."

"It was a slip of newspaper. You mean it had been carefully cut out from the page?"

"Yus, that's abaht wot I mean."

"And what did it refer to?"

"Can't say. Remember seeing some think abaht a crown, that's all."

"About a crown! Did it have the date at the top?"

"No, it didn't—only the day—Thursday."

"Was it a big slip of newspaper?"

"Weren't very big—abaht three inches long, I should say."

"And that's all you can tell me about it?"

"That's about all. You see mighty curious abaht that there slip of noosepaper, Mr- Blake."

The criminologist smiled dryly at this remark, and got up from his chair. He seemed suddenly impatient to be off.

"Are you sure there's nothing else you've omitted to tell me, Kelly?" he asked.

"Nothing, Mr. Blake—there's my oath on it."

"And I suppose it's useless asking you where I can find your friend, Jim? Yes, I see it is. Honour among thieves—eh? Well, I won't press you on that matter at the present moment. Are you living all alone? Isn't there anyone to look after you?"

"Reckon I can look arter meself!" growled the old lag. "An' there's Mary here; she's a good gal."

"She's your daughter, Kelly?"

"Well, she is and she isn't. She's the ole woman's girl."

"I see; your stepdaughter. And where is your wife?"

"Dunno; ain't seed the ole woman since I came outer stir yusterday. But there's Mrs. Brown upstairs; she's allus good to Mary when there ain't no one about."

"What domestic bliss!" muttered Blake, exchanging glances with Tinker. "Well, I think I'd better send a doctor round to have a look at you, Kelly," he added.

"No, yer don't!" was old Kelly's fierce reply. "I ain't 'aving no doctor a-nosing around here. Reckon I can lick me own sores, as I've done afore."

With a gesture of perplexity, Blake turned to the stubborn old man's stepdaughter, who was squatting in the corner, treasuring her precious chocolates.

"Mary," he said, "have you ever seen a pound-note before? No, I can see you haven't. Well, here is one. It is worth twenty silver shillings, and with twenty shillings you can buy quite a lot of things. Take great care of it, and also take care of your father until he is well again."

Blake raised a threatening figure to the injured old man.

"You dare to spend that money in drink, Kelly," he added, "and I'll pack you off to hospital. You shall have something on account each day. Wiser not to give you a lump sum down; it would be all gone by the morning. Now I must be off. I will look you up to-morrow."

Tinker followed his master from the poverty-stricken room. They came out into the dimly-lit street, and Blake set off briskly in the direction by which they had come. They reached Mare Street some few moments later, neither of them having made any remark.

"The Rutland Hotel's somewhere near Paddington, I think," said Blake, suddenly stopping. "Let's get hold of a cab."

He did not speak again until the two of them were seated in the taxi speeding westwards. Then he turned to Tinker somewhat eagerly.

"That explains how our friend Falcon vanished so

quickly to-day," he said. "Obviously, he must have hidden himself, and waited until I came out, then followed me to London Fields. The mysterious Mr. Falcon is a crafty knave."

"But why should he follow you, guv'nor?"

"For obvious reasons. He comes to me thinking I am about the only man likely to be able to get on the scent of his stolen property. But he doesn't want me to read what is written in that wallet, so he makes no mention of it and asks me to recover the key.

"He followed me to London Fields, obviously with the intention of finding out what fence had handled his property, meaning then to make stealthy enquiries himself concerning the stolen wallet. As events turned out, however, his task was simplified. He must have seen me accost Mick Kelly, and may have guessed I passed the job on to him. From that moment Mick Kelly's movements must have been watched.

"Of course, there's more than this man Falcon in the plot. Probably it wasn't he, but one of his confederates that followed me. It appears to be quite a cunning little intrigue."

"It certainly seems to have possibilities," agreed Tinker. "Got any idea of what the game is, guv'nor?"

"It is difficult to say as yet," replied Blake. "There is just a chance that I may get hold of this man Lipsky at the Rutland Hotel and learn something from him. In the meantime, I want you to follow up another possible clue."

"And what is that, guv'nor?" asked Tinker eagerly.

"The clue of that newspaper cutting from the 'Daily Mail.' It may tell us something, it may not. You heard what Kelly said. It was a Thursday issue of the paper, the article was about three inches long, and it refers to a crown. I'll drop you in Fleet Street. Go on to Carmelite House—the 'Daily Mail' offices—and search backwards through the files. Remember, you need only look at the Thursday issues."

"I've got you, guv'nor," nodded Tinker.

"We are at Ludgate Circus," said Blake. "You'd better get out of here. So long for the present. Probably I will find you at Baker Street when I return."

Tinker hurriedly dismounted, and the cab went on again. Some twenty minutes later it dropped Blake at Paddington.

The Rutland Hotel was situated quite close to the station, in one of those narrow streets almost entirely given over to small hotels of a cosmopolitan character. Entering the vestibule, Blake walked up to the reception-office.

"Is Mr. Lipsky staying here?" he inquired of the clerk inside.

"What, Lipsky the waiter, sir?" asked the clerk, with a quick glance at his inquirer.

"That is probably the Lipsky I wish to see," rejoined Blake.

"Just a moment, sir," said the clerk, and vanished into a back office.

Moments later he reappeared, this time accompanied by a stout man with a broad expanse of shirt-front, whom Blake at once took to be the manager.

40

"You are inquiring for Lipsky, sir," said this individual, drawing Blake aside confidentially. "Are you a friend of his, may I ask?"

"Merely an acquaintance," replied Blake evasively. "But I should like a word with him if he is here."

"He is not here," said the manager. "He was suddenly taken ill last night in the dining-room. A rather peculiar affair. He collapsed and had to be sent home. This morning he did not turn up, and when later I sent round to make inquiries he seemed to have vanished."

"Um-m! That's curious. What was the nature of his illness?"

"A heart attack, I should think. He was waiting in the dining-room at the time; we were rather busy. Then he suddenly swayed and fell to the floor. Caused rather a commotion." The manager hesitated, as if meditating a further disclosure, then felt in the pocket of his waistcoat and took out a scrap of paper in a somewhat crumpled condition.

"Lipsky was clenching this in his hand," he added. "I don't know if you can read what is written on it. I can't. I am intending to hand it over to the police or somebody, in case it's important."

Blake smoothed out the paper with some interest. On it was pencilled just three words in the Czech language— "The Seventh Key."

Without showing anything of the surprise he felt, Blake merely said:

"It is rather important. I'd like to keep it, if you'll allow me."

THE FOURTH CHAPTER

The Lost Clue.

"The Seventh Key!"

What precisely was the meaning of this cryptic reference? It appeared obvious from this that the key bearing the figure seven, of which John Falcon had spoken, was vitally concerned in the mysterious plot. But Sexton Blake did not betray the fact that he understood the brief communication. He glanced at the hotel manager and shook his head doubtfully.

A queer language!" he muttered. "What nationality was Lipsky?"

"A Swiss, so he said. I do not know much about the man. He came here about a year ago. I engaged him for a week only, as we were very busy, and, therefore, did not insist on references. But he proved a very good waiter, and so he stayed on."

"Where is he living?"

"At 14, Parmoor Buildings. Not far from here—in

Mellin Court, just off Craven Road."

"What was Lipsky like?"

"A man of about thirty-five, rather short, clean-shaven, and with a scar over his right eye. But you know him, sir, do you not?"

"I am wondering whether it is the same man," replied Blake casually. "Was he married?"

"Not as far as I am aware, sir."

"Thank you. I'll make inquiries at Parmoor Buildings and let you know the result," said Blake, and with a nod he left the hotel before the manager could ask his identity.

Blake's face wore an intrigued look as he stepped outside. With some eagerness he turned in the direction of Craven Road. Ten minute's sharp walk brought him to Mellin Court.

Parmoor Buildings proved to be a huge block of flats situated in a somewhat dingy neighbourhood, and evidently occupied by poor and needy families whose breadwinners were mostly employed in the hotels and theatres of the West End.

A large, bare, stone-flagged entrance-hall gave access to the building, and a stone staircase wound up to the floors above, which Blake proceeded to climb, coming across Flat No. 14 on the second floor.

The door was locked, and there was no answer in response to Blake's summons. He had scarcely expected there would be, and, with a swift glance to right and left to make sure no one was in sight, he slipped a skeleton-key into the lock, noiselessly turned it, and stepped inside, closing the door behind him.

For a moment he stood there listening, but no sound reached his ears. Assured that the apartment was unoccupied, Blake switched on his pocket-torch and swept the white beam of light around.

A small, square room met his gaze, furnished in the usual conventional style—a table, a few plush-seated chairs of varnished wood, a writing-desk, a cheap and somewhat gaudy carpet, with some meretricious pictures in gilt frames hanging about the walls.

So much Blake saw at a glance, and then the thin beam of light rested upon the huddled form of a man lying close to the writing-desk against the wall in the corner.

Blake's lips compressed grimly. He had scarcely been prepared for such a discovery as this. Noiselessly he crossed the room, and dropped on his knees beside the motionless figure.

That the man was dead he saw at a glance; had apparently been dead for the last twenty-four hours. He had been fatally stabbed, the downward thrust of the blade having penetrated the left shoulder. Flashing the torch in his face, Blake recognised him as the waiter, Lipsky, from the description he had received from the manager of the Rutland Hotel.

This was a sinister discovery. The plot had suddenly assumed a deeper and graver aspect. What was the motive that had impelled this murderous act? Lipsky had been recognised last night at the Rutland Hotel; he had been followed to his rooms, and had there been attacked. So much was evident. But the motive of the crime was still a mystery.

Was there any clue to be discovered in the dead man's pockets? Blake wondered. He proceeded to search them. But a brief scrutiny assured him that he was too late. The pockets were empty; they had been rifled.

Blake rose to his feet, and quietly went round the room, making a close inspection. It was scantily furnished, and beyond the writing-desk there was nothing to arouse his interest. Opening the drawers, one by one, Blake found them also empty. Whatever contents the desk might have contained had been removed.

Two other apartments adjoined that in which the dead man lay. The door of one was closed, and on opening it Blake found it led to a tiny little kitchen, containing a gas-stove and the usual cooking utensils. After a brief inspection, Blake crossed to the other door, which was half open.

This led to a small bed-room, and at the first swift glance, Blake's interest was aroused. Some sort of struggle had taken place here, he saw immediately. The signs of disorder bore mute witness to that fact. And lying on the floor was an open suit-case, in which some articles of clothing had been hastily flung.

In the opposite wall was a window. Crossing, Blake cautiously glanced out onto a large asphaltic courtyard below. Slightly to the right of the window a spiral iron staircase ran up the side of the building, placed there obviously in case of fire. The catch of the window, Blake noticed, was broken.

Had Lipsky's assailant, or assailants, entered by this means? Blake wondered. It was very probable that such was the case. And the suit-case, lying open on the floor, seemed to argue that Lipsky was hastily packing in preparation for a hurried flight at the moment when he had been attacked. Obviously the crime had occurred last night. He had been followed from the Rutland Hotel to his flat.

The struggle had occurred in this room. The kitchen and the room adjoining bore no signs of disorder. Lipsky apparently had been struck down here. How was it, then, that he came to be lying dead in the adjoining room?

The question intrigued Blake. Having glanced over the garments lying in the suit-case, and discovered nothing from them, he began a more careful scrutiny of the room. And on the counterpane of the narrow iron bedstead, he came across a significant brown stain.

The counterpane was also disarranged, and on the faded strip of carpet immediately beneath was another sinister brown patch. Evidently Lipsky had fallen on the bed when he had been stabbed, and then slithered to the floor. So Blake reasoned. And yet the dead man was now lying in the other room. Had he been carried there, and if so, for what reason?

Again the question aroused Blake's curiosity. By the look of that brown smudge on the carpet it seemed that the unfortunate man had lain there for some time. Had he been unconscious, and later recovered sufficiently to drag himself by his own efforts into the other room?

There should be evidence still remaining to answer that question, and, using his torch circumspectly, Blake quickly found it—a trail of blood crossing the room to the door, crossing also the adjoining room to the very spot where the dead man now lay. The unfortunate Lipsky then had regained consciousness after his unknown assassin had left, and had crawled from one room to the other.

Had any definite motive prompted that last effort of the stricken man? He was now lying close to the writing-desk. Had the writing-desk been his objective, to reach which he had summoned up that final supreme effort? But the writing-desk was now empty; its contents, whatever they might have been, had been removed.

Blake glanced down speculatively at the motionless man, pondering the problem in his mind. Lipsky was not in front of the writing-desk, but lying at the side against the wall. His right arm was reaching forward; he must have been reaching out for something at the moment he expired.

Reaching for what? The fingers of Lipsky's right hand were inserted between the writing-desk and the wall. Was it something at the back of the writing-desk that he had endeavoured to possess himself of?

Blake pulled the desk away, and searched with his torch. But there was no sign of a secret drawer at the back of the writing-desk, as he had swiftly supposed. Then the tell-tale smudges of bloodstained fingers on the wall behind attracted his attention. So Lipsky had been groping on the wall, not on the back of the writing-desk!

Again Blake thought of a secret recess, and he tapped the wall with his knuckles. But it sounded perfectly solid, and there was no sign of a crack or crevice. At the spot where Lipsky's fingers had groped, however, was a seam in the wallpaper, where one length overlapped the other. And the seam at that particular place appeared at some time to have been stuck down again after having been raised.

Instinctively Blake prised up the paper. It came away from the wall quite easily. And behind, flattened to the wall, so that its presence remained unsuspected, was an oblong slip of blank white paper. Somewhat eagerly Blake lifted it and glanced at the other side. It was a printed form made out in the Czech language.

Kneeling there, Blake proceeded to decipher it by the aid of his torch, when suddenly a furtive tread sounded behind him. Instantly he was on his feet; but a moment too late. A blow caught him on the head as he turned, and the paper was snatched from his fingers.

Reeling back under this unexpected attack, Blake recovered himself in time to see a dark figure springing towards the door of the bed-room. He plunged blindly after his unknown assailant, and reached the door just as it was slammed violently in his face.

Wrenching it open, Blake dashed across the room to the open window, clambered out onto the iron fire-escape, and sped down it. A woman, evidently one of the tenants of the building, was standing below staring after the fleeing figure just vanishing through the entrance to the courtyard. At Blake's swift appearance she suddenly raised a shrill scream of alarm.

Blake brushed past her, and sped towards the entrance. Reaching it, he dashed out into the road, still fiercely resolved to overtake his unknown aggressor. He thought he saw the man vanishing to the right, and flung himself in pursuit. But, reaching the top of the street a few moments later, he could no longer discover any sign of his nimble quarry.

Then Blake paused, realising that further pursuit was hopeless. He caught at the railings and recovered his breath. The blow he had received, although he had avoided its full force, had been no light one. He was feeling its effects now, and for a few moments he experienced an unpleasant sensation of vertigo.

Then a sudden fierce anger surged up within Blake. He had been fooled, cheated, outwitted. There could be only one explanation to account for the startling attack. His unknown assailant must have been concealed in Lipsky's flat all the time. And the kitchen was the only possible hiding-place. He had been hidden in the cupboard.

What a fool he was not to have glanced inside that cupboard! Blake choked back his mortification. He had been caught napping like a simpleton. However, it was futile to waste time in vain regrets. It was now a matter for the police; they must be advised of the sinister crime that had taken place at Parmoor Buildings.

Pulling himself together, Blake proceeded to retrace his steps.

But as he approached Parmoor Buildings he discovered that there was no longer any necessity for him to inform the police. The alarm had already been raised, and outside the entrance to the building which a few moments before had been deserted, a crowd of people was collecting talking together in excited tones and running to and fro.

At the same moment a policeman came hurrying across the road and pushed his way through the excited throng.

It was probable that the woman who had screamed at Blake's sudden appearance from the window of the unfortunate Lipsky's room had raised the alarm, doubtless thinking that a burglary had taken place. At any rate, the secret of that sinister room on the first floor had now been discovered without Blake's direct intervention.

Blake crossed to the other side of the street and walked casually past the scene of the commotion. His obvious duty, of course, was to inform the police of what had transpired. Yet he was reluctant to do that and thus reveal the part he himself had played in the mysterious affair. The knowledge of how he had been outwitted still rankled with him.

Besides, he wanted to think, to puzzle things out. The sinister discovery he had just made in Parmoor Buildings had added a deeper significance to the intrigue. And his brain was still a little confused from his recent unexpected attack.

Still undecided, Blake presently found himself outside Paddington Station. Then a taxicab happened to crawl by and settle the question for him.

"To Baker Street," he said, and climbed inside.

Tinker had not yet returned when Blake arrived at his chambers. Dropping into the chair at his desk, Blake cupped his chin in his hands and lapsed into thought. He remained thus for nearly half an hour, then suddenly rose to his feet, with an air of decision, and went into his bed-room.

When Tinker, looking somewhat dissatisfied, put in an appearance shortly afterwards, he found his master just finishing packing his suitcase.

"No luck again, guv'nor," he announced. "I searched through the 'Daily Mail' for the past year, but I couldn't find anything about a crown. I should think old Kelly must have been mistaken. Probably it was some other day but Thursday."

"Probably so," assented Blake; "or the cutting may have been some years old. Never mind, it can't be helped."

"Did you also draw a blank, guv'nor?" asked Tinker. Then suddenly, noticing the packed suitcase, added "Hallo! Where're you off to?"

"Off to Prague first thing in the morning," said Blake, snapping the bag shut and pushing it aside.

"Prague!" echoed Tinker. "What, the capital of Czecho-Slovakia?"

"You've got it, my lad. We'll talk it over in the other room."

Filled with curiosity, Tinker followed his master from the bed-room; and, having made himself comfortable with his ancient briar, Blake proceeded to acquaint his assistant with the dramatic events that had occurred after the latter had got out of the cab in Fleet Street an hour or so before.

Tinker listened to his master's recital with eager attention, and at the conclusion gave a low whistle of astonishment.

"We seem to have got mixed up in a sticky business, guv'nor," he said. "What could that fellow have been doing in Lipsky's rooms?"

"Looking for that printed form I discovered hidden behind the wallpaper," replied Blake. "They didn't find it in Lipsky's wallet as they hoped, and so one of them came back to search for it."

"And without your help he would probably never have found it, guv'nor. What a pity you didn't have time to read what it was all about!"

"I managed to read some of it," said Blake; "enough, at any rate, to decide me to pay a hurried visit to Prague. That printed form was a banker's deposit receipt issued by a bank at Prague some time in the year nineteen hundred and sixteen. I remember the number of that receipt, and the name of the bankers. That will be sufficient to enable me to trace it once I get to Prague."

"And you think it is an important clue, guv'nor?"

"I'm convinced that that deposit receipt is the key to the whole mystery," rejoined Blake. "How this fellow Lipsky got hold of it I don't know, nor who he is. But the fact that he took such precautions to conceal it proves not only that he had no right to it, but also that he anticipated that an attempt might be made to steal it from him."

"And that strange reference to the seventh key, guv'nor—what can that mean?"

"I can't say," confessed Blake. "Probably I shall solve that problem also when I reach Prague. But it is evident that that brief reference to the seventh key was enough to give this fellow Lipsky a nasty scare. He returned to his rooms last night with the intention of slipping off at once, but his enemies caught him before he could make his getaway."

"And they've got hold of this deposit receipt now, guv'nor?"

"Unfortunately, yes. And now they've got it they'll make for Prague as quickly as possible, if I'm not greatly mistaken. That's why I'm slipping off in the morning without dropping a hint to Scotland Yard. That would only delay my departure, and probably serve no useful purpose. But I want you to follow up the case while I've gone, Tinker, and if any new facts emerge to wire me in our usual code at the Moravia Hotel, Prague."

"I'll do that, guv'nor," nodded Tinker. "And how about old Mick Kelly? When he hears about this fellow Lipsky being found dead he'll feel a bit scared."

"See Kelly," said Blake, "and tell him to keep his mouth shut. I dare say he'll do that without any telling. Also, supply him with some ready cash to keep him going. And make him disclose the identity of his friend Jim. Probably Jim may know more about this business than we think. However, I'll leave you to act on your own initiative, Tinker. In the morning I'll have a final word with you. Now I'm going to tumble in and snatch a few hours' sleep. Good-night!"

"Good-night, guv'nor," said Tinker, and proceeded to follow his master's example.

THE FIFTH CHAPTER

An Old Friend Turns Up.

EARLY THE FOLLOWING morning Tinker accompanied his master to Victoria Station and saw him off by the boat train.

He turned away with some reluctance, feeling a little lonesome at Blake's departure. If Tinker had had his wish he would have boarded the train with his master and accompanied him on his long journey across Europe.

Entering a restaurant near by, Tinker ordered some breakfast, and proceeded to eat in gloomy silence. There was only a brief reference in the stop-press column of the morning papers to the crime at Parmoor Buildings. The Press had evidently not received fuller facts in time for publication.

Having at length finished his meal, Tinker proceeded to act on the instructions he had received from his master. His first step, he decided, was to pay a visit to Mick Kelly at London Fields. And thither Tinker wended his way.

On arriving at Mick Kelly's squalid abode, he found the old lag already recovering from the effects of his rough handling, and in quite a cheerful frame of mind.

"Top o' the mornin' to yer, mister!" he cried. "Come right in an' make yerself at 'ome. Well, yer see, I'm on me stumps ag'in, only this blamed leg's still giving me gippo."

"Probably it'll keep you out of mischief for a bit," replied Tinker unsympathetically. "Have you seen the papers?"

"Wot papers?" asked Kelly with sudden suspicion.

For answer Tinker pointed to the brief paragraph in the stop-press column.

A scared look crept into old Mick Kelly's battered face as he read it.

"W'y, it's the cove whose name was on the envelope in that wallet!" he muttered. "Looks like a swinging job. Yer know I ain't got nuffin to do with it, mister."

"I know you haven't. Kelly. But how about your friend, Jim?"

"Jim? He ain't got nuffin to do with it, neither. I'll take my oath on it!

"All the same, I want a word with friend Jim," said Tinker, "Where can I find him?"

"I ain't giving away a pal," replied old Kelly stubbornly. "I tell yer Jim knows nuffin about it."

"Then he's got nothing to be afraid of," said Tinker. "Come, if you're wise, Kelly, you'll tell me where I can find him, for your own sake, as well as his."

Mick Kelly hesitated.

"Promise me you won't shop him?" he asked.

"Mr. Blake has already given his word on that matter, Kelly."

"Well, I can't tell yer where yer can find Jim," said Kelly, "but he'll be along 'ere this arternoon."

"At what time?"

"About three o'clock, though I can't say for certain."

"Well, then, I'll call back here a little before three," said Tinker. "If your friend turns up before I arrive keep him here, Kelly."

"Right y'are; do that, mister."

Leaving Mick Kelly's sordid surroundings, Tinker returned to Baker Street. There he proceeded to deal with Blake's correspondence, intending afterwards to pay a visit to the "Daily Mail" offices and have another search through the files, as Blake had instructed him.

But his master's correspondence occupied Tinker longer than he had anticipated, and it was well into the afternoon by the time he had finished, so that he had to postpone his visit to Fleet Street. Hastening from the house, he took a cab to London Fields, hoping that he might be able to glean some information from Mick Kelly's light-fingered friend.

Mick Kelly, however, greeted his visitor with a dubious shake of the head.

"Sorry to disappoint yer, mister," he announced, "but Jim's sent along word that he ain't turning up. Reckon he's seed that there noose in the paper an' got the wind up."

"Then where can I find him?" demanded Tinker in ruffled tones.

"If yer comes along 'ere about nine o'clock this evening I'll take yer to a little pub where yer likely to find him," said the old lag.

"Right, I'll be here!" said Tinker curtly, and after a further brief exchange of remarks departed in none too good-humoured a frame of mind.

Feeling somewhat irritated at the further waste of time, he came out into Mare Street, Hackney, and stopped to board an approaching bus, when suddenly a hand fell on his shoulder and a deep, familiar voice spoke in his ears.

"Hallo, Tinker, my lad! Where're you off to?"

Tinker swung round, to find himself confronted by a big-framed, broad-shouldered man, with a strong mouth, rugged, determined features, and a pair of queer blue eyes.

One needed only to take a quick glance at him to appraise him for what he was—a globe-trotter, a scout of fortune, a knocker-up of adventure, who had met life halfway and conceded the odds to Fate on scores of untrodden back-trails in the red-raw places of the earth. And such he was, too—known as "Granite" Grant, King's Spy, one of the most trusted agents of the British Secret Service.

"Why, you, Mr. Grant!' cried Tinker, considerably astonished at this unexpected meeting.

"That's my name," laughed the other. "Catching this bus? So am I. Come on!"

Tinker followed his big companion up the stairs and sat down beside him.

"You're the last person I expected to meet down in this part of the world, Mr. Grant," said Tinker.

"That's where I'm generally to be found—where you least expect me," observed Granite Grant drily. "Well, how's the guv'nor?"

"Quite fit," said Tinker. "He left for the Continent this morning."

"Um-m! Must have passed him. I came across by the midday boat. Have a smoke?"

Granite Grant opened a rather bulky cigarette case, which evidently also served as a pocket-book, for one pouch was stuffed with visiting cards and various other odds and ends, including newspaper snippings.

And as Tinker's gaze rested casually on one of these cuttings, sticking above the rest, the printed heading happened to attract his attention.

"May I look at that?" he cried with sudden excitement as Granite Grant was just about to close the case.

"Look at which, sonny?" asked Granite Grant, glancing swiftly at his youthful companion.

"At that newspaper cutting," said Tinker, reaching out and taking the slip of paper from the case.

And with eager eyes he proceeded to peruse the following:

"CROWN JEWEL MYSTERY.

"Strong doubts have arisen at Prague as to whether the Bohemian crown jewels, of very great value, are really still in the treasure chamber of St. Wenceslaus' Chapel, at Prague, where they have been kept since 1625. Before the War they were kept locked up, with locks, the keys of which were entrusted to seven individuals. For many years the treasury has not been unlocked, and rumours were current that the jewels were removed to Vienna during the War. Some of the key-holders and keys are missing, and there are excited demands that the treasure chamber should immediately be forced to see if the jewels are still there."[1]

Before even Tinker had come to the end of this interesting news item he knew he had found the very article for which he had searched so fruitlessly the night before. And the reason of his failure was explained—the cutting had been taken from a Tuesday's issue of the "Daily Mail," and not a Thursday's, as Mick Kelly had said.

So here was the solution of the strange plot in which he and his master had become involved! In his excitement at this startling discovery, Tinker quite forgot all about his companion. But Granite Grant quickly reminded him of his presence.

"Well, sonny," he asked jestingly, "can you tell me anything about the Bohemian Crown jewels?"

"It's astonishing!" said Tinker, in excited tones. "Why, that fellow, Lipsky, must have had one of those missing keys! That explains the mysterious reference to the seventh key. And the guv'nor's gone off to Prague—"

Tinker got no farther. Granite Grant gripped his arm and spoke with sudden vehemence.

"What are you saying, sonny?" he demanded. "Sexton Blake's gone to Prague? He knows something about these Crown jewels? Come, give me the facts, as briefly as possible!"

With an effort Tinker mastered his excitement and

proceeded to acquaint his companion with all that had occurred since the visit of the mysterious Mr. Falcon to Baker Street, the previous day.

Granite Grant's rugged face grew a shade grimmer as he listened to the story, but he made no comment until Tinker mentioned the finding of the deposit receipt concealed behind the wall-paper in Lipsky's room. Then he broke in sharply.

"What was the name of the bank?" he asked.

"A bank in Prague, but I can't tell you the name," replied Tinker. "The guv'nor knows; that's why he suddenly decided to go to Prague."

"You're sure you can't tell me anything more about that deposit receipt, sonny?"

"Unfortunately, I can't. Even the guv'nor only knows the number and the name of the bank."

"And he crossed to Calais this morning. That means he'll travel by the Orient Express and change at Vienna for Prague?"

"That's the route he's taking," nodded Tinker.

The bus was approaching the Bank of England. Granite Grant rose to his feet with sudden decision.

"I must get hold of Blake before the Orient Express leaves Paris," he said. "So long, sonny!"

But Tinker was not to be so easily shaken off. In the circumstances he felt he had scarcely been treated fairly. Following his companion off the bus, he caught him up just as he was jumping into a cab.

"Where're you off to, Mr. Grant?" he cried.

"Croydon aerodrome, sonny."

"You're flying across?"

"That's the ticket. Can't stop, sonny!" Granite Grant waved his arm, and the cab sped off, leaving Tinker standing there staring after it with flushed face.

But he only remained thus a moment. Suddenly he started into activity, dashed after another cab, and, shouting "Baker Street" to the driver, clambered inside.

Tinker sat fretting with impatience during the next quarter of an hour. At Baker Street he only stayed long enough to find his passport, slip on a heavy travelling coat, and stuff a few things into a small bag. A few moments later he also was speeding in a taxi in the direction of Croydon.

When Tinker arrived at the aerodrome, breathless and excited, a machine was just being run out of one of the huge hangars. Close by stood the tall, familiar figure of the King's Spy.

"Only just in time, Mr. Grant!" cried Tinker, running up to him.

"Lawks!" exclaimed Granite Grant. "What're you doing here, sonny?"

"Coming across with you," said Tinker.

"Nothing doing! Sorry, but you'll be in the way on this little trip."

"Listen!" said Tinker desperately. "You'll miss the guv'nor without me. I've just remembered that he's leaving Paris by another route."

"What other route?"

"Tell you when we're in the air."

Granite Grant hesitated, but only for a moment.

"Jump in!" he shouted, as the engine suddenly started to roar.

It was not until they were soaring some thousands of feet above the earth, and London was already fading in the mist, that Tinker was compelled to confess the deception he had practised.

"Now, what's this other route Blake's taking?" demanded the King's Spy. "Don't know of any other route, sonny."

"Neither do I," replied Tinker in subdued tones.

Granite Grant glanced at him sharply, then broke into a grim chuckle.

"I've a good mind to chuck you overboard," was his only comment.[2]

Tinker was only too thankful to get away with it so lightly as this. And observing that his big companion was in an uncommunicative mood, he made no further remark, much as he wished to put a few pressing questions.

During that swift rush through the air Granite Grant glanced constantly at his watch, while his face wore a look of strained suspense. From his manner Tinker concluded that the issue of the race on which they had embarked hung in the balance, and that success or failure was but a matter of moments.

Dusk was falling when the twinkling lights of Paris were sighted and the machine began to descend into Le Bourget Aerodrome just outside the gay city. Granite Grant sprang out before even the machine came to rest.

"Touch and go!" he cried, and pelted towards the main entrance, with Tinker in hot pursuit.

There a precious moment or two were wasted in a discussion with the Customs officials, so that Granite Grant was compelled to adopt somewhat forcible methods of persuasion. Taking advantage of the confusion, Tinker slipped through the barriers, and was lucky enough to secure a cab.

"To the Gare de l'Est!" he shouted to the driver, as the King's Spy came dashing from the Customs office. "Well done, sonny!" he cried, clambering inside. "I think we'll just manage to do it now." And thrusting his head out of the window, he urged the driver to desperate efforts by a promise of treble fare.

But, unfortunately, Granite Grant's hopes were not realised. Arriving at the Gare de l'Est, he sprang from the cab and, followed closely by Tinker, dashed frantically for the departure platform of the Orient Express, only to find the barriers closed when he reached them. The Orient Express had left on its long rush across Europe half a minute before.

Granite Grant stood there, with his lips compressed tightly, glancing down the empty platform. The look on his rugged, hard-bitten face was so terrible that Tinker kept out of his way, fearing a violent explosion.

But his fears in this respect were not justified. Granite Grant merely stuck a cigarette between his teeth and struck a match.

"Unlucky!" was all he said. "Let's go in search of something to eat."

THE SIXTH CHAPTER

Two Tricks to the Enemy.

THE ORIENT EXPRESS is a sort of magic carpet that whisks one from the grey sombre skies of London to the sunlit glamour of the Golden Horn.

If one takes the eleven o'clock train from Victoria to Calais Maritime Station, one finds waiting there a number of long, brown carriages on whose sides hang strings of names that sound like a list of European crises—Vienna, Belgrade, Sofia, Bucarest, Athens, and Constantinople. This is the Orient Express, which is about to start on a four days' run—Europe's longest railway journey—into parts of the Continent where people still wear raw-hide shoes and homespun cloth as they did in the days of Alexander the Great.

It was the Orient Express that Sexton Blake boarded that day a few hours before Tinker's unexpected meeting with Granite Grant in Mare Street, Hackney. At a quarter past six that evening the Orient Express reached Paris.

The train was a little late in leaving Paris—if its departure had been delayed few more moments Sexton Blake might have been saved several exciting adventures. As it was, however, he left Paris behind without the slightest suspicion of the surprising encounter which he had so narrowly missed.

So the massive train, with its half-dozen or more sleeping coaches, restaurant car, and huge engine, settled down to a sustained rush—that hypnotising rumpity-rump-rump of the big Continental expresses—which showed that it meant business. And Sexton Blake settled himself comfortably in the corner of his coupe with a heap of magazines and journals which he had been prudent enough to bring with him.

Blake anticipated no further trouble to relieve the monotony of his long journey. Nevertheless, he determined to keep a cautious eye open in case of mischief. Although he was unaware of the real extent of the plot which he was bent on frustrating, he knew enough to convince him that he was dealing with daring and crafty foes. And it was quite possible that one or more of the gang were on the same train as himself.

Therefore Blake remained on his guard, and took careful stock of his fellow-passengers.

But he saw nothing to arouse his suspicions, and the hours that followed passed uneventfully. There is little one can do on a long railway journey beyond reading and smoking and occasionally stretching one's legs in the corridor. All of which expedients Blake tried. And, later, he wandered along to the restaurant car for dinner, over which meal he lingered for an hour or more.

Afterwards he spent another hour in the corridor, smoking his beloved briar and staring out into the darkness at the fleeting landscape. Then, returning to his "sleeper" once more, he read for a short time, and finally tumbled into his bunk.

Possessing the happy faculty of being able to sleep when and where he willed, Blake dropped off into a restful slumber as soon as his head touched the pillow. He awoke once during the night, and realised that the train was making terrific speed. Glancing out of the window, he saw the lights of a station flash past like the wink of an eyelid. They were passing through South Germany, he judged.

Hoping that they might not hit anything at that hurtling pace, Blake decided to go to sleep again, leaving the rest to Fate.

"One hundred and twenty-five kilometres (78 miles) an hour we were doing," said the chef-du-train next morning when Blake questioned him. "The engine could do more than that, monsieur, but we should be off the rails if we did."

"Um-m! Shouldn't like to fall out at that speed," said Blake, and went off in search of breakfast.

But as they entered the restaurant car he was surprised to hear his name being called by one of the stewards.

"Monsieur Sexton Blake!" cried the man, glancing about him expectantly and holding a telegraph envelope in his hand.

"That is for me, I think," said Blake, approaching.

"Picked up at Munich, monsieur," explained the

steward, handing over the missive.

With some curiosity Blake tore open the envelope and extracted the flimsy. The brief message it contained was in code, a code only known to him and Tinker, and for that reason Blake knew at once that it had come from his assistant, although the sender's name was omitted.

"Keep your eyes skinned," he read.

Thrusting the missive into his pocket, Blake sat down to his hot coffee and rolls. His face betrayed nothing of the thoughts that were speeding-through his mind. Nevertheless, Tinker's brief warning message was causing him considerable speculation.

The telegram had been despatched from Paris the previous night. That was queer. So Tinker was in Paris! And he could only have reached Paris thus early by one means—that was by air. What had occasioned his sudden flight from London? Blake wondered.

There was but one answer to this question. Tinker must have made some important discovery, and had attempted to reach his master before the latter left Paris. Failing that, he had sent this warning telegram. Tinker wouldn't have sent that brief message without urgent cause.

What did it mean precisely? Had Tinker discovered that his master was being followed? That seemed the most likely explanation. Blake decided to be extra vigilant for the remainder of the journey—the more so since, in a measure, Tinker's warning had defeated its object. The steward had been shouting his name all over the train; if any of his stealthy foes had been unaware of his presence before, they probably knew of it now.

Blake glanced surreptitiously at the other occupants of the restaurant car. They were cosmopolitan crowd, men mostly, of all nationalities, types, and creeds.

He ate in silence, still speculating over Tinker's strange telegram. Without a doubt, he would find a more lengthy message from his assistant awaiting him at the Moravia Hotel when he reached Prague. Probably then the mystery would be explained.

Having finished his breakfast, Blake proceeded to stretch his legs in the corridor, still keeping a watchful eye on his fellow passengers. But no incident occurred to arouse his suspicions, and about midday the Orient Express arrived at Vienna.

It was here that Blake had to change to catch the connection to Prague. Mingling with the bustling crowd, he passed the barriers, and outside took a taxicab to the north station. Arriving there, he found he had a couple of hours at his disposal before the Prague train was due to start.

Knowing the discomfort of railway travelling in Central Europe, however, Blake took the precaution of booking his seat in advance, and left his suitcase in charge of the guard, whom he generously tipped. He then went off to renew his acquaintance with Vienna, a city of which he was very fond.

Once Vienna had been the gayest capital in Europe. Blake remembered it in those pre-war days. Yet to the casual glance the city showed few outward scars of the revolution and turmoil through which it had passed. Gaiety and music were still enthroned in its fine boulevards, its brilliant cafes and its beautiful public gardens. Vienna hid her rags. The Kartner Strasse and Opern Ring, along which Blake passed, were flocked with well-dressed people, many clad in costly furs, for there had been a heavy fall of snow, and the wind was bitterly cold.

Deeply interested in all that was going on about him, Blake forgot the passing of time. Glancing presently at his watch, he was surprised to discover that over an hour had gone by. He must hurry if he wished to have something to eat and be back at the station in time to catch the Prague train. Slipping into a near-by restaurant, therefore, he sat down at a little marble-top table and ordered a hasty meal.

Another man took the vacant chair opposite him a moment later—a short, stout individual with a Semitic cast of features. Beyond a casual glance, however, Blake took no further notice of the newcomer, who buried himself behind a newspaper.

His requirements were soon served, and Blake hurried over the meal, with one eye on the clock. Towards the end of the repast his attention was distracted for a few moments by a seedy-looking individual, striving to earn a living by selling picture-postcards, who had entered the restaurant.

Blake took pity on the man, for he read in his careworn and ravaged face signs of birth and breeding, and guessed that he had seen better days when Vienna witnessed the pomp and ceremony of the imperial court. So he purchased some of his postcards, for which he paid him a sum out of all proportion to their value, and received the unfortunate man's extravagant expressions of gratitude.

The fat man opposite got up hurriedly and as if he were afraid of being asked to dispense charity, and, knowing that he had little time to spare, Blake also prepared to make his departure.

Beckoning the waiter, he settled his bill, and, casually picking up his glass, raised it to his lips to finish the contents. But as Blake swallowed a mouthful of the sparkling wine he fancied it had a strange, bitter flavour, which he certainly had not noticed before. He set the glass down at once, and rose to his feet. There was no time to inquire into the matter. Hurrying outside, he hailed a cab and drove off to the station.

But Blake had scarcely climbed inside than he experienced a strange feeling of dizziness. Immediately a queer suspicion flashed to his mind. Exerting all his will-power, he strove to throw off the heavy stupor that was creeping over him, and struggled to rise to his feet. But his strength seemed to have deserted him, and with a deep sigh he dropped back on the seat.

During the interval that passed Blake did not quite lose consciousness. His mind was dazed, and he could not stir himself in his own behalf. Yet he was convinced that only a few moments had elapsed when suddenly he roused himself and stared vaguely around.

The cab had stopped, the door was open, the driver was stooping over him splashing his face with cold water, and a little knot of curious people had collected outside. Suddenly thought rushed in upon Blake's mind, and he staggered to his feet.

"The station!" he cried. "I'm all right—get there as quickly as you can!"

"We are at the station, sir," answered the driver in puzzled tones. "You've had a fit or something. Better sit here for a bit and—"

Blake interrupted him with a swift gesture, thrust some notes into his hand, sprang from the cab, scattering the surprised spectators right and left, and dashed for the departure platform of the Prague train.

To his surprise he found the platform deserted, and there was no sign of the train to be seen.

"Where's the train for Prague?" he demanded of a passing porter.

"Gone, sir," came the reply. "Left twenty minutes ago."

Utterly incredulous, Blake turned and glanced up at the clock. The porter had spoken the truth, there was no mistake about it; he was exactly twenty minutes late. Dismayed by this unlooked-for calamity, Blake dropped into a seat and buried his face in his hands.

He had been tricked. There could be no doubt of that fact. He had been drugged—more probably an attempt had been made to poison him. The wine that had tasted bitter was the cause of his strange malady. It had been tampered with while for a moment or two his attention had been engaged with the vendor of picture-postcards.

And the fat Semitic man, who had sat concealed behind his newspaper, must have slipped something in the wine. Fortunately for Blake, he had only swallowed a mouthful, otherwise the affair might have had a more sinister ending.

But it was bad enough as it was. If his stealthy foes had failed in their murderous attempt, they had at least succeeded in frustrating his purpose—that was to reach Prague in time to prevent their presenting the deposit receipt at the bank.

Blake chuckled grimly at the thought. He had been caught napping in spite of Tinker's warning message. His crafty foes had managed to hoodwink him just when his journey seemed likely to meet with success. The knowledge was too humiliating to be endured.

Was there yet no way of turning the tables on his cunning enemies? Blake roused himself at the question. Perhaps even now there might be a means of reaching Prague in time to achieve his purpose. The train that he had just missed arrived at Prague somewhere about nine o'clock that evening. The bank would be closed then; the conspirators must wait until it opened in the morning. Could he arrive in time?

Urged to action by this possibility, Blake made his way swiftly to the inquiry bureau. The official there at first shook his head in reply to question, but on being tipped for his pains stirred himself to consult the time-tables.

"There is a slow train leaving the West Station at eight o'clock this evening, sir," he said. "It goes a long way round, and doesn't arrive at Prague before six o'clock in the morning."

"That will do," said Blake eagerly, and, thanking the man, he was just turning away when he suddenly remembered his suitcase.

"I left my bag in charge of the guard on the train that

left for Prague a half-hour ago," he explained. "It has the initials S.B. Can you make inquiries at the other end?"

"That will be all right, sir,' came the reply. "I'll telephone along the line and get them to drop it on the local at Brod, then you can pick it up at Ritstadt."

Blake thanked his informant again and came out of the bureau. He was feeling well pleased with this hopeful turn of events, and quite sanguine again of being able to put a spoke in the wheel of his unseen foes. Little he guessed that at that very moment one of them was in the bureau he had just left, making polite inquiries concerning himself and his intentions.

But although he was unaware of this fact, Blake remained on his guard against further possible stealthy attacks on him, and determined not to be caught a second time. He was still feeling the effects of the doped wine he had drunk, and he decided to rest for the next few hours in order to refresh himself for the tedious all-night journey that was in store for him.

He therefore directed his steps to an hotel near the West Station, and made himself comfortable in the lounge, where a stringed orchestra was playing. There he had tea, and stayed until close on half-past seven, then prepared to make tracks for the train, determined not to miss it this time.

But before entering the station Blake purchased a bag and one or two other articles, in case his own suitcase should not turn up at Ritstadt—an emergency for which he was quite prepared.

The train was already crowded—trains are always

crowded in Central Europe both day and night—and there was only standing room left. Blake took up his position in the corridor, and prepared himself for a long and uncomfortable journey.

The night was bitterly cold, snow had commenced to fall again, and the landscape was shrouded in a thick white mantle. The train crawled, stopping at every little village and hamlet, where rustic-looking folk got in and out. Blake's feet soon felt like blocks of ice, and he proceeded to stamp vigorously in an attempt to restore their circulation. This kind of travelling, he sadly reflected, was somewhat different from the warmth and luxury of the Orient Express.

Nearing midnight, however, the train became less crowded, and Blake was able to find a seat, much to his relief. They had now crossed the Austrian frontier into Czecho-Slovakia, and the snow-covered countryside looked very bleak and desolate in its mantle of white. Some time later, when the train had stopped at a wayside station, Blake happened to notice the guard passing outside. Leaning out of the window, he called to him.

"I am expecting to pick up a suitcase at Ritstadt," he said. "It has the initials S.B. Will you be on the look-out for it?"

"Very good, sir; I'll keep my eyes open for it," replied the guard, and blew his shrill whistle.

The train crawled on once again, and an hour or more passed, with several stops in between. The carriage was too dimly-lit to enable Blake to read, and all his fellow-passengers were dozing to an accompaniment of deep snores. Blake found himself nodding once or twice, and it was on one of these occasions that the door was suddenly flung open and the guard aroused him.

"You were inquiring about a suitcase, sir," he cried. "I think it's just been put in my van."

Blake jumped up instinctively and sprang on to the platform. It was a tiny station built of rough wooden planks, at which the train had halted, and without stopping to think, he concluded that it must be Ritstadt.

Running along to the guard's van, he climbed inside. And at that same moment a stunning blow on the head, delivered by some unseen hand, knocked him senseless.

THE SEVENTH CHAPTER

Two On the Trail.

GRANITE GRANT, AS has been seen, was possessed of a philosophical temperament. Having missed the Orient Express at Paris by such a narrow margin, and just failed to overtake Sexton Blake, he did the wisest thing he could do in the circumstances—he went in search of something to eat. For there is nothing like a good feed to take the edge off one's exasperation—especially if that good feed happens to come from a Parisian cuisine.

And over the meal that followed in the cheerful environment of a first-class hotel, Granite Grant became a little more communicative than he had been during that hurried flight from London.

"Lucky I should run up against you in Mare Street, Hackney, to-day, sonny," he observed. "I had just drawn a blank, too."

"Then you went there for a purpose?" asked Tinker, thirsting for further information.

"Reckon I never go anywhere without a purpose, sonny," was Granite Grant's reply. "Yes, I went there to find a certain gentleman named Blenkoff, living just off Mare Street. But friend Blenkoff had 'beat it' without leaving his new address."

"And who was this fellow Blenkoff?"

"It's a long story, sonny, but I'll just give you a few facts. You read that newspaper cutting about the Bohemian Crown jewels being locked up in the treasure chamber at Prague for the last three hundred years, that there was a rumour of them having been removed to Vienna during the War, and that several of the seven keyholders and keys are now missing?

"Well, that's the plot, and it's been keeping me busy on and off for some months—the Continental police as well—searching for the missing keys. The keyholders appear to have died natural deaths, but the keys they had charge of have vanished. Then I got wind of the fact that a certain gang of Continental swindlers, with this fellow Blenkoff at the head, was also interested in those missing keys.

"Blenkoff's headquarters were in Paris, and I had him watched. A few days ago he received a wire from a fellow at Hackney—evidently your mysterious friend Falcon, and one of Blenkoff's gang. Blenkoff slipped across to London at once, but, unfortunately, he wasn't trailed. I only arrived this morning, an hour or so before I ran up against you in Mare Street, and, of course, I drew a blank.

"That's the story, sonny. And from what you've told me, I'm thinking the plot's a bit deeper than I suspected. My idea was that Blenkoff was trying to get hold of duplicates of those seven keys in order to get at the stuff in the treasury at Prague. A bold scheme that! But that deposit receipt Blake found—and lost—puts a rather different complexion on the affair. Blenkoff was after that for a certainty."

"And how does this fellow Lipsky figure in the plot?" asked Tinker.

"Can't say for certain just yet—and the poor beggar will never be able to answer the question. But somehow he managed to get hold of the seventh key and this deposit receipt as well. Obviously, he was recognised by one of Blenkoff's gang, the fellow who sent him the wire. And Blenkoff followed him to his rooms and knifed him.

"However, the main thing at the present moment is to stop Blenkoff presenting that deposit receipt at the bank. He's on the way to Prague now for a cert—probably on the same train as Blake. And Blake will never reach Prague if friend Blenkoff can help it. That's why I was so anxious to overtake your guv'nor—to put him on his guard."

"You think the guv'nor's in danger?" asked Tinker anxiously.

"I do. You can bet Blenkoff's aware of his movements—and he won't stick at trifles."

"Then I must send a wire to the guv'nor," said Tinker, with decision. "He'll get it somewhere along the line."

"I thought of that,' replied Granite Grant. "But we don't want to delay Blake. Everything depends on his reaching Prague as quickly as possible. And I'm still hoping to overtake him at Vienna."

"How can you manage that?"

"By the same means we employed to get here, sonny. We're leaving for Vienna by aeroplane first thing in the morning."

"But something might happen to the guv'nor between here and Vienna," said Tinker. "I think I'd better wire him."

"Well, do as you like; only don't say anything about meeting him in Vienna, in case we don't get there in time. In that case Blake might wait, and so miss the Prague train. Now, I must fix up about this machine in the morning. See you again later. So-long!"

Feeling anxious concerning his master's safety, Tinker also left the hotel with his big companion, and went off to the station to send that warning telegram to his master, which Blake received on the Orient Express as has been seen.

By the time Blake was reading Tinker's warning, the youngster and Granite Grant were already approaching the frontier of South Germany, some thousands of feet above the earth, having left Le Bourget Aerodrome at daybreak with the same machine and pilot who had flown them from London on the previous day.

That seven-hundred-mile flight Tinker ever afterwards remembered as one of his most unpleasant experiences. Soon after leaving the ground he was numbed with cold, and he remained in that frozen state until the end of the trip. A landing, he believed, was made somewhere near Munich, but he had little recollection of the fact; and when at length Vienna was reached, it was with difficulty that he could climb from the machine.

There that same rush was made for the station as had occurred in Paris the previous night, and in the taxicab Tinker began to warm up.

"D'you think we shall do it?" he asked of the King's Spy.

"Just manage it, I think," said Granite Grant in suppressed tones. "Here we are! Hop out, sonny!"

Tinker hopped out, and followed his big companion as best he could. The shrill whistle of the Prague train was just sounding as they arrived on the platform, and the porters were slamming the carriage doors.

"Blake's bound to be somewhere on the train!" cried Granite Grant, making for the nearest carriage. "See if you can find him."

Tinker bundled in after him and proceeded to hurry along the corridor, glancing in at each compartment in search of his master, while the train jerked forward and glided out of the station, momentarily gathering speed. But he presently reached the foremost carriage without seeing any signs of Blake.

Thinking that Granite Grant may have discovered his master in one of the end compartments, Tinker proceeded to retrace his steps. But when presently he met the King's Spy he saw at once that he had been no more successful.

"Haven't you seen him?" he asked impatiently. "But he must have caught this train. There isn't another one that he could have gone by. He's on it somewhere. We'll look until we find him."

They went off in opposite directions again, this time Tinker searching the rear carriages. The train was crowded, and it was easy to miss a person among all those passengers, so that Tinker went about his task very slowly. But he met with no better success than before. There was certainly no sign of Blake's being on the train. And Granite Grant at length returned with the same negative result.

"It beats me," he muttered. "I was dead sure we'd find Blake here. Seems we're unlucky again. Wonder if he could have caught an earlier train? I'll ask the guard."

The train had just stopped at a station and was on the move again as Granite Grant went off on his errand. While he was gone Tinker renewed his search, being loath to believe that he had missed his master a second time. When, however, after an interval, Granite Grant rejoined him he saw at once from his face that he had discovered something.

"Blake missed the train," he explained. 'His suit-case is in the guard's van. A message came through at the last station from Vienna asking for his bag to be sent on to Ritstadt when we reach Brod. He's catching a train from the west station this evening. It goes a long way round, and doesn't reach Prague until six in the morning. But that'll be time enough to get to the bank before it opens."

"Then we'll meet the guv'nor at Prague in the morning?" said Tinker.

"I'll decide that later, said Granite Grant, speaking in low tones. "It is quite probable that our friend Blenkoff is on this train. I've only seen him once, and he's almost certain to be disguised, so I doubt if I should recognise him. But I'm going to have a prowl round. You find a seat, sonny, and make yourself comfortable."

Tinker managed to find a seat, while Granite Grant proceeded to prowl around. During the hours that followed Tinker saw him occasionally passing in the corridor, but it was not until about half-past seven that evening that the King's Spy stopped outside and beckoned to him.

"Don't see any signs of our friends!" he muttered. "I've decided to get out at Brod and go on to Ritstadt with Blake's bag. I'm rather anxious to have a word with him before he reaches Prague. But you can stay on this train if you like, and put up at the Moravia Hotel to-night."

"No; I'd rather come with you," said Tinker promptly.

"Very well; then we'll keep together. Brod's the next station, I think, so you'd better wait here in the corridor."

The train stopped at Brod twenty minutes later, where Granite Grant and Tinker got out, Blake's bag was placed in charge of the stationmaster, the guard refusing to hand it over to Tinker or his companion. After over an hour's wait the Ritstadt train came puffing in, and Granite Grant and Tinker took their seats.

Being a small local train, its accommodation was of the worst description possible, and the discomfort of the interminable cross-country journey that followed made Granite Grant regret that he had undertaken it.

But it came to an end at last, about one in the morning, when Ritstadt was reached.

Ritstadt proved to be quite a small village, and it was with difficulty that Granite Grant succeeded in getting served with some hot beverage, for which they were both grateful. The train by which Blake was arriving was not due in until some hours yet, and Granite Grant and Tinker spent the latter half of that tedious interval stamping up and down the snow-covered platform in an endeavour to keep warm. Then at last, to their infinite relief, they saw the lights of the approaching train.

"Run along to the front!" cried Granite Grant, as the train drew up beside the platform. "Blake's bound to get out to look for his bag."

Tinker obeyed, and hurried along to the engine, expecting momentarily to see his master. Reaching the engine, and not meeting him, he proceeded to retrace his steps more slowly, until he was nearing the rear of the train. And there he came across Granite Grant, the stationmaster, and the guard of the train, apparently having an argument. The guard was scratching his head in a puzzled fashion, and glancing down at Blake's suit-case, which the stationmaster had charge of.

"Very curious!" he was saying. "The gentleman told me soon after we left Vienna that he expected to pick up his bag here. But there was a bag for him at the last station; one of the porters said he'd put it in my van. So I told the gentleman about it, and I think he jumped out of the carriage and ran along to the van."

"There's a mistake somewhere," said the stationmaster. "His bag couldn't have been up the line if it came from Brod. Anyway, here it is."

At this point in the discussion a passenger, leaning out of the carriage window close by, put in a word.

"The gentleman didn't come back," he said. "He was sitting opposite me until the last station, where he jumped out. He's left a bag here on the rack."

Tinker glanced up at the bag in question. It was a new one, and he concluded at once that his master must have bought it in Vienna before he left. He turned to Granite Grant and met the latter's puzzled look.

"This is a bit suspicious, sonny," he said. "Let us have a peep into the guard's van."

They hurried along to the end of the train, the guard and stationmaster following. Climbing into the van, they glanced about them with the aid of the lantern. And suddenly Tinker caught sight of something lying half hidden by a heap of luggage. He picked it up, and recognised it instantly. It was a felt hat, with the crown crushed in as if from a violent blow.

"It's the guv'nor's hat!" he cried sharply.

Granite Grant's mouth tightened grimly as his gaze rested on the damaged headgear.

"Dirty work!" he muttered. "I suspected as much." Suddenly he turned on the stationmaster. "What's the name of the last station?" he demanded.

"Tadwitz, sir—about seven miles up the line."

"Is that train just passing going there?"

"Yes; but it's a goods train, sir."

Granite Grant wasted no further breath in words; but, seizing Blake's suit-case from the astonished stationmaster's grasp, flung open the other door of the van and leapt out on to the line. Tinker followed his example, and plunged after him as he dashed for the train on the up line that was already nearly through the station. Clambering on to one of the trucks of timber, Granite Grant grasped Tinker's hand and hauled him safely on board.

"Lucky for once!" he cried. "We'd had to walk if this hadn't come along!"

"D'you think we shall find the guv'nor at Tadwitz?" asked Tinker anxiously, when he had recovered his breath.

"We shall see!" was Granite Grant's grim reply.

And they lapsed into a gloomy silence.

The goods train took over half an hour to do those seven miles, and it did not slacken speed at the next station, which was in total darkness. Granite Grant and Tinker jumped off the truck and stood there while the lumbering train rattled by them.

"Well, this is a ramshackle show with a vengeance!" muttered Granite Grant, glancing about them.

His remark was certainly justified. Tadwitz Station could scarcely be called a station; it consisted merely of a raised platform on either side constructed of rough planks, which were now concealed beneath the heavy fall of snow. And an intense silence brooded over the place. There was no sign of any other human presence.

"We must have made a mistake!" muttered Tinker. 'This can't be Tadwitz Station."

"Reckon it is, sonny. At any rate, we'll have a look around. If Blake were attacked in that van and chucked out of the door on the other side, as seems likely, we ought to find traces in the snow. This way!"

Followed by Tinker, he crossed to the down line, and proceeded to walk along it towards the rear end of the platform.

"This is about where the guard's van must have stopped," he muttered, and walked slowly on.

"Ah!" he cried, a moment later, pointing. "This is where it happened!"

Granite Grant had not spoken without cause. To Tinker also the sinister evidence was only too clear. At that particular spot the white blanket of snow was disturbed as if by an inert body and trampled down by footprints. Obviously, here a man must have jumped from the guards'-van, dragging a heavy burden with him.

The footprints led on up the centre track, with another trail brushed in the snow beside them. Granite Grant commenced to follow them, with Tinker keeping close. They walked in silence, the same grim suspicion occupying both their minds.

Suddenly Tinker glanced ahead, and drew a sharp breath.

"That sounds like a train!" he cried.

As the words left his mouth the lights of an engine suddenly appeared round a steep bend in the line ahead. Granite Grant uttered a hoarse cry, and raced forward. Twenty yards or so farther on he came across a mound of snow covering one of the metals. He stooped, and began frantically raking it aside with his hands, the rumble of the approaching train growing rapidly louder.

Tinker joined him a moment later, and the heap of snow quickly disappeared before their combined efforts, revealing the body of a man lying there, bound and gagged, with his neck resting on the railway-line.

They grasped the inert form, and staggered back with their burden—just as the heavy goods train went rumbling past.

THE EIGHTH CHAPTER

In the Forest.

IT WAS A hair-breadth escape! The very nearness of the thing caused Tinker a violent trembling. No need for him to doubt that this helpless man who had so narrowly missed being decapitated was his beloved master. A sigh of thankfulness escaped his lips.

Granite Grant was already stooping over the prostrate form, swiftly unfastening his bonds.

"He's all right!" he muttered, in suppressed tones, and took a flask of spirits from his pocket.

Sexton Blake was not unconscious, but dazed and numbed with the cold. He gulped down the strong stimulant, then glanced inquiringly from one to the other, and a faint smile of puzzlement crept into his face.

"Don't talk now! Help me to lift him!" said Granite Grant sharply.

Tinker lent a hand, and together they proceeded to carry his master back towards the station. A short

distance beyond a small brick cottage was standing—
the only sign of human habitation within sight. It was
in darkness, and Granite Grant nearly burst in the door
before it was opened by a surly-looking old Czech in his
nightshirt, who was evidently the stationmaster, porter,
and booking-clerk rolled into one.

He greeted his visitors none too affably at first, but
Granite Grant soon had him bustling about, aided by
an old woman who was obviously his spouse. In the
room behind a welcome fire was quickly blazing and
in its cheerful warmth Sexton Blake speedily recovered
from the severe ordeal through which he had passed.
Fortunately, his hat had saved him from the full force of
the blow that had stunned him, and the injury was but
slight. A steaming-hot bowl of soup, of which Granite
Grant and Tinker also gratefully partook, helped to put
matters right.

But even then the King's Spy would not permit Blake
to talk.

"Tumble on to that couch, old man, and forget
everything!" he commanded. "Never mind how I come
to be here. We'll talk later."

"Don't bully me," murmured Blake, with a weary smile.
"I'm incapable of resistance."

And he did as he was told. Tinker was also feeling
fagged out, and, wrapping himself in a blanket, lay down
in front of the fire.

Only Granite Grant's indefatigable spirit would not
rest. Drawing his sleepy host aside, he spoke in eager
tones.

"When is the next train for Prague?" he asked.

"Not until eight o'clock in the morning, Excellency."

"Too late. Is there another goods train?"

"The last one passed just before you arrived here, Excellency."

"Then how can I get to Prague immediately?"

"It is impossible."

"It must be done, my friend. Can I get a car anywhere?"

"Perhaps in the village, Excellency. But a car will be useless in this heavy snow."

"We shall see. How far away is the village?"

"Nearly a mile along the road, Excellency."

"Show me the direction," said Granite Grant, and went outside, accompanied by the old man.

The latter returned a few moments later, and bolted the door behind him. During the two hours that followed silence brooded over the cottage, and Tinker and his master scarcely stirred. Then suddenly a muffled drumming of hoofs sounded outside, and the next moment impatient blows beat upon the door.

The old man cautiously drew the bolts, and Grant stepped inside—his giant figure muffled to the ears in a sheepskin jacket and leggings. In his hand he grasped a stout hunting-crop. Crossing to Sexton Blake, he shook him by the shoulder.

"Tell me the name of the bank and the number of the deposit receipt, old man," he urged. "Quickly—there is no time to lose!"

Blake sat up and shook himself. He seemed now quite recovered from his misadventure.

"What's the game, Grant?" he asked, surveying his friend with a look of interest.

"Listen. Prague's forty miles from here by rail, and scarcely thirty cross-country. There's no train, and I'm going by road. I shall just manage it in time, I think, with a little luck. Now, tell me the name of that bank at once, then you can tumble off to sleep again."

"Tell you when we get to Prague," was Blake's rejoinder. "I'm ready!"

"But you're not coming, man; I won't hear of it!"

"Then I'm not telling you the name of that bank."

"Madness! I tell you I've only got one horse."

"Plenty more, I dare say, where that came from."

"But—" expostulated Granite Grant, then shrugged his shoulders in despair. Without further argument he turned to the door.

Tinker, who had also been aroused, hurriedly followed his master outside. There he found waiting, tethered to a post, a great dun mare, who was restlessly pawing the snow, impatient to be off.

"You ride her to the village," said Granite Grant curtly, turning to Sexton Blake.

"No; it's your mount," remonstrated Blake, drawing back.

Granite Grant wasted no further time in words, but caught Blake in his arms and chucked him into the saddle.

"Hang on the other side, Tinker," he ordered, and grasped the near stirrup-iron.

"You've certainly got a way with you, my friend!" chuckled Blake, glancing down as he caught at the bridle.

The old railwayman approached Granite Grant as he was about to give the word to start.

"Be careful, Excellency," he muttered warningly; "there are wolves in the forest. A few days ago a pack of the hungry brutes attacked a train not far from here."

"It's the two-legged wolves I'm more concerned about," was Granite Grant's significant reply. "All ready?" he cried. "Then off we go!" and cracked his riding-whip.

The great dun mare wanted no second bidding; had not Blake's restraining hand on the bridle held her in check she would have been off like a streak of lightning. He curbed her to a loping trot, and, hanging to the stirrups on either side, Granite Grant and Tinker kept pace with her.

The pale gleam of dawn was just creeping across the white-mantled countryside, and the utter stillness of everything appeared uncanny in the ghostly light. A brief five minutes' run brought them to the village of Tadwitz— merely a handful of scattered cottages in which not a sign of life appeared.

"Go easy!" cried Granite Grant. "I'll tell you the shack when we get to it. Just a few yards farther on."

The shack proved to be a group of farm buildings at the farther extremity of the village, and there Blake pulled up his spirited steed. Granite Grant beat loudly upon the door of the wooden homestead, and his summons was quickly answered by a bearded man carrying a swinging lantern in his hand.

"What, back again, Excellency?" he asked in surprise, holding the lantern aloft and peering closely at his visitor.

"Back again for horses for my two friends," answered Granite Grant shortly. "Hurry, my good fellow; we've no time to waste."

The man muttered dubiously, shaking his head. Granite Grant grasped him by the arm and dragged him outside.

"Come, don't talk!" he cried impatiently. "There's half a dozen horses in the stables. I saw them."

The farmer came reluctantly, evidently impressed by the strength of Granite Grant's iron fingers. They made their way round to the back of the premises, Sexton Blake and Tinker following behind.

There were several animals in the stables, four in all— sturdy Czech ponies, full of stamina and courage.

"They'll do! Saddle up a couple of them," said Granite Grant. Suddenly he turned swiftly on the farmer. "Where're the other two?" he demanded. "There were six here a short while ago."

The farmer drew back, muttering sullenly. Granite Grant did not wait for an answer to his question, but thrust the man roughly aside and ran out into the yard. In a moment he was back again.

"Who's gone out with those other two horses?" he shouted fiercely. "They must have left just after me; their tracks are plain in the snow. Who took them out, I say?"

With an angry snarl the farmer whipped out an ugly knife and drew back threateningly. But Granite Grant sprang upon him, twisting the weapon from his grasp and gripping his throat with the other hand.

"Ah, would you!" he hissed. "Speak, you rascal, or I'll squeeze the breath out of your body!"

"Mercy, Excellency!" gasped the man. "I will tell you the truth. Yes, they came directly you left. There were two of them. They said they wanted to overtake you. I thought they were friends of yours, Excellency."

"And took money from them to keep your mouth shut, eh?" said Granite Grant scornfully. "Better stick to the truth, my friend. Which way did they go?"

"They have gone to Prague, Excellency; and there is only one road to Prague."

Granite Grant turned to Blake and his assistant.

"Your two nice friends, Blake," he muttered aside. "Two of Blenkoff's gang—the rascals who tied you to the line. I knew they must be somewhere in the neighbourhood, and I had a notion that I was followed here."

Blake nodded thoughtfully.

"D'you think they're hanging about on the watch?" he asked.

"We'll see where their tracks lead to," replied the King's Spy, taking a heavy Service revolver from his pocket and looking to the smooth working of the mechanism.

"Have you two got guns?" he asked.

Both Blake and Tinker felt for their trusty automatics and placed them in readiness.

"Good!" nodded Granite Grant. "Looks as if we may want 'em. Now you'd better borrow some of those sheepskins and leggings in the corner over there, while I lend a hand with the animals."

His two friends complied, and by the time they had attired themselves for the long ride their mounts were ready. They climbed into their saddles, and Granite Grant stayed a moment to have a final word with the farmer.

"If you've any further treachery up your sleeve, my friend, you'll be sorry," he said. "When these beasts get back here you'll be paid for your trouble, and not before. And that won't be until I reach Prague in safety. Just go and think over that."

"I know no more than I have told you, Excellency," answered the man in more subdued tones. "Keep your eyes open along the road through the forest."

"Never fear, I sha'n't go to sleep," was Granite Grant's rejoinder, and feeling the touch of his rider's heels, the great dun mare sprang forward through the gates.

Sexton Blake and his assistant were waiting in the road outside, their two spirited mounts prancing impatiently and chafing at their bits.

"Our two friends have gone this way," said Blake, pointing to the tell-tale hoof-prints in the snow.

"And that's our way, too," replied Granite Grant grimly. "Off we go!"

The mare broke into a sharp canter, the two Czech ponies following suit. Granite Grant rode slightly in advance of his two friends, keeping a watchful eye on the white-carpeted ground in front of him.

"Rather fortunate that you didn't set out alone—eh?" Sexton Blake cried to his friend.

"Perhaps you're right!" grunted Granite Grant.

After that none of them spoke again for some time. Only the rhythmic drumming of the three pairs of hoofs broke the stilly silence. The road led across an open plain, and all about them gleamed a great white plateau. The pace was exhilarating; the three beasts, as well as their riders, seemed to be enjoying the experience. To Blake and his two companions, however, was added a spice to their adventure by the knowledge that somewhere on ahead lurked two stealthy foes, bent on frustrating their purpose. But while their tell-tale hoof-prints remained discernible there was no immediate danger of falling into a trap.

The road, after crossing several miles of open country, began to pass straggling clusters of bushes and trees, while farther ahead of them a black shadow crawled upon the mantle of snow, intimating that they were approaching the forest. Suddenly Granite Grant, who had kept in advance of his two friends, reined in his mount, bringing the great mare back on her haunches.

"Our two wily friends have left the road here!" he cried, when Blake and Tinker joined him a moment later. "Just hold the bridles, Tinker, while we see what their little game is."

Tinker complied, and together Blake and Granite Grant proceeded cautiously to follow the tracks of their two cunning foes, keeping their eyes skinned in case they should be lurking close at hand. After tracing the hoof-marks through some snow-covered shrubs, however, they suddenly came out on the shelving bank of a shallow, trickling rivulet.

"What have they done?" asked Granite Grant, stopping. "Forded it, d'you think?"

"Probably," nodded Blake, "although I can't see their tracks on the other side. They may have taken to the water for some distance; it's certainly not above a foot deep even in the middle."

"What's their game, then?"

"Doubtless making a detour to get on in front of you and await your coming. Don't suppose they suspect there are three of us."

"You're right, I think. We'll stick to the road, and see what turns up. Are you agreed?"

"Yes; I think that's the best plan," said Blake.

And the two of them returned to the horses.

They rode off again, and some ten minutes later reached the outskirts of the forest. There Sexton Blake called a halt.

"I've got a little scheme to work off against our crafty friends," he said. "Probably they'll be lying in wait somewhere ahead, and it's better to let them think there's only one of us. I'll ride on in advance of you two fellows, and when the fun starts you can slip in and catch them by surprise."

"The very notion I was revolving in my own mind," cried Granite Grant; "only I guess I'm the fellow who's taking the lead in this little venture. If you don't agree, Blake, I'll race you for it!"

Blake glanced at his friend's great dun mare, and answered with a shrug of his shoulders.

"You've won, Grant!" he said. "Carry on!"

Without further argument, Granite Grant urged his mount into a swinging trot. Blake and Tinker gave him a hundred yards' start, then followed after him. The forest of trees closed about them, and between the thickly rising trunks wound a ribbon of white, beaten snow.

Feeling now that an attack might be made upon them at any moment, a strained silence fell upon Tinker and his master, and they rode forward with their eyes looking ahead, catching occasional glimpses of Granite Grant's stalwart form in front as the path straightened out.

After some miles had been covered in this fashion without incident, however, their tension somewhat relaxed, and Blake turned to his assistant with a smile.

"We haven't even exchanged greetings yet," he said. "I got the telegram you sent from Paris. Well, how does our friend Grant come into the story? Better tell me all about everything; it'll help to pass away the time."

Nothing loath, Tinker proceeded to relieve his master's curiosity, and his recital occupied them for the next five miles or so. Suddenly, however, when he had almost reached the conclusion of his interesting story a dramatic interruption occurred. Across the heavy silence there came the sharp crack of a revolver-shot, followed instantly by another, and the brooding forest of fir and pine trees awoke to a thousand echoes.

For a brief moment both Blake and his companion stiffened; then simultaneously they dug their heels into their two mounts and sent them leaping forward. The next moment, as the path straightened out, they caught a fleeting glimpse of the great dun mare vanishing in the dim distance ahead, while sprawling upon the snow lay Granite Grant's giant form, motionless as if he were dead.

The spectacle affected Blake like a physical blow, and a choking cry came from his lips. At the same moment he caught sight of two men come running from the cover of the trees on either side, making for their prostrate victim with the evident intention of rifling his pockets. So intent were they on their object that they failed to notice the approach of the other two horsemen until they were almost upon them; then, firing at random, they attempted to escape.

And suddenly Granite Grant leapt into life, with a mocking shout, and flung himself upon one of the ruffians. The other Blake rode down, and, swinging from his saddle, grappled with the man as he was picking himself up from the ground. A blow between the eyes from Blake's fist sent the fellow to the ground again, and this time he did not attempt to rise.

Turning swiftly, Blake was just in time to observe Granite Grant beat the other ruffian to the ground. He ran towards his friend with outstretched hands.

"What a shock you gave me, Grant!" he cried. "I really thought they had plugged you that time!"

"Just a little trick!" laughed the King's Spy. "I tumbled from my saddle when the first shot was fired. They fell to it nicely." He glanced down at his two would-be assassins, and added: "Well, what shall we do with the rascals? Leave 'em here, I think, and take their horses along with us."

"That's not a bad notion!" agreed Blake.

"Where are their horses? I see them—tethered in the trees over there. You'll want one yourself, Grant, since your mare's gone off in a panic."

He paused suddenly as a faint, discordant cry sounded from the depths of the gloomy forest of trees.

"Wolves!" he muttered. "Listen! More of them, too! The sooner we get out of here the better!"

Tinker had fortunately managed to prevent his master's mount from following the mare's example, and with the horses of their two vanquished foes they had now one to spare, which Granite Grant led by the bridle.

Those sinister howls were growing louder in the forest, and the animals were becoming restive. Leaving the two ruffians to fend for themselves, our three friends pressed on once more, and a mile or so farther on came upon the great dun mare, now recovered from her fright, patiently awaiting their approach. Granite Grant was only too pleased to transfer his giant frame to a more comfortable seat, and after that their progress was not disturbed by any further exciting incident.

Half an hour later the trees suddenly began to fall away on either side, the forest gave place to the open country once more, and very quickly the three riders found themselves entering the main street of a village of clustering, dirty, white-washed habitations.

THE NINTH CHAPTER

What Happened at Prague.

THE VILLAGE AT which our three friends had so unexpectedly arrived was but four miles from Prague, and the road beyond fit for wheeled vehicles. At the village inn they were able to procure a motor-car—a somewhat antiquated machine, but, nevertheless, good enough for their purpose. Their steeds had earned a rest after the long and hard ride, and they were placed in charge of the ostler.

The three stayed just long enough to gulp down some hot beverage. There was not a moment to lose; even now it was doubtful if they would arrive in time to achieve their purpose. So they pushed on once more, with a Czech driver at the wheel.

A brief ten minutes' run brought them to the outskirts of the town, the car passed through a narrow gateway set in a fortress wall, and immediately below the whole city of Prague lay spread out beneath a mantle of snow—its spires and roofs, river and bridges, parks, gardens and palaces, glittering in the cold morning light.

Blake had already given the driver the name and address of the bank for which they were making, and the man, who was evidently well acquainted with his whereabouts, drove on without hesitation. The car descended the slope and proceeded to twist its way through the narrow, corkscrew streets of the ancient city, crossing the river and presently coming to a stop outside a grey stone building, behind a cab that was waiting there.

Granite Grant sprang out and hastened up the steps to the building. It was a little before ten o'clock in the morning, an early hour for business to be transacted in Prague, and it seemed that few members of the bank's staff had yet put in an appearance.

At the farther end of the front office was the manager's room, to which Granite Grant directed his steps, followed by Blake and Tinker. But before he could reach the door it suddenly opened, and two men emerged, carrying a black deed-box between them. The one was a sharp-featured individual, with a rat-trap mouth, dressed in clothes of a most fashionable cut; his companion a flat-faced man with a drooping reddish moustache—none other than the mysterious John Falcon!

He recognised Blake at once, and in his surprise he dropped the deed-box, stopping dead, with his mouth gaping open in astonishment. His companion also stopped with a sharp exclamation, and glanced with quick suspicion at the newcomers. Then, as if divining the situation, he suddenly grasped the deed-box and made a dash for it.

But Granite Grant was too smart for him. With a neat movement he tripped him up, and the deed-box went clattering to the floor.

"Not so fast, friend Blenkoff!" he cried. "What's all the hurry about?"

Blenkoff was on his feet in a moment, and, uttering a snarl of rage, whipped out a revolver. Granite Grant caught his wrist and twisted it as the weapon exploded, shattering a pane of glass in the dome above, then dealt him a stunning blow on the chin with his bunched fist.

In the meantime "Mr. Falcon" had recovered from his first surprise and flung himself upon Blake. Startled cries were raised in the bank; excited clerks came running from all directions, and the manager's frightened face appeared at the door of his room.

But the commotion was all over in a few moments. The discomfited Blenkoff and his companion found themselves with their backs to the wall and with their fronts threatened by two menacing weapons. Livid with anger, the master-swindler, who had been so long sought by the Continental police, tried to assume the role of righteous indignation.

"This is an outrage!" he protested, glaring malevolently at his captor, and addressing himself to the circle of scared officials he cried: "Why don't you throw yourselves on this bank robber?"

Granite Grant laughed dryly.

"Bank robber yourself, friend Blenkoff!" he mocked. "But this time you haven't quite managed to pull it off. Fetch the police, someone. I fancy they'll be rather interested to know what's in that deed-box."

* * *

THE CONTENTS OF that deed-box did prove somewhat interesting. For when it was opened it was found to contain a part of the Bohemian Crown jewels—much to the bank manager's amazement, who had been led to believe that it merely held legal documents, as the entry in his safe custody book stated.

The deed-box had been deposited with him during the War by Mr. John Falcon, whose real name was Lupinov, and who was a member of Blenkoff's gang of swindlers.

The waiter Lipsky, whose share in the plot cost him his life, was suspected to have been formerly a valet to one of the key-holders of the Prague Treasury who had since died.

The precise details of the plot will never be known; but it is evident that, during the turmoil and confusion of the War, some of the Crown jewels were taken from the Treasury for removal to Vienna, and that Lipsky, at Lupinov's instigation, succeeded in exchanging the deed-box in which they were stored.

Lupinov then deposited the deed-box at the bank, meaning to get it out of the country at the first opportunity. But Lipsky apparently stole the deposit from him and fled, managing somehow to reach England after the War.

He no doubt intended one day to return to Prague and possess himself of the jewels, but, fearing discovery, delayed the attempt. In the meantime, Lupinov had spent several years in prison for some other offence, but on coming out proceeded to track Lipsky down and extract vengeance.

Such are the facts concerning the mystery of the Bohemian Crown jewels, revealed in this story for the first time. And had it not been for the combined efforts of Sexton Blake, Tinker, and Granite Grant, it is probable that the mystery would never have been solved.

THE END

Notes

1. This is inspired by facts. The Bohemian Crown Jewels really exist and are, in truth, protected by seven locks with seven keys and seven key holders.

2. The Sexton Blake authors often worked against tight deadlines and the stories rarely went through anything resembling a rigorous editing process. Sometimes, the hurried writing showed. In this case, Granite Grant's use of the word "sonny" was so tediously frequent that it required a judicious excision here and there so as not to annoy modern readers.

GHOST MOBILE

THE FIRE POPPED and Pedro emitted a deep sigh.

Sexton Blake returned the Union Jack to the binder's top sleeve. He leaned back, smiling, and said, "Those were the days!"

"Do you miss them?" I asked.

"I might do were it not for one thing."

"Which is?"

"That these are also the days."

"And how does Mr Sexton Blake function in our skeptical modern world?"

I realised my mistake immediately. Current status classified! I raised a palm. "My apologies."

"One must change with the times," he murmured. He turned to the next issue. "Ah! Ruff Hanson."

"Larger than life."

"Indeed so. As was his author, Gwyn Evans. Whenever I undertook a case that became particularly, shall we say, colourful, I passed my notes to Gwyn. He had a knack, an ability to capture the strangeness that often emerged from the Credibility Gap."

"In terms of fellow detectives," I said, "at home, you had numerous Scotland Yard allies. William Spearing was the first, Detective-Inspector Coutts was the most popular, then there was Harker, Lennard, Martin, Widgeon, Thomas, Venner—"

Blake issued a derisive snort.

Superintendent Venner—who featured throughout the 'forties in issues of The Sexton Blake Library—had been portrayed by the author Anthony Parsons as a pompous and vain man who rode on Blake's coat-tails. An accurate depiction, to judge from the detective's reaction.

I went on, "But in the USA, it was Hanson, a private investigator, who offered you perhaps the most notable assistance."

"If you mean notable in the sense of memorable, then yes, you're probably right. Hanson was a blunt man who, though ill-suited to delicate situations, somehow always managed to blunder through them without breaking anything that didn't need to be broken."

He took out the story paper and opened its near-century old pages.

"The newspaper man Splash Page was involved in this one, too," he observed. "Along with some remarkably progressive technology!"

GHOST MOBILE

by Gwyn Evans
UNION JACK issue 1,467 (1931)

THE FIRST CHAPTER

The Ghost of Hangman's Hill.

KLAXON SHRIEKING, MOTOR throbbing, tyres skidding, the great grey limousine swept round the corner at sixty-five. Yellow headlights cut a savage slash through the gathering darkness on the new arterial road. It picked out dark thatched farms, fallow fields, clumps of dark trees with skeleton branches bordering the river in Mandeville Vale.

An Austin Seven squawked like a frightened chicken and swerved to the ditch to avoid the roaring grey monster.

At the wheel a grim, tight-lipped man crouched, eyes glaring into the darkness.

Speed!

The man's face was white and tense with the thrill of the desperate pace. The night wind screamed as he hurtled ahead. On the dashboard the needle hovered around seventy-five. He gave a short, savage laugh.

Speed!

The ether had crackled less than half an hour before

with an urgent SOS, and this wild ride through the night was John Gorman's answer.

On through the night he hurtled, fear gnawing at his heart. Less than an hour ago he had been dancing at the Blue Dragon night club without a care in the world. The band had played a lively melody and his partner was more than usually desirable and attractive. He had turned into the bar for a cocktail; then had come the summons, the SOS of the wireless.

Brief, simple, and urgent.

"Will John Gorman, of Wenford, return home at once as his mother has met with a bad accident and is seriously ill."

That was all. John Gorman had gulped down his cocktail, nodded a curt farewell to his dancing partner, and started up his powerful grey car. He had been up in town for a week, and now—

He glanced at the dial. The needle quivered between seventy and eighty. A grey mist hung over the bleak hillsides. The road ran in deep, wide curves down the Chilterns as he flashed like a streak through the darkness. He was aiming for the long, straight road of the valley.

Gorman tried to think of nothing but his driving. He did not dare conjecture what had happened to his mother, that dear, grey-haired old lady in the manor house at Wenford. The pressure of his accelerator foot increased. Through the gloom, a twinkle of yellow lights showed where Mandeville in the Vale, that thriving and new village, was situated.

Gorman gripped the steering-wheel until his knuckles shone bone-white as the car skimmed the brink of the last turn before he neared the straight.

Suddenly, with an involuntary gasp, he had made out an unsuspected black gash at the side of the white road—a side turning. Savagely he swung the steering-wheel. The dim shape of an enormous lorry loomed towards him. The brakes went on gently, gradually, but at that speed they screamed.

After that wild momentum the car seemed to crawl. But the needle of the speedometer showed forty.

The lorry grew larger. Gorman, peering ahead through the windscreen, felt the flesh crawl on his scalp. The great truck had not given him right of way. It advanced towards him like a vast juggernaut. Before he dimmed his headlights he glimpsed the figure of the driver. His mouth grew dry with sudden fear.

Death at the wheel!

For a split second he saw it. Two bony hands, fleshless; beneath the driver's cap, no face—simply a white, grinning skull.

John Gorman cried out just once. With a mighty effort he jerked his car past the rear wheels of the truck. Too late. His rear wings caught the rear of the lorry's body, swinging his automobile in a sweeping semicircle, and almost wrenching his arms from their sockets.

For a moment or two the giant limousine seemed to hang poised on two wheels, its tortured motor seemed to whine and scream in agony—then the splintering crash as the car overturned. A great gout of flame leapt up.

Silently—not even the throb of an engine—the lumbering lorry with its skeleton driver continued on its way. It was swallowed up a moment later in the grey, impalpable mist. So swiftly had it come and gone, so unnaturally silent was it, that in those last seconds of life Gorman had no time to decide if he had actually seen it.

Suddenly, above the fierce roar of the flames, a long drawn-out shriek echoed eerily in the hills, and a wild, fantastic figure appeared from behind the matted hedgerows, screaming in a shrill voice:

"Death! Ha, ha, ha! Death rides abroad to-night! Blood and flame at Hangman's Corner!"

In the crimson glare of the fire the gaunt figure of an ancient crone stood etched in black against the flaming background. She held aloft her skinny arms. Her hair was long and matted; it streamed over her shoulders. She was clad in tattered rags. Her two yellow fangs were bared in an exultant smile as she capered and gibbered on a little knoll above the blazing car.

"Death!" she screamed again, and flung back her head.

From her slavering lips a scream of bubbling, high-pitched hysterical laughter welled.

In the roadway a thousand-guinea car blazed; the crone capered madly round Jack Gorman's funeral pyre.

GAT MASTERS, GANGSTER, was in an ugly mood. In his own crude way Gat was not a bad burglar. He operated for five years before landing in the police net—which is not a bad average for a second-rate hoodlum. It was when he met Emerson Freece that he tripped up and took a seven year jolt at the Big House in Ossining—Sing Sing.

Released from Sing Sing, Gat Masters was a little greyer, a good deal tougher, and stiffer in the finger joints. But he was a lot more cunning, and in his heart, nursed for seven long weary years, the flame of vengeance glowed.

On the other hand, Emerson Freece, known in Chicago's underworld as "Rainy Day" Freece, had slipped through the law's fingers. He was a wise guy and, as his sobriquet indicates, had been wise enough to put by the proceeds of the million-dollar stick-up in the Farmer's National Bank.

Gat had been the unlucky one. His mouthpiece, a shyster lawyer named Aronberg, had done his best, but the District Attorney was out for a clean-up, with the result that Gat went up the Hudson to Sing Sing for seven years.

Emerson Freece, wise in his generation, had faded out with the boodle. Gat Masters had heard that he had slipped to Europe immediately after the trial, and that he himself had been left to hold the baby. And now, his penance done, Gat Masters, gun-man, released on parole, faced the world again. His mood was as ugly as his battered face.

He gravitated naturally towards his old haunts in Chicago's underworld. Most of his erstwhile companions had vanished, shot in feuds or gone to the pen, Gat felt no regrets about them. His whole life was preoccupied by and dedicated to one mission—to find Rainy Day Freece.

For seven years he had brooded on the injury. Freece had promised him a thirty-seventy split, and to see him through if it came to a showdown. The hold-up itself had been admittedly Freece's planning. It was audacious, cold-blooded and, up to a point, successful. Very little bloodshed, too. Freece had shot a bank messenger and winged one of the tellers while Gat had only found it necessary to club a cashier with his rod.

But for a stupid oversight, both crooks would have got away with it, but Gat got drunk and indiscreetly told 'Frisco Sal, his girl friend, that from that night on he was living on Easy Street.

This information reached the sharp ears of Detective O'Dare. Gat was pulled in, and Rainy Day Freece stirred not a finger to help.

Gat Masters had hoped against hope during the trial that Freece would turn the trick, but a cynical message delivered to him by a stool-pigeon from his fellow-crooks undeceived him. On the day Gat Masters changed his name for a number he learned that Rainy Day Freece had left New York for Europe, and with him the proceeds of the million-dollar stick-up.

Gat served his seven years, giving little trouble. He was released one grey day in February, caught the P. & A. for Chicago, and gravitated naturally towards Lou's Pool Parlour on the east side of the Windy City.

Lou was there, unchanged even after seven years. His lean, rat-like face was smooth and unwrinkled as ever. His patent leather hair slicked back with the same fastidious care from his sloping forehead. He greeted Gat with a nod as if he had seen him only yesterday.

"Hallo, Gat!" was all he said.

Gat Masters nodded.

"I wanna drink, Lou, an' a doss."

"Sure," said Lou the accommodating. "Y'r know y'r way in."

He jerked his head towards the dingy plush curtains which screened the Pool Parlour from the hideout beyond.

Gat Masters lurched through and found himself in a small room with several tables, at which sat half a dozen furtive-eyed, pasty-faced men, each of whom glanced at him suspiciously. They spoke in undertones without moving their lips. Gat Masters ordered a drink from a Chinese waiter.

A thin, emaciated young man, with eyes unnaturally bright and nostrils twitching incessantly, lurched over to the table.

"Hallo, Gat!" he greeted.

The ex-convict glowered at him suspiciously. He recognised the type, one of the innumerable hop-heads that infest Chicago's underworld; dope addicts. The man was a killer, one of the human vermin who fortify themselves with cocaine before bumping off their victims.

"Beat it," Gat growled, his ugly, brooding eyes lowering savagely.

"Aw, come off it, Gat!" said the other, with an insolent drawl. "Say, you still sore with Rainy Day Freece? Remember me, Gat, Italian Larry?[3] I see you in the Big House three years back."

Recognition dawned in Gat Masters' eyes, He grunted ungraciously, then made a place at his table.

"Sit down."

The dope fiend accepted with alacrity.

Gat Masters poured out four fingers of rye whisky and

drained it at a gulp.

"It's a dud life," said Larry. "Wot's a guy gonna do to make a livin'? The cops is gettin' wise to Lou's place. Wot's yer game now, Gat?"

The gagster shrugged his shoulders.

"Me—I ain't gotta game," he said. "Me nerve's gone. I can't lift a poke 'thout takin' the rap." He laughed discordantly. "Me, Gat Masters! Eff it hadn't been for that double-crossin' rat, I'da been on Easy Street now."

"Say, listen, Gat," said Larry. "Howdja like me to grubstake you till you find Freece? I got the wire that Rainy Day's quit the crook game. I met Flash Grey in N' York last fail. He wised me up that Freece is on the up an' up over in England, with a swell house and rolling in coin.

"This side's gettin' kinda too hot ter hold me, an' I've always had a hankerin' after Europe. The Spieler is crossin' over next week an' takin' me with 'im. How about taggin' along with the bunch? You used ter be pretty useful in the old days."

Gat Masters poured himself out another drink.

"The Spieler, eh?" he said reflectively. "Does he still tell as good a tale, Hoppy?"

Larry grinned evilly.

"You betcha," he remarked. "I've gotta date with him. He's on a sure fine graft, an' I don't mean maybe."

He looked up suddenly as four light taps sounded at the door. Instantly silence fell on the group of crooks.

FOR JUST A second Gat Masters' pasty, pock-marked face changed colour. He wetted his dry lips. Though he knew

120

it was one of the gang, seven years at Sing Sing had frayed his nerves, and he drained his drink at a gulp.

"Who's that?" he growled.

A greasy-faced Greek slouched to the door and pulled back a small flap at eye-level in the panel. He peered out, then grinned his shoulder at the group.

"The Spieler," he announced.

Italian Larry chuckled.

"Let him in."

The Greek pulled back the catch, and a moment later Spieler MacBride, one of the slickest-tongued men in America, strode elegantly into that smoke-laden room.

Gat glanced up at him from beneath his penthouse brows. They were poles apart, these two, the squat, thick-set Gat, and the elegant confidence-man in his smart tailored suit, and with his clean-cut face and sensitive hands. They possessed but one thing in common, and that was their attitude towards society. Each held that the world was his oyster, but whereas Gat Masters cracked his by brute force, the Spieler used charm and finesse.

The Spieler was, in his way, a figure of mystery even in the underworld, and the rougher element went in awe of him.

He paused for a moment on the threshold, and wrinkled his nostrils with disgust as he sniffed the stale air.

"Larry," he drawled, and there was the faintest hint of an American twang in his voice, "you do choose the most deplorable hangouts. Phew!"

He drew out a silk handkerchief and fanned himself delicately with it.

"Aw, can that high-hat stuff, Spieler! Meet Gat Masters."

The Spieler glanced sharply at the gangster, placed his soft hat and gloves on the table, and sat down.

"Charmed, Mr. Masters," he said. "And how are things up the river?"

"Rotten," returned Gat curtly. "An' don't you high-hat me!" he added truculently.

"You seem to be suffering from a grouch, my friend," said the Spieler.

"A grouch!" growled Gat Masters, and a vein throbbed dully in his low forehead. "I'll tell the cock-eyed world I've gotta grouch. Ever heard of Rainy Day Freece?"

"Often," said the Spieler. "He cleaned up a million on that Farmer's National stick-up, didn't he?"

"Yep, the dirty, double-crossing twister!" snarled Gat Masters. He thrust both ape-like hands towards the elegant crook. "See them mitts!" he growled.

The Spieler adjusted his monocle. It was typical of his status in Chicago's underworld that no one dared to laugh. He saw the broken nails and the thick, calloused fingers, and shuddered slightly.

"One day," snarled Gat Masters, "these mitts are gonna be dug in Freece's t'roat!"

"I see," said the Spieler softly. "Put by for a rainy day!"

Three smart raps sounded at the door, and again silence fell.

"Who's that?" snapped the Greek, cautiously opening the sliding panel.

"It's me!" grated back a voice. "Open up. The cops is comin'."

Italian Larry's face changed colour. Gat looked up

suspiciously. If he wished to avoid any one kind of individual more than another, it was policemen.

The door burst open; a cold draught swirled from the hallway. On the threshold stood a slim figure, masked and menacing. In his hand a blue-nosed automatic.

"It's a frame-up!" squealed a flabby-faced crook near the door. "Look out, Larry!"

The man at the door fired point blank at the speaker. But he dropped as the bullet whistled over his head and phutted into the wall. Instantly Larry's gun started to jet flashes of flame.

A clatter of overturned tables. The crack of bullets.

The Spieler, vaulting gracefully over a big divan in the corner, took cover. Larry, crouching behind a marble-topped table, fired spasmodically. Blood oozed from his shoulder. Gat Masters, yellow teeth bared, hurled the bottle full at the gunman. It splintered an inch above the killer's head.

"Croak him!" he spat.

Larry lunged across the room, but stopped in mid career. He spun round and slid to the floor. A neat, round hole was drilled in the centre of his forehead.

The gunman's automatic crackled twice again. The Greek squealed and crumpled beneath the table. With a howl of fury Gat Masters leapt across the room. He made for the door and slammed it shut. Bullets splintered the panelling, and Gat cursed as he felt a tearing, searing pain in his right shoulder.

A whistle shrilled somewhere, to be followed by a long and ominous silence. For nearly four minutes no one spoke. Only the Greek moaned horribly from underneath the table.

An immaculate figure emerged from behind the divan. He passed his handkerchief lightly over his lips, glanced down at the lifeless figure of Italian Larry, and shrugged his shoulders.

"Larry's got his," the Spieler said calmly. "We can let up now, I guess."

Gat Masters, cursing his wounded shoulder, glared savagely round the room.

"Have a drink," said the Spieler.

Less than ten minutes later the body of Larry had been removed, and the gang of crooks were playing poker.

Larry had got his—that was all. It was a mere incident in Chicago's underworld. In a city where three murders are committed a day, the sudden end of a notorious killer caused very little stir.

The gang gave him a funeral three days later. Amongst the wreaths was one that cost the whole of a hundred dollars from Tony Spinelli, chief of the Stove Pipe Gang, his murderer.

They take their murders lightly in the Windy City.

A week later Tony himself was riddled by machine-gun bullets in broad daylight at the corner of Madison and State Street. Both gangs called it square.

The Spieler had left Chicago by the Twentieth Century Limited half an hour before, in the company of Gat Masters. He was tired of Illinois. Europe called, and Gat Masters would be a useful henchman now that Larry had been bumped off.

THE SECOND CHAPTER

Twelve Red Dots.

SPLASH PAGE WAS sitting in his usual negligent attitude on his untidy desk in the news-room of that go-ahead newspaper, the "Daily Radio." He lit a gasper, yawned with boredom, and scanned the news flimsies on the spike.

He was known as "Splash" Page on the Street of Ink because his stories were usually splashed with enormous headlines across the front page of Britain's liveliest newspaper.

Good journalists are born, not made. There was a legend in Fleet Street that Splash was created with printer's ink in his veins. He had an uncanny nose for news, but to-night was an off night and Splash was feeling disgruntled.

So also was that important person, Julius Jones, the night news editor.

He sat at his desk sucking noisily at the clay cutty he affected, then called out suddenly in a stentorian voice that quivered the glass walls of the news-room.

"Splash!"

"Did you call, sweetheart?" asked Page demurely.

"Yes, indeed. See here, hold this. Get on to the story and see what you can do with it."

Julius forthwith handed him a telegram from the Wensford correspondent of the 'Radio.' Shorn of its journalese and telegraphic contractions, it ran as follows:

AN AMAZING SERIES of accidents on the lonely stretch of road three miles from Mandeville in the Vale, a pleasant little model village in the Chilterns, now appear to be related in an astounding fashion.

At the inquest held yesterday on John Gorman, 32, who was killed on this mysterious spot which bears locally the ominous name of "Hangman's Hill," evidence was given that a big vehicle backed out of a lane in front of Mr. Gorman's car.

The coroner stated that there was no opening at this spot from which any vehicle could have emerged. He described the mysterious lorry as being a phantom. It was revealed to-day that each tragedy of this ominous road is preceded by an apparition of a ghostly motor-lorry.

For the past two years this stretch of road has been the scene of numerous motor accidents. An amazing feature is that it has been found impossible to discover any real explanation of the mystery. Pedestrians have been run down and killed or seriously injured.

On every occasion the driver has declared that the victims were invisible to him until it was too late to avoid them.

Mr. Wilfred Butler, the licensee of a lonely inn some quarter of a mile away from the scene of the smash, stated to-day that two or three times he has seen a phantom lorry on the road.

He states that the ghost vehicle makes absolutely no sound and that it vanishes into thin air after proceeding about three hundred yards. The coroner invited members of the jury to visit the ill-omened spot at midnight to see if they could discover any supernatural manifestations.

The greatest excitement prevails locally. The jury returned a verdict of "Accidental Death," but local feeling insists upon a further investigation of the mystery.

Splash Page laid down the telegram, and his keen, alert face was very thoughtful.

"Julius," he said, "this looks like being a peach of a story. Not that I believe in ghosts, but it's queer that all these unexplained accidents should take place on that spot."

"Go to it," said Julius Jones. "Find out if any of them have been insured by the 'Radio.'"

"STRAWDONARY! MOST STRAWDONARY, what! When I was in Poona in '84, a subaltern of mine named Faunceroy told me a story about a phantom rickshaw. I thought the fellah had been liftin' his elbow too much at the time, but now I realise that there are more things in heaven and earth, as Shakespeare says—or was it Kipling?—than are dreamt of in our philosophy."

Colonel Hannibal Smith, J.P., F.R.A.S., puffed at his cheroot and blew a pungent cloud of smoke to the rafters of the roof of the spacious club-room on the Mandeville golf links.

Young Maltravers stifled a yawn.

The colonel's yarns were apt to be tedious, but it would have been almost lèse-majesté[4] to have interrupted him in his reminiscences, for Colonel Hannibal Smith was a person of some consequence in Mandeville in the Vale.

There were half a dozen members in the club smoking-room. Young Maltravers, twenty-four, a slim, athletic figure in plus-fours, was the son of an eminent City man, Hector Maltravers, who lived at Beach Dene, the nearest house adjoining the colonel's estate.

Mandeville in the Vale is unique.

It is a modern village, built and run in the spacious manner of Tudor times. Situated a little more than forty miles from Charing Cross, close to the Chilterns, it had been established little less than four years. As the colonel had said when he had broached his scheme to Mr. Carrington Lang, the architect:

"Damme, sir, when I came back from India I expected to find at least a little corner of the old country unspoilt by jerry-built bungalows, obscene petrol pumps, and cinemas. And what do I find? The whole of the Chilterns a rash of bungaloids. No decency, no privacy, and a cursed Bolshevist spirit rampant amongst the working class! Yes, sir—rampant!"

And he snorted like a war horse.

They were sentiments with which Mr. Carrington Lang cordially agreed, both from policy and conviction. The colonel was a very wealthy man, and when he broached his scheme of the erection of a model estate with houses built suitably to accommodate professional men of means, Mr. Lang was in whole-hearted agreement.

"Nothing tripperish; nothing jerry built!" had been Colonel Hannibal Smith's instructions.

Carrington Lang interpreted them, and Mandeville in the Vale materialised. It was a pleasant spot, and though the colonel's outlay on the estate had been considerable, the result had justified his expectations.

The place possessed no railway station, the railway served the little town of Mandeville Magna some four miles distant from Mandeville in the Vale.

The inhabitants of the latter spot were not inconvenienced however, for each possessed an automobile, except young Maltravers, who more than made up for the deficiency by being the proud owner of a Moth plane.

Mandeville in the Vale prospered and grew, and life there was easy and pleasant, provided one conformed to Colonel Hannibal Smith's benevolent despotism. There were no shops nearer than Mandeville Magna, but there was an excellent golf course handy, and some good shooting on the colonel's estate.

It was a contented, prosperous community. An ideal dormitory and playground for the captains of industry who spent most of their time in the City during the day.

If Colonel Hannibal Smith was inclined to be somewhat of a Pooh Bah in the district, the fact caused very little friction.

This evening the golf club-room fireside was filled with the leading citizens of Mandeville in the Vale.

First there was the colonel himself, a spare, wiry man with a lean, tanned face, and tough as whipcord. He had piercing blue eyes beneath bushy white eyebrows, which latter were rather more abundant than his small, close-clipped moustache.

Lounging in an armchair sat the designer of Mandeville in the Vale, Mr. Carrington Lang, a tubby little man with an egg-shaped head, and a round, chubby face. Next to him, tall, black-haired, and scholarly, with a shrewd, clean-shaven face ornamented with wispy sideboards and wearing a pair of heavy shell-rimmed spectacles, sat Dr. Ivan Novak. He was a celebrated psychiatrist, with a considerable practice in Harley Street as a mental specialist.

In addition to young Maltravers, Mr. Walter Nesbit of the old-established firm of Nesbit, Wister, Appleton and Nesbit, solicitors, sat pulling a reflective pipe.

The conversation had turned naturally on the topic of the tragedy of Hangman's Hill. The inquest had been held that day by the coroner, Dr. Walford Wells, at Mandeville Magna. The colonel had been present and had retailed to the others, who had just returned from town, a more or less detailed account of the affair.

"But dash it all, colonel," broke in young Maltravers, "it seems so beastly silly, somehow. What I mean is, one always associates ghosts with moated granges, clanking chains, an' all that. A really respectable ghost is never less than a hundred years old. What do you say, doc?"

Dr. Novak's grave face relaxed into a smile.

"That is the popular conception," he remarked.

"I don't see," said Maltravers, lighting a cigarette, "how on earth a mechanical prosaic thing like a motor-lorry can have a ghost? Admittedly that bend at Hangman's Hill is a nasty, eerie sort of spot—I remember when I had my motor-bike I often thought I saw a motor-car with

130

headlights, and yet when I looked again it wasn't there—but I don't think there was anything supernatural about it. The light's very tricky at night."

Carrington Lang cleared his throat.

"I'm not so sure," he said gravely. "About two months ago I was driving slowly along the road—I wasn't doing more than twenty—when I suddenly saw the back of a large open lorry turn out from a side turning I never remember seeing before. I swerved suddenly and I was almost thrown out of the car. They told me—or at least Constable Pierce told me when I met him close by the Wheatsheaf—that I couldn't possibly have seen a lorry—yet I'm positive I did."

"Humph!" said the colonel. "Frankly, gentlemen, I don't know what to make of it. I heard a very queer story down in the village this morning. Do you remember about six years ago there was a terrible accident on that very spot?

"A motor-lorry belonging to the Chiltern Provision Co. skidded and overturned, the petrol tank burst into flames and the unfortunate driver, a young fellow named Haggarty—who was to have been married in a week's time—was burnt to a cinder in the debris?"

The lawyer nodded.

"Yes, I certainly recall it," he remarked. "He was the only son of widow Haggarty of Scrubb Wood Farm; and incidentally, Novak, this is something in your line," he added, turning to the doctor. "The poor old soul has never been the same since the accident. She was ill for months with brain fever and I'm told that she is non compos mentis. She wanders about at certain times, especially when the moon is full, and frightens everybody in the village."

"Indeed?" said Dr. Ivan Novak. "Has she no one to look after her?"

The lawyer shook his head.

"No. She owns the farm—it is only a small holding. I'm afraid she will be having the sanitary inspector after her; I'm told it's in a shocking state. The poor creature is quite harmless, though local people credit her with being a witch."

"Hrmph—nonsense!" broke in the colonel. "Silly yokel's gossip!"

Dr. Novak's strange greenish eyes rested speculatively on the colonel's mahogany, weather-beaten face.

"I think it would repay me if I dropped in some time at Scrubb Wood Farm!" he said. "I've always been interested in rustic superstition, especially in its relation to witchcraft!"

"Stuff and nonsense!" said Colonel Hannibal Smith. He turned to the lawyer. "Nesbit, my boy, what about a rubber of bridge?"

A tap sounded at the door, and Fenton, the club steward, entered.

"A letter for you, colonel!" he said, handing over a buff-coloured envelope.

The colonel glanced at the superscription and opened it with a murmur of apology. While the others moved towards the card tables he opened the missive. The envelope contained no letter, but a small object.

With fingers that shook, the colonel extracted therefrom a little ivory domino with twelve scarlet spots—the double six.

For a moment or two he stared wide-eyed at the envelope, then gasped hoarsely:

"Who—who brought this, Fenton?"

"Jenks, sir," replied the steward— "one of the caddies. He tells me a stranger gave him a shilling to deliver it."

"I see!" said Colonel Hannibal Smith dully.

He replaced the ivory oblong in the envelope and put it in his pocket.

His eyes were haunted. He turned with an effort to join his companions. Nesbit had just opened a new pack of cards. The colonel helped himself to a stiff whisky-and-soda.

Suddenly he paused and the glass clattered against his teeth. A wild scream rang out from the darkness. Then a burst of mocking, maniacal laughter that turned his blood to ice.

"What's that?" gasped young Maltravers.

The group was frozen into immobility as the echoes of that ghastly laugh died away on the chill night breeze.

For a full minute no one spoke.

Young Maltravers was the first to rise to his feet. He dashed to the door of the club-room, opened it, peered out. A chill wind moaned eerily over the common. The echo of that ghastly laugh had died away on the misty downs.

Fenton, the steward, white-faced, peered over his shoulder.

"Did—did you hear it, sir?"

"Hear it?" echoed Maltravers. "Gosh, I'll never forget it! Tell you what, Fenton, this is an occasion for a long, stiff drink!"

He gave one last glance at the fog-filled night; then, with obvious relief, turned into the club again.

Colonel Hannibal Smith glanced at him sharply. Nesbit was shuffling a pack of cards.

"Probably an owl or something," said Maltravers.

"Owls don't laugh!" growled Novak.

It cannot be said that the rest of the evening was a particular success. A sudden damper had fallen on the little group. It was only Novak, the scientist, who ventured any rationalistic explanation of that eldritch yell.

"It is either one of those confounded new motor sirens that Jerry Wiltshire delights in, or it may be our nocturnal friend, the hag, Haggarty."

The gathering broke up suddenly shortly after ten. Colonel Hannibal Smith went home in his little Bentley two-seater, a silent and badly scared man. He was not thinking of screams or ghostly laughs, but of twelve red dots.

THE THIRD CHAPTER

Visitors at the Wheatsheaf.

DEREK PAGE'S INFALLIBLE method of procedure when tackling a news story was: "When in doubt, try the local pub."

He arrived at Mandeville Magna in his rakish roadster, which Tinker, Sexton Blake's young assistant, had nicknamed the "Red Peril," shortly after half-past nine.

He found it a straggling hamlet, nestling in the shadow of the Chilterns. Found, also, it boasted of five public houses, one parish church, and one Baptist chapel.

He chose the most comfortable-looking of the buildings. He needed more spirituous than spiritual ministrations, for it was a foggy night.

Mine host of the Wheatsheaf—a tall, slow-moving man named Amos Ayres—greeted the journalist with a deferential nod. Splash entered the crowded tap-room and ordered a room and a drink. He scanned the sanded, oak-beamed bar. Its customers, he noted, consisted of small tradesmen and one or two ruddy-cheeked yokels.

The landlord breathed heavily on a pewter tankard he was polishing and replaced it on the rack.

"Eff you'd like the zaloon-bar, zur," he ventured. "Zo as you could zign the register—"

"Right-ho!" said Splash. "And you might get me something to eat as well."

The landlord touched his forelock, and Splash followed him into the adjoining room. It was a cosy little place, with a cheerful fire blazing in the grate. The room was occupied by a lone figure in a settle seat at the corner.

Splash warmed his hands at the blaze and nodded a greeting. The other inclined his head in acknowledgment and resumed the perusal of a local paper. The journalist sized him up when the landlord had bustled out to prepare his supper. The stranger was dressed in a comfortable suit of grey moleskin, a somewhat uncommon suit, Splash noted, for it was cut on the lines of plus fours. He had a tight-lipped mouth and close-clipped moustache. His grizzled hair was cut short and stood up like the bristles of a brush.

But it was his eyes that held Splash. Hard as agate, with something of that stone's greenish hue. No smile softened the austerity of his stern features. He looked like a man of indomitable and inflexible will. Not once did he glance up from his paper. Splash Page wondered who he was.

He engaged the landlord in conversation when that worthy had brought his meal.

"How far is Mandeville in the Vale from here?" he inquired.

"Matter of four miles, zur. It be a rare foggy night to go a-motoring," he added. "Would you be stayin' here long?"

"Oh, a few days, I should fancy," answered Splash. "They say you can get some fairly decent golf round here." He raised his voice for the benefit of the man in moleskin, who continued reading and evinced no sign that he had heard.

"You're right," added Splash; "it's a foul night for motoring. Hardly see your hand before your face. Incidentally, I heard there's been a shocking accident somewhere near here."

"Ay, that's true, zur; an' it ain't the first nor yet the last, I'm thinkin'."

"Indeed?" Splash Page did not hurry the man.

It was not his way when angling for information. He resolved to adjourn after supper to the four-ale bar and engage the local yokels in a friendly game of shove-ha'penny or darts. He had already decided that he would obtain very little conversational change from the taciturn man in the corner.

The landlord moved away to attend to his more vociferous customers in the tap-room, and Splash continued his meal in silence.

Supper over, he lit a cigarette and strolled over to the adjoining room, just as the inn door opened suddenly and a wild-eyed, dishevelled figure burst into the bar.

"A brandy—quick!" gasped the newcomer in a shaking voice. He swayed, and would have fallen had he not clutched the counter.

* * *

IT WAS THEN that Splash noted that the man had a wooden leg, a peg strapped to the stump of his corduroy trousers. His face was ghastly white. It was obvious that, despite his deformity, the man had been running with desperate haste. He was frightened to the marrow.

"Quick—a brandy!" he repeated, with chattering teeth.

Amos Ayres glanced sharply at the cripple.

"Now, what's all this, Jem Chance?" he said sternly. "You know you don't drink sperrets—"

"But I see'd it!" gasped the shaking man. "Three miles back on the Wriklin road. The Ghost Lorry!"

Splash Page flung a coin on the counter.

"Have it with me," he said. "You seem to have had a shock, old man."

Jem Chance seized the tumbler greedily. It rattled against his tobacco-stained teeth as he gulped the brandy down gratefully. A tinge of colour crept back to his ashen cheeks.

"Naw, then," said the landlord, "pull yourself together! Comin' in with all them wild yarns!"

A silence, tense and dramatic, fell on the crowded tap-room and for once Jem Chance, the local poacher, found himself in the pleasant position of having everyone in the pub hanging on his words. He was not exactly a popular customer. He had long been disliked for what the locals called his "artfulness."

"Thank 'ee kindly, sir," he said to Splash Page. "If you'd see'd what I've see'd to-night, you'd understand."

"But what did you see?" broke in the landlord's impatient voice.

Jem Chance lowered his voice and glanced fearfully over his shoulder.

"The Ghost Lorry," he repeated. "An' as true as I stand 'ere, it 'ad a skelington a-drivin' of it. It came along by 'Angman's 'Ill so quiet an' so sudden—just like a howl swoops down on a mouse. I were takin' my dog—Tray, that is—an' goin' for a stroll where the old chalk-pit be."

"An' where they little old rabbits be, too!" chuckled the landlord maliciously. "You been drinkin', that's what, Jem!" he said.

The poacher scowled. He slapped his stick against his wooden leg with a hard crack.

"Drinkin'?" he said. "S'welp me, I ain't had a drop all day!"

He turned for encouragement to Splash Page.

"I tell 'ee, sir, would I be lyin'? I that 'ad this 'ere leg took off a year ago an' near killed all on account of the Ghost Lorry at 'Angman's 'Ill! I—I tell 'ee all, 'ere an' now, there be a curse on the place, an' I wouldn't go near it again, not for a million pounds!"

The dead silence that followed the man's words was shattered by a long-drawn-out hoot of a klaxon horn and the harsh grinding of brakes in the High Street.

For a moment no one spoke, Jem Chance shivered violently.

Rat-tat-tat! Three loud, imperious knocks reverberated through the ancient inn.

"For 'evvin's 'sake don't open the door!" he begged, and there was stark horror in his tones.

Splash Page's keen, journalistic brain sensed at once the

dramatic effect of that thunderous clamour on the door.

It was close on ten o'clock, but it was obvious that Ayres would have a difficult job in getting rid of his customers in accordance with the law. The landlord's big, heavy-jowled features reddened and it was with reluctance that he advanced to open the outer door which gave on to the saloon bar. The tap-room had a separate entrance of its own. He was spared the ignominy of retreat, however, for the door opened with a swish and two figures stood on the threshold, followed by a swirl of fog.

IN THE HALF light in the passage they looked monstrous and grotesque in their heavy coats. One of them, the taller of the two, wore a flying helmet, the goggles of which were pushed up over his forehead, giving him the uncanny appearance of having two pairs of eyes.

His companion, a burly, thick-set man, looked to Splash Page like a pugilist.

"Say," drawled the man in the goggles, "can you tell me where abouts we are? This doggone fog has got us down. Have you got a garage and an apartment for me and my valet?"

Amos scratched his chin dubiously. Americans were rare visitors at this time of year to Mandeville Magna.

"Well, zur," be began doubtfully, "it's jest on closing-time, an' I dunno as 'ow—"

"Forget it, son! Eff you're full up, we can flop down anywhere," said the stranger. Ostentatiously he opened his leather coat and took out a bulging note-case.

From it he extracted a couple of notes, and Splash

noticed that he took good care to reveal a thick wad of money. The sight of the note seemed to reassure the landlord. He glanced significantly at the clock, but his voice was not so peremptory as usual when he called out: "Time, gentlemen, please!"

"Will you have a drink with me?" said Splash Page. "I'm staying here," he added, when the last tardy yokel had lumbered out into the night.

He heard the thud of Jem Chance's wooden leg and his shrill, complaining voice die away in the distance.

"I guess that's real handsome of you, sir," said the American, with a smile which revealed two glistening gold teeth. "My name is Skinner—Flaxman P. Skinner of Hertford, Connecticut. Say, Budd, see if you can forage round and get some eats," he added to his battered-visaged companion.

Under the mellowing influence of a second whisky, the genial Mr. Skinner grew expansive. After anathematising the fog, he announced that he was in England on a little business proposition, and was thinking of hiring a house in the district which would be handy to London and give him a real opportunity of seeing the English countryside.

Splash found him affable, amusing, and undoubtedly intelligent. That subtle sixth sense of his warned him not to take the man at his face value, however.

When he at length followed his ill-favoured valet in the wake of the landlord, Splash was left to cogitate on the strange things that had happened within an hour of his arrival at the village.

First there was the taciturn man in moleskin. A

surreptitious glance at the registration book revealed very little about his antecedents. Just a line of entry:

"Challoner, C. E., ret., London. Nationality, British."

He learned from the landlord that Colonel Challoner had arrived after the inquest and had retired to bed shortly before closing time.

Next, there was the scared poacher and his ghost story; and finally the arrival of this pair of Americans at this quite unlikely time and place.

Splash was puzzled. Whether it was the grey fog and the air, or constraint about the landlord, he could not define; but an impalpable atmosphere of mystery and evil seemed to brood over the Wheatsheaf.

HAD HE BEEN present in the bed-room at the end of the corridor some distance from his own room, he would have realised that his hunch about the strangeness of the Americans was justified.

The elegant Mr. Skinner divested himself of his outer garments, revealing a dandified suit of pewter grey. He lit a cheroot and turned to his valet.

"Waal, Gat," he drawled, "I reckon you an' I are on Easy Street. We've found him, and we've tipped him off."

Gat Masters' flaccid mouth twisted into a grin.

"You've said it, Spieler," he remarked. "But I reckon this is a hole of a country to be landed in on a foggy night."

"Patience, have patience, Gat," replied the confidence man. "In the morning you'll be able to behold all the beauties of this fair and sylvan landscape."

It was typical of the Spieler to use a British accent when talking to his henchman, and an American accent when in conversation with Englishmen. He knew to a nicety the psychological effect it would create.

"Aw, shucks!" said Gat Masters. "I tell you, Spieler, that I'm gonna settle with Rainy Day Freece first, an' then we'll pull this trick o' yours."

"You'll do nothing of the sort, my dear fellow," said the Spieler, menace in his smooth voice. "Don't forget that Scotland Yard are not fools, and that they hang a man very quickly in this country."

"Huh!" grunted the gangster. "Eff things don't move soon, I guess I'll pull out on this deal."

"Don't be a fool," returned the other. "I tell you there's a cool million dollars in this if you stick by me. I brought you over, and what's the use bumping off Rainy Day Freece till we've got a chance of getting hold of some of the cash?"

Gat Masters grinned crookedly. With his low beetle brows and harsh accent, he was a queer specimen to be found in an English wayside inn.

That night Amos Ayres slept badly, but Splash Page slept not at all. He was busy arranging his assignments for to-morrow. The strange story of the Ghost Lorry had gripped his imagination. Jem Chance's narrative had held the ring of truth. What strange malign influence was at work in this sleepy Buckinghamshire village? What was the explanation of this phantom car—this ghost automobile? Ghostmobile! The word flashed into his head; it had just the snappy ring for a headline.

He made a mental note of it as he stared into the darkness of the inn bed-room. To-morrow promised to be an exciting day.

THE FOURTH CHAPTER

The Man From Bleakmoor.

SEXTON BLAKE, THE celebrated detective, came out of the fog-laden air of Baker Street into the cosy warmth of his consulting-room, and found his assistant, Tinker, sitting on a hassock, reading a copy of the 'Daily Radio.'

The youngster looked up with a smile of greeting.

"Well, guv'nor, any luck?" he inquired as the detective doffed his hat and coat.

Blake glanced at the clock. It was nearly 2 p.m., and as he exchanged his overcoat for the comfort of his dilapidated dressing-gown, he reached for his briar.

"A tedious and tiring morning," he said. "Did you find those Morrison cuttings, young 'un?"

Tinker grimaced.

"Yes, guv'nor, and that was a tedious and tiring job, too. Gosh! I wish something would turn up! This Morrison business seems to be all routine and no action!"

Blake smiled tolerantly as he lit his pipe.

145

A tap had sounded at the door. Mrs. Bardell entered at Blake's response, with an orange envelope in her hand.

"Which there's a telegraft arrived for you, Mr. Blake," said the worthy woman. "And I wishes you would use your influenza with the Postmaster General about those audacious young limbs, the telegraft-boys, and the way they pulls my bell almost out of its sukket!"

Blake's lips twitched as he ripped open the radiogram. Mrs. Bardell's English seemed to get weirder and more wonderful as the years went by.

The message was laconic and typical:

"Howdy hitting London eight to-night.—RUFF STUFF HANSON."

Blake saw that it had been wirelessed from the Aquitania. He tossed the missive across to Tinker.

"Hold that one, young 'un!" he remarked. "That ought to stop your worry about routine and action!"

Tinker grinned delightedly as he read it. The wire was from their old friend, Ruff Hanson, the dynamic American gunman sleuth.

"Gosh! That sounds good, guv'nor!" he said, with a chuckle. "I wonder what the old big stiff's coming to England for now?"

Blake shrugged. A visit from Ruff Hanson invariably indicated a certain liveliness. Hanson was one of Blake's New York agents—a very welcome colleague.

"I say, guv'nor!" remarked Tinker a few moments later, looking up from his resumed reading of the 'Radio.' "It's a funny business this phantom motor-lorry affair down in

Bucks! I see Splash Page has gone down to investigate it!"

He handed the newspaper over to Blake, and pointed to the heavy scare headlines of Splash Page's feature, eminently typical of that ebullient journalist.

"TERROR IN BUCKS.

GRIM LEGEND OF HANGMAN'S HILL.

THE GHOSTMOBILE.

By Derek Page.

"Mandeville Magna, Wednesday.

"The Phantom Lorry, which was graphically described by the coroner, Dr. Walford Wells, on Monday, at the inquest held on John Gorman, who was burnt to death in a mysterious car accident, has again spread panic and terror in this quiet Chiltern village.

"What is the mystery of this strange Ghostmobile? And what malign curse hangs over the ill-omened Hangman's Corner? To-day I have interviewed a score of reputable witnesses, and each has strange stories to tell of this sinister spot. I have carefully compiled a list of accidents that have occurred here during the past two years from the official police reports.

"It is an appalling record. No fewer than thirteen serious motor accidents, seven of which ended fatally, are tabulated. I have personally investigated, both at night and in broad daylight, this ominous corner, and, though a rational explanation will undoubtedly be found, the mystery has not yet been satisfactorily explained.

"The inhabitants of the district are terror-stricken. Jem Chance, a labourer who was knocked down by a motor-cycle combination and severely injured nearly a year ago, stated emphatically last night that for the second time he had encountered the Phantom Lorry. He gave a graphic description of this weird vehicle."

Blake looked up from the report.

"Typical Splash Page stuff!" he remarked, with a smile. "I'm afraid, however, I am rather sceptical about the Ghostmobile. There is such thing as collective hallucination, and I am not impressed by the number of witnesses. Crowds are just as liable to be inaccurate as the evidence of one."

The phone bell shrilled, and Blake reached for the receiver. His eye-brows lifted quizzically as he recognised the vibrant, eager voice of Splash Page himself.

"That you, Blake, old man?"

"Speaking. What's the matter now? Have you solved the Ghostmobile mystery?"

"Solved it?" said Splash. "By Gosh, Blake, this is the weirdest and most uncanny story I've ever handled! The devilish thing has taken a toll of another victim!"

"Not so much of the Fleet Street jargon!" said Blake. 'Do you mean that somebody else has—"

"Yes!" replied Splash. "And, what's more, Blake— here's the staggering part of it—the Ghostmobile was seen to-day—an hour ago—in broad daylight by at least three witnesses, who all swear that the dashed thing vanished

148

before their eyes. What's more, the body of a man was found frightfully mangled at the side of the road within a few minutes of the Ghostmobile's passing! Can't you come over and look into this business? This is right in your line. I've phoned the 'Radio,' and they are keen on having you! The paper will pay all expenses, of course!"

Blake hesitated.

"It sounds interesting, Splash; but I've just had a radiogram from Ruff Hanson, saying he'll be here by to-night's boat-train."

"Ruff? Oh, good man!" said Splash enthusiastically. "Bring him with you!"

"Who is the victim that has been—er—taken toll of?" asked Blake.

"A chap named Challoner; he's a retired colonel, I believe. Secretive sort of devil. I met him last night, but he was very stand-offish. Poor devil! He'd come down for the sake of his health, I understand. Probably a retired Indian Army man. I'm just following up his history."

Sexton Blake pursed his lips for a moment; then:

"I—I think I can save you the trouble," he said. "I knew Challoner well!"

"Eh?" ejaculated Splash, in astonishment. "I thought his face looked vaguely familiar. One of your crook friends, Blake?"

"On the contrary," said Sexton Blake. "But he has lived surrounded by crooks for the past seven years!"

"Lived amongst crooks?" echoed the journalist.

"Precisely," said Sexton Blake dryly. "He used to be the Governor of Bleakmoor Prison!"

IT WAS WITH a very thoughtful expression that Splash Page emerged from the post office in Mandeville Magna and entered his vermilion roadster.

He was frankly puzzled. He had spent the morning gossiping with the local villagers, and an hour before had paid a visit to Mandeville in the Vale. Here he had found himself a welcome guest at the golf club. He knew young Maltravers slightly, and had been introduced into that select coterie which made the synthetic Tudor village one of the most exclusive communities in the South of England.

He would have liked to have met Colonel Hannibal Smith, but that far from happy warrior had been called up to town on urgent business. The plump Mr. Carrington Lang, however, had been delighted to air his views, not only on the Gorman tragedy, but on the diverse subjects of architecture, town planning, modern drainage, arterial roads, the recent General Election, the Gold Standard, the 'Evening Standard,' and the standard of living.

Splash, with the patience that Fleet Street journalists have acquired, listened on the off-chance of gaining a grain or two of wheat from the chaff of the architect's verbiage.

He found Mandeville in the Vale a picturesque enough spot. Carrington Lang had done a fairly good job, and the houses, if a trifle garish without the mellow touch of time, seemed to be large and well-planned.

Colonel Hannibal Smith's home dominated the estate. It was on a low hill, half-timbered gabled structure with a long, broad driveway and a glade of beech and fir trees. Splash learnt that the gallant colonel's hobbies were both earthy and heavenly, but that they both had to do with spheres. Golf and astronomy.

Carrington Lang, proud of this local landmark which added such tone to the place, pointed out the observatory, a domed tower on the crest of the hill, adjoining the colonel's house.

Splash was interested to learn that the famous Dr. Ivan Novak was a member of the community. But though both Maltravers and Lang had been willing enough to open up about Mandeville's inhabitants, he found very little material to go on regarding the Ghostmobile. He had returned to the Wheatsheaf shortly after lunch, and it was then that the amazing news reached him that the phantom motor-lorry had again been seen on Hangman's Hill.

He phoned the preliminary details and was now on his second visit to the local police station. The body of Challoner had been removed to the local mortuary. The doctor, a tall, grey-haired, bearded man, had just emerged from the mortuary when Splash Page entered. He was accompanied by Inspector Graves, of the local constabulary.

The inspector, Splash was pleased to note, was one of the new type of official; brisk, assured, and unexpectedly youthful.

"Ah, Mr. Page," he said. "Bad news travels fast. You've heard the latest, of course?"

Splash nodded.

"The whole village is agog with it, inspector," he said, and with the ease born of long practice made himself affable to officialdom.

"What exactly is the real low-down on this, inspector?" he asked when Dr. Wells had taken his departure.

They were both seated in the inspector's little room at the back of the local police station. For answer, the other pointed to the official buff forms on the desk.

"If you will treat this matter in confidence, Mr. Page," he said, "I don't mind you having a look at these. I don't hold with the old-fashioned notion of excluding journalists. I believe that the Press and the police should work in harmony."

"Quite," said Splash. "If only a few more at headquarters were of the same sentiment, inspector, I think there would be fewer unsolved mysteries. You can rest assured that I won't put my foot in it."

He proffered his cigarette-case and scanned the curt official documents with interest.

"I see that the preliminary medical report is that deceased met his death about six hours ago. That's strange."

The inspector smiled grimly.

"That's not the only strange thing about the case."

"But I thought he was killed by the Ghostmobile," said Splash, puzzled. "And I find our dear old friend 'some blunt instrument' was present at the time. This is extraordinary."

"I thought that would startle you, Mr. Page," said Graves. "It startled me. But Dr. Walford Wells is a pretty sound man. The unfortunate Colonel Challoner was clubbed by some blunt—"

He hesitated.

"Go on, say it," said Splash. "A fortune awaits the man

who invents an alternative phrase for that. It means, of course, that Colonel Challoner was murdered at eight this morning. What on earth was he doing out so early?"

"That's just what I'd like to know," replied the inspector. "The landlord of the Wheatsheaf told me he got up at six."

"Did he take his golf clubs with him?" asked Splash.

The other shook his head.

"No, he said he was going to take a brisk walk as far as the golf links, though."

"H'm!" said Splash thoughtfully. "I suppose you know who he was?"

"Well," the inspector hesitated. "I haven't been all through his papers yet, but he seems to have been a person of some consequence judging by—"

"Well, then I can save you some trouble," broke in Splash, echoing Blake's own words to him. "He was the ex-governor of Bleakmoor prison."

"*What!*" gasped the startled inspector. "Good lor', Mr. Page, now I remember why the name sounded so familiar. The ex-governor of Bleakmoor murdered here in Mandeville: it seems almost incredible!"

"Incredible or not," returned Splash, "it's true! The point is why was he murdered! Prison governors are not as a rule very popular people, but—I suppose you haven't any ex-convicts living in the district?" he added as an afterthought.

The inspector looked startled.

"Well—er—no," he said slowly. "Unless, of course, you consider Jem Chance one. He got six months hard for poaching a while back."

"Jem Chance?" echoed Splash Page. And his face grew very thoughtful as he recalled the white-faced shaking man who had gabbled his incoherent story of the Ghostmobile at the Wheatsheaf the previous night. "Well, yes—perhaps."

"Now, look here, inspector," said Splash in a sudden burst of frankness. "Let's get this straight. Do you or do you not believe in this phantom motor-lorry?"

Graves rubbed his chin thoughtfully and hesitated.

"Well, between you and me, sir, I don't know what to say," he said. "I'm not a superstitious man, but there have been so many queer happenings on Hangman's Hill that I'm beginning to think there's some truth about the place being haunted. Of course, driving at night is always a tricky business, but so many people have sworn that they've seen this queer ghost car that there must be some foundation for the story."

"But this is the first time it's been seen in broad daylight," said Splash. "Who was it that actually saw it?"

The inspector smiled.

"Three independent and perfectly reliable witnesses," he remarked. "I have their statements here if you care to see them. One is Mr. Carrington Lang. The second is a man named Mockser, who is a driver for the local gravel merchants in Mandeville quarry; and the third is an American gentleman named Skinner—let me see—yes, Flaxman Skinner."

Splash Page glanced at the brief reports. In substance they were all the same. The sum total was that a strange lorry, making no noise, swept round the bend of

Hangman's Hill at between forty and fifty miles an hour. The lorry driver, Mockser, stated that his vehicle swerved violently for a reason he could not explain. Each witness was emphatic about the silence, and that the lorry seemed to disappear after travelling little more than five hundred yards round the hairpin bend.

"I met this Mr. Skinner last night," said Splash. "He seemed a level-headed sort of bloke. I think I'll go round and interview him. He's staying at the Wheatsheaf.

"And if I were you, inspector," he added, "I'd keep an eye on Jem Chance."

"You leave that to me," replied the official grimly. "My men are already out photographing and searching the spot where poor Colonel Challoner's body was found. At first glance it looked as if he had been run over, but Dr. Wells is positive from the type of the injury that he was clubbed to death before the wheels of the car passed over him."

"It must be a pretty solid ghost," interjected Splash Page, "if its wheels can be responsible for such injuries."

Hardened newspaper man though he was, he shivered slightly as he replaced the doctor's detailed medical description.

He rose to his feet.

"By the way, inspector," he added, "I'm expecting a very good friend of mine down this evening. I hope you won't mind him looking into the matter? His name is Blake."

"Not Sexton Blake?" said Graves, and his face lit up with a smile.

"Yes, Sexton Blake," said Splash.

"But that's splendid!" commented the other. "I met Mr. Blake when I was a sergeant in the Y Division. He helped me out of a very nasty mess once," he added reminiscently.

Splash Page chuckled inwardly. Things were moving according to plan. Usually the provincial police were prejudiced against outside interference, but it was obvious that the inspector would welcome Sexton Blake's assistance.

It was in a very thoughtful frame of mind that the journalist returned to the Wheatsheaf. The problem of the phantom motor-lorry was growing more and more obscure. What was it that had brought an ex-prison governor to this quiet Buckinghamshire village? What sinister menace brooded over Hangman's Hill?

These and other problems occupied his mind as he retraced his steps to the inn. More than ever he realised that some dark and sinister mystery hung over this peaceful valley in the Chiltern Hills, and he longed impatiently for the advent of Sexton Blake.

A surprise awaited him on his arrival at the Wheatsheaf. He learnt from the landlord that the two American gentlemen had taken their departure half an hour before.

"Gone to Lunnon, they said," Ames volunteered. "They both zeemed kind o' upset like, an' ter tell yer the truth, zur, I wasn't sorry to see the back o' them."

THE FIFTH CHAPTER

Dr. Novak's Client.

DR. IVAN NOVAK, the celebrated mental specialist of Harley Street, polished his already shining finger-nails, and smiled blandly over his mahogany desk at the sturdy man who sat opposite to him.

The latter seemed to be the last person in the world to need the psychological treatment for which the doctor was renowned. He looked, in brief, the picture of rude health.

The physician regarded him gravely through his shell-rimmed glasses.

Dr. Ivan Novak was the personification of professional prosperity. From the crown of his sleek black hair to the tips of his spatted, patent leather shoes, he was immaculate. He had a long, rather lean face, but it shone with that healthy pinkness that only a gourmand or an athlete possesses. His dark eyes rested speculatively on his client for a moment or two. They were set somewhat close together, but that was a detail one overlooked whenever the doctor was disposed to be charming—and that was often.

"I am very distressed—very distressed indeed, Mr. Mullins," he said, in his well-modulated voice. "But at the risk of sounding trite, I must say that even amongst us professional men, business is business. I am paying you a certain sum of money for definite information. You choose to withhold the most vital part of that information, and you expect me to fulfil my part of the bargain."

"Now, look here, Dr. Novak," broke in the visitor truculently, "you might be able to put it across a lot o' these neurotic Society women, but you're not going to put it across me. Megantic sails from Liverpool on the sixteenth, and as for the route of—"

"My dear fellow, pray modulate your voice," broke in Novak. "Though the walls of this consulting-room have heard many strange secrets, there is no necessity for you to repeat what we both already know. I shall expect you to keep to your bargain, and inform me within twenty-four hours of the exact movements of the—er—merchandise, and, as promised, I shall pay you the stipulated sum."

Mr. Mullins gnawed nervously at the edge of his draggled moustache.

"But look here," he burst out explosively, "think of the risk. If it was to leak out that I—"

Dr. Novak checked him with a gesture.

"After the sixteenth there will be no risk, my friend," he announced. "Just you carry on as usual—and mind you let me know at once if there is any change in the schedule."

The man named Mullins lumbered to his feet. He glanced helplessly at the doctor.

"Well, I'm in it up to the neck!" he said, with an air of finality.

Novak's green eyes gleamed satirically behind their glasses.

"Yes—up—to—the—neck," he said with slow emphasis.

The other man's florid face turned grey. He murmured something incoherently. Novak's slim fingers reached for an ivory bell-push on his desk and the door of the consulting-room opened. A nurse appeared.

"Good-morning, Mr. Mullins!" said Dr. Novak. "Don't worry!" He turned to the nurse and smiled. "Will you show the next patient in, please?"

The nurse glanced at the little memorandum tablet in her hand as Mullins passed out.

"Will you see Mr. Freece, sir?" she said.

Dr. Novak smiled.

"Show him in, nurse!"

A moment later Rainy Day Freece entered the consulting-room.

THE GREY PANTHER purred rhythmically at a level forty on the Watford by-pass, with Tinker at the wheel.

On the rear seats Sexton Blake and his American colleague, Ruff Hanson, puffed at their cigars in silence.

Ruff had arrived, as he had said, on schedule. They did not speak much, these two old friends, as the Rolls Royce sped onwards towards the Chiltern Hills. Theirs was the comradeship where silence and a good smoke was more eloquent than words.

Blake's eyes were half closed. Just before leaving Baker Street he had skimmed through the late extra of the 'Evening Wireless,' and Splash Page's hurriedly telegraphed report: of the latest Ghostmobile development.

Tinker, as always, joyed in the response of the Grey Panther to his touch at the wheel.

Ruff Hanson, his ugly, good-humoured face shadowed by the brim of his enormous Stetson hat, surveyed his square-topped boots complacently.

"Some bus!" he said laconically, at length.

Sexton Blake switched his thoughts back with a jerk.

"We ought to be in Mandeville Magna in about twenty minutes," he said.

In the light of the tonneau lamp he traced out the route from a map on his knees.

"When you get to Rickmansworth, Tinker," he said, "let me have the wheel."

The youngster nodded. Ruff Hanson looked curiously at his colleague.

"Goin' to have a shot at this Ghostmobile to-night, Blake?" he ventured.

The detective nodded.

"With luck!" he replied.

"Say, listen! Wise me up to this spook truck!" said Ruff Hanson. "As fer as I can make out it seems to be goin' round slaughtering jay walkers twice nightly. I'll tell the world I didn't expect to go snoopin' around after spooks, Blake, as soon as I arrived. I told you that I was actin' on

160

behalf of the Metropolitan Guaranty Fund? Headquarters advised me that Spieler MacBride arrived in England three days back with a thug named Gat Masters. Spieler held up the Guaranty Trust for ten grand before he made his getaway. He's a slick guy all right, the Spieler.

"We wirelessed his mug and fingerprints to Scotland Yard, so guess it won't be long before we pull him in."

Blake nodded.

"I think you can safely leave that to Coutts, Ruff." he said. "After all, there'll be tedious extradition formalities to go through before you can take him back, and if I know anything about you you'll be bored to death hanging around. This Ghostmobile business promises a little excitement, anyway."

"Oh," said Ruff Hanson, patting his hip pockets, in which reposed his two heavy six-guns. He had affectionately christened them Willy and Wally. "Excitement's my middle name and shootin' is the fondest thing I is of—as they say down in Harlem."

Near Rickmansworth Tinker slowed down and Blake changed places with him. They branched to the left. The night was inclined to be misty. A fitful and watery moon shed a tricky half light on the landscape.

Blake drove steadily at thirty, his keen eyes alert and watchful. Near Mandeville in the Vale he allowed the speedometer needle to drop to twenty.

Hangman's Hill was about a mile from the village, and Blake's senses were now keenly on the alert. He had formulated no definite theory as yet from the versions he had read in the night's papers. Subconsciously, he noticed, however, the pseudo Tudor houses of the colony, and a quirk of amusement played round his lips at Mr. Carrington Lang's essay to escape modernity.

The Grey Panther swung round the bend. The signpost raised skeleton arms against the grey sky. On either side the bleak fields were wreathed in a dank ground mist and visibility was bad.

Then suddenly—it happened.

Even Blake, used as he was to quick judgments, was taken momentarily aback.

Round the bend, in the centre of the road, there materialised the blurred outline of a large motor-lorry. It had come into focus so suddenly and so silently that for an instant Blake thought it was some trick of light. He swung his steering-wheel round to the left.

"Look out, guv'nor!" cried Tinker involuntarily.

It almost seemed as if the ghostly vehicle would crash into them. It was only Blake's iron self-control and superb handling of the car that prevented them from turning over.

They skidded violently almost into the hedge; and then, just as it seemed they must crash, the car swung round on its axis in a circle and Blake pulled the monster up facing the way from which they had come.

Tinker laughed shakily, but Blake slipped in the clutch, and the car rolled forward in the wake of the juggernaut lorry as it sped onward without a sound and rounded the bend.

At this instant two jets of flame flashed from the surrounding darkness. The offside window of the Grey Panther was starred and splintered at the same moment.

"Holy Heinz!" roared Ruff Hanson, and his blue eyes blazed. "Stop the car, Blake! Stop! I'm gonna get that guy who's shooting at us!"

As if by magic, two heavy revolvers appeared in his ham-like hands. They were Hanson's pets, Willy and Wally. Blake, torn between two impulses, stopped. The lorry had vanished, anyhow, and these shots certainly demanded attention.

"Open that door!" Ruff rasped to Tinker. "And keep under cover, buddy!"

Tinker slammed back the catch. With a joyous bellow, the gunman-sleuth leapt into the roadway.

Crack!

Again the darkness was stabbed by flame. A bullet phutted unpleasantly past Ruff Hanson's cauliflower ear.

Ruff Hanson's gun spoke once. The light was none too good.

"Steady on, Ruff!" came the cool voice of Sexton Blake.

Bang!

Wally spoke this time, and sound of the shot echoed thinly through the hills. Then silence.

"Got 'im, I guess!" said Ruff.

"Come on, Blake; let's have a look-see!"

Gun in hand, he raced towards the low hedge that skirted a culvert on the left of the roadway. Even as he did so he tripped and fell sprawling. He swore luridly below his breath.

Sexton Blake helped him to his feet and peered ahead into the darkness. About two hundred yards away across the bleak common an oblong of yellow light shone.

Blake's face was tense.

"The shot came from that clump of trees to the right there," he muttered. "We'd better investigate."

He switched on his electric torch.

Ruff Hanson brushed his knees and cursed again.

"Quite a warm reception," said Sexton Blake. "I wonder what exactly—"

The rest of the sentence was drowned by a shrill burst of unnatural laughter, and into the full beam of his torch whirled a wild and fantastic apparition.

"Waddyou know about that?" demanded Ruff, as the capering figure of a woman in a tattered cape, with long, grey, matted hair streaming over her shoulders, staggered towards them.

"Depart from here: the time is at hand! I am the flail of the Lord!" shrieked the hag in a shrill, unnatural voice. "The ungodly shall perish." Her voice rose to a scream. "Beware of the wrath of the Lord, whose handmaiden I am."

She advanced towards them fiercely, yellow fangs bared, her eyes wild with madness.

"Bughouse," said Ruff Hanson laconically.

Blake's face was grim as he flashed his torch into the woman's face. She was obviously in a high state of frenzy or hysteria. He grabbed her suddenly by her skinny forearm.

"Be quiet, woman!" he said, and his stern eyes were compelling. "Get back at once!"

Whether it was the sternness in the detective's voice or the blinding glare of the torch they did not know, but the half-crazed creature stopped suddenly and began to whimper as she fell on her knees.

"Look after her, Ruff. I believe she comes from that tumbledown cottage over there," said Sexton Blake, moving abruptly to the right towards a small, dark coppice from which the shots had come.

His torch cut a questing swathe through the darkness. Cautiously he advanced when he neared the trees, every nerve taut, an automatic in his left hand.

Had Ruff Hanson's bullet found a billet?

Not a sound save for the melancholy hoot of an owl disturbed the night's oppressive silence.

Blake flashed his torch downwards and gave a sharp exclamation. Beneath a gorse-bush he made out a round, black object. He approached it cautiously. He strained his ears, but could detect no sound of any lurking enemy.

The gorse, with its yellow bloom intensified by the yellow glare of his torch, was thick, and made an admirable ambush.

"Come out of that!" snapped Blake.

Silence.

Then he saw. A sprig of the yellow broom was damp, but not with dew. It was fresh blood, brown in the lamplight against the yellow of the gorse.

Ruff Hansen had not missed.

Blake stooped over the round object and picked it up. It was a cloth cap of check tweed. He turned it over and gave a soft whistle. On the label within was the maker's name:

> "Myerstein,
> East 35th St.,
> Chicago."

He straightened to his full height and his fingers trembled ominously on the trigger.

"Stick 'em up," he snapped, "or I'll shoot!"

No reply came from behind the gorse-bush. He pressed forward, and the rays of his torch illuminated a motionless, shapeless figure on the ground.

It was very still, weirdly grotesque in the moonlight.

Blake drew in his breath sharply. There was something uncanny about the body's natural attitude. It was that of a man clad in corduroys. But what added to the fantastic horror of death was the man's left leg—a wooden stump pointing grotesquely to the sky.

THE SIXTH CHAPTER

The Face at the Window.

"PRRMPH."

Colonel Hannibal Smith trumpeted belligerently into his large bandanna handkerchief. He glared round the smoke-room of the club-house on the Mandeville Golf Links.

Nesbit was there, and the faithful Carrington Lang. Young Maltravers and Jerry Wiltshire had not yet arrived from town.

"You were saying?" said Nesbit helpfully, when the colonel's purple face emerged from behind his purple handkerchief.

"I was saying it was disgraceful, sir—downright disgraceful!" said Colonel Hannibal Smith. "A man of your intelligence, Lang, saying you actually saw this Ghostmobile in broad daylight!"

The architect polished his pince-nez.

"I tell you I did," he repeated firmly. "And the body of

the poor devil, Challoner, was lying frightfully mangled in the culvert at the side of the road."

"Heaven save us all!" broke in Nesbit, a dry, precise little man. "When I took this place, colonel, I expected to have found somewhere where I could spend my declining years in peace. And now here we are, plunged into the most appalling crimes and mysteries that it has ever been my lot to—"

Bang! Bang! Bang!

He jumped visibly in his chair. With one accord all leapt to their feet and rushed for the window.

"More shooting!" groaned Nesbit. "What does it all mean? I'll tell you what, colonel, I'm certain there's a homicidal maniac loose in the district."

Colonel Hannibal Smith's ruddy face paled as he craned over Lang's shoulder and peered through the darkened window over the misty moors.

"Where's Novak?" he demanded roughly. "He said he'd meet me here at seven. It's nearly eight o'clock now. If there's a maniac loose in this district, it comes into his province."

Fenton, the club steward, entered at that moment.

"A Mr. Page would like to see you, colonel," he announced. "He won't detain you long, but he would be glad if you could spare him a few minutes."

"Page? Page?" repeated the other. "Who is he?"

"Oh, quite a decent cove," broke in Carrington Lang. "A journalist fellah. I showed him round the estate this morning. Seems a most intelligent young man with very sound views."

"Eh? What's that?" demanded the colonel. "I tell you, Lang, I won't have it. A lot of cursed newspaper reporters snooping around, poking their inquisitive noses into business that doesn't concern 'em!"

"The gentleman is waiting for an answer," reminded Fenton tactfully.

The colonel wheeled round on him savagely, eyes snapping beneath his shaggy eyebrows.

"Did you hear those shots?" he demanded sharply.

"Yes, sir, but I thought maybe it was young Mr. Maltravers or Captain Wiltshire out pigeon shooting in the beech woods."

"Pigeon shooting, my foot!" said the colonel. "I reckon I know a revolver shot when I hear one. Show this fellow in, Fenton," he added.

A moment later Splash entered, smiling and debonair as usual. He nodded agreeably at Lang and Nesbit, and held out his hand to the colonel.

"Good-evening, gentlemen!" he said. "Sounds as if there's a certain liveliness on the Mandeville front," he added with a chuckle. "I'm sorry I missed you this morning, Colonel Smith. I have long been acquainted with your work on the origin of nebulae. Mr. Carrington Lang was showing me your observatory this morning when he was good enough to take me over the estate."

"What's that, what's that?" barked the colonel. "You know something of astronomy?"

"Certainly," said Splash unblushingly. "I had the privilege of listening to your paper on the galactic nebulae at the annual meeting of the Royal Astronomical Society last year."

"H'm!" said the colonel, somewhat doubtfully. "Sit down, young man. Have a drink? One does not associate a modern journalist with the study of stars—other than film stars!" he added dryly.

Splash smiled and stretched his hands towards the blaze of the fire.

"To tell you the truth, colonel, it was not exactly on astronomical subjects that I called to see you. Your man told me you would be at the club-house at seven this evening and I dropped in to see if you had any statement to make regarding the Mandeville Terror."

The colonel snorted.

"The Mandeville Terror? Is that what they're calling it now? By heavens, Lang, this is an outrage! This matter must be sorted and sifted to its foundations. The whole peace of this place has been ruined since that fool doctor Walford Wells gibbered about ghost lorries at the inquest."

"Precisely!" agreed Splash blandly. "And it is in order to put an end to these stories and get at the truth that my paper has sent me here, colonel. I am investigating the mystery from a purely rationalistic point of view."

"Huh!" grunted the colonel. "You think there is a rationalistic explanation, then, young man?"

The little lawyer smiled secretively at Splash Page's adroit handling of the fire-eating Hannibal Smith. Splash was a wily bird.

"I'm sure you, as a scientist, colonel, discount a supernatural theory?"

"I think it's all silly schoolboy rot!" exploded Hannibal Smith.

A tap sounded at the door, and again Fenton entered apologetically. The steward's face was chalky white.

"Beggin' yer pardon, sir," he began hesitatingly, "but there's been a bad accident again on Hangman's Hill, and there's a gent 'ere as would like to use the club telephone. There's a man been shot, an' the—er—Ghostmobile 'as appeared again."

"WHAT?" SPLASH PAGE leapt to his feet, an eager light in his eyes.

The other three glanced at each other significantly.

"Pray pardon my intrusion, gentlemen!" said a cool voice from the doorway.

Splash turned round and gave a pleased grin of recognition.

"Why, Blake, old man—you!" he said in surprise. "When did you get here?"

"Ten minutes ago," said the criminologist quietly. "Pardon the liberty, gentlemen, but I must phone the local police. A man has been shot dead on the common within the last quarter of an hour."

Colonel Hannibal Smith glanced in astonishment at the famous detective's clean-cut, impassive face.

"Murdered!" he ejaculated. "Good heart alive!"

"It looks like murder!" said Sexton Blake quietly.

The detective's softly made announcement had a staggering effect on Colonel Hannibal Smith. Blake noted that the man was utterly dumb-founded by the news.

"Of course, of course you may use the phone, my dear fellow!" Smith said effusively when Splash had completed the introductions.

Blake crossed over to the instrument and called up the police station at Mandeville Magna, telling them briefly of the details. "Let me offer you a whisky-and-soda, Mr. Blake?" said Carrington Lang hospitably.

Blake nodded his thanks and sank into an armchair to await the arrival of the local constabulary. He had left Tinker in charge of the Grey Panther, and Ruff Hanson had carried the half-fainting crone back to her wretched cottage on the common.

"What happened, Blake?" demanded Splash, intent on the story.

Briefly the detective gave a concise account of his encounter with the Ghostmobile. The others listened in silence.

"Then you have caught no sight of the man?" inquired Carrington Lang.

Blake shook his head.

"The ground mist is very tricky!" he announced. "I made a rough search, but it was next to impossible to find any tracks!"

Little Mr. Nesbit shivered.

"Bless my soul! It's positively dangerous to be abroad, Mr. Blake!" he remarked. "I'll tell you quite frankly, Lang, that I'm not going home alone to-night!"

"Nor I," said Carrington Lang, with a nervous giggle.

Colonel Hannibal Smith pushed out his chest. From the hip-pocket of his plus-fours he withdrew a heavy Smith & Wesson.

"Heaven help anyone who comes into line with this to-night!" he said grimly. "Have you formed any theory at all, Mr. Blake? You are a level-headed man, not given to fanciful ideas. What is your impression about this so-called Ghostmobile?"

Blake shrugged his shoulders.

"I never form definite opinions without definite data, colonel," he said. "My impression was certainly that the lorry was a tangible thing. I invariably leave the supernatural theory as a last hypothesis, and I usually find it isn't needed at the finish!"

There came the sound of a motor-car on the gravelled lane that led to the club-room, and a few moments later Inspector Graves, accompanied by a sergeant, two constables, and the police surgeon, entered the club-room. They had hurried over in response to Blake's call.

Colonel Hannibal Smith stood with his back to the fireplace, and nodded a trifle condescendingly.

"You've been very quick, Graves. It's a cursed nuisance all this, to say the least! Judging from Mr. Blake's description, that poaching fellow, Jem Chance, has been shot. I knew he would come to a bad end," he added, shaking his head sagely.

The inspector turned with marked deference to Sexton Blake.

"I'm very glad, as I told Mr. Page this morning, that you're looking into this matter, sir," he said cordially. "Can you tell me what's happened?"

Blake lit a cigarette.

"Certainly, inspector. If you'll get on the phone right away and send a message with the description I shall give you, I think there is a chance of you nabbing the man responsible!"

"Great Scott! Did you see him?" ejaculated the inspector, in surprise.

Blake shook his head.

"No. But I do not think you will go far wrong if you advise county headquarters to detain on suspicion a middle-aged man, with short, close-cropped grey hair, about five feet seven inches tall, possibly wounded, speaks with a marked American accent, and has, presumably, recently arrived from America."

"Good lord!" ejaculated Splash Page. "I know a chappie whose description that fits very well—the fellow who was at the Wheatsheaf last night, Flaxman Skinner's valet. How in the name of Mike did you deduce that, Blake?"

For answer, Blake pulled out the cloth cap which he had picked up near Jem Chance's dead body.

"A simple matter, Splash!" he remarked. "This cap, as you will see, is comparatively new. It is a little too small for the owner, I should fancy, judging from the hairs which are adhering to the inner band, and which, as you see, are grey and closely cut. He has left several unmistakable footprints near the body, and it is simple to reconstruct a man's height from the length of his stride!"

"That being the case," said Splash, "I can supplement your description. I got an eyeful of the fellow last night. He looks a hard-bitten plug-ugly, with a broken nose and cauliflower ears!"

Colonel Smith drew out his virulently hued bandanna, and Blake's keen eyes noted that his face went ashen grey.

Suddenly he leapt to his feet and gave a strangled gasp.

"Look! Look!" he shouted hoarsely. "There he is! Grab him quick, inspector!"

With a shaking finger, he pointed to the club-room window overlooking the links. For an instant a face was pressed against the pane—a battered, ugly face that seemed decapitated from the body.

"Quick!' snapped the inspector to the sergeant; and together they tore open the door and raced out into the night.

The face vanished, and Sexton Blake laughed out loud.

Colonel Hannibal Smith looked like a man who has been sentenced to death.

THE SEVENTH CHAPTER

Sorting Things Out.

"AND THAT, MR. Blake, is the sum total of the facts we have up to date!"

Inspector Graves closed his black official notebook with a decisive snap of its elastic band and glanced inquiringly at the man from Baker Street.

It was after midnight. Through Splash Page's instrumentality, rooms had been booked at the Wheatsheaf for Ruff Hanson, Blake, and Tinker. At the moment the four friends, with Inspector Graves, were seated in the cosy saloon bar after a hectic three hours on the common, and, for Blake, a somewhat unpleasant half-hour in the local mortuary.

"Waal, dog my cats!" broke in Ruff Hanson, "Eff that ain't the bee's knees, inspector! How many accidents do you say have taken place at the corner by Hangman's Hill?"

"Up to Wednesday last, forty-three, seven of which

ended fatally, Mr. Hanson!" he answered. "We now have two more to add to the list, if we include the murder of poor Chance and the attack on you this evening."

Ruff Hanson rubbed his scrubby chin thoughtfully. An idea seemed to strike him.

"Let's give the description of this Yank the once over again," he remarked. "I've got a notion that his mug sounds familiar!"

Graves read out the brief description, which had been wired to all the police stations in England.

"I'm afraid it is hardly a compliment to you, Ruff, dear old son, when you peeped in at the window, for us to take you for the alleged murderer," said Splash.

Ruff Hanson's humorously ugly face widened into an engaging grin.

"I ain't no Ramon Novarro,[5] kiddo," he chuckled. "I jest peeped in to see if Blake had got back all right after I'd taken that poor crazy Jane back to her cottage."

Ruff Hanson smiled reminiscently at the consternation which his weather-beaten face had caused in the golf club-room.

"As I was sayin'," continued the American gunman-sleuth, "I ain't ever claimed to be an oil-paintin', but durn my hide, I reckon I'm a mite more human lookin' than this guy."

From his bulky wallet he suddenly extracted three photographs, on the back of which was stamped the official mark of the New York Central Criminal Bureau.

"That's one o' the guys I'm trailing," he announced. "Reco'nise him? He's a tough egg. Monicker, Masters—Gat

Masters, an' he's tailin' around with Spieler MacBride."

Splash Page whistled softly.

"By Gorge, that's the fellow who was in here last night," he announced. "I'll swear it! It looks as if your job is likely to be simplified, inspector."

"Well, I'll be goldarned!" said Ruff. "It looks as if I'd blundered right in on it, Blake. I wonder if the skunk recognised me, and that was the reason for to-night's little shootin' match?"

Sexton Blake slowly filled his briar.

"I doubt it, Ruff," he remarked. "In the first place, he'd hardly have learnt of your arrival in England, and in the second place, he would need exceedingly sharp eyesight to recognise you in the car."

Inspector Graves meditatively sipped his drink.

"I don't mind admitting to you, Mr. Blake, that I'm quite baffled," he said. "I hardly know where to begin. The issue is so obscure. First we have accidents—and we're not quite sure whether they are accidents, and then on top of that these two wanton and seemingly purposeless murders within the last twenty-four hours. Quite frankly, I'm right out of my depth."

Blake settled himself back comfortably in his chair and puffed slowly at his pipe.

"The great thing in affairs of this sort," he began, "is to separate essentials from the irrelevant. Now let us try and line up all the available facts at our disposal. The first time that the so-called phantom lorry received semi-official publicity was on Monday at the inquest on the unfortunate Mr. John Gorman.

"We must be careful here not to confuse an expression of opinion with a matter of fact. Assuming the credibility of the witnesses, the coroner, Dr. Walford Wells, was doubtless justified in drawing the jury's attention to the phenomenon. But I think he exceeded his duties when he attributed a supernatural origin to the ghost lorry."

Blake paused and turned to the inspector.

"You told me, I believe, that Dr. Wells dabbled in spiritualism?"

"That's so," agreed Graves. "His wife is a medium—or claims to be."

Blake smiled.

"Then obviously his opinion is coloured. Now there is no doubt about it," continued the detective, ticking off the points on his lean fingers, "Hangman's Hill bears an unenviable reputation for accidents. It is a dangerous corner. Whether those accidents are due to negligent driving or to supernatural phenomena we have as yet not sufficient data to decide. The tangible evidence that we have is unfortunately of a negative quality in one sense.

"FIRST, THE ARRIVAL of Colonel Challoner, ex-governor of Bleakmoor. He is a stranger in the vicinity, and is undoubtedly murdered within twenty-four hours of his arrival. He was murdered either by a homicidal maniac, or by a person who knew him and bore him a grudge. Robbery was undoubtedly not the motive, as a search of his pockets showed.

"Ruling out for the moment the lunatic theory, we are brought up against a secret enemy. In his position as the

180

prison governor, Challoner undoubtedly made many enemies.

"It is therefore reasonable to assume that the man who murdered Challoner was an ex-convict who has passed through his hands. I am not building on the theory yet until I have more evidence, but simply using it as a working basis."

"I see your point, Mr. Blake," said the inspector. "But the only gaol-bird, as I have said, we have round here was Jem Chance—and he, poor devil, was shot to-night. And he was not really a convict from a convict prison. He only did six months."

"And durned lucky for me," broke in Ruff Hanson, "that the bullet you found in his bean was a .38 automatic. I always use a .45 myself."

Blake smiled.

"I was rather afraid myself, until after the doctor had examined the wound, that in your impetuosity you had shot him. But let us keep to the point. We will assume that Colonel Challoner came down here simply to rest and play golf, as he explained to the landlord. He is recognised by an ex-convict who has served under him at Bleakmoor."

"But—but there aren't any convicts in the district," objected the inspector.

Again Blake smiled.

"Do not be too sure of that. You would be surprised how many notorious prisoners are living down their past in an odour of respectability. Only the other day in Norfolk I met a charming old local preacher who was highly respected as the fairy godfather of the village. No one even suspected that he had served twenty years for strangling his wife."

"By Jove!" broke in Splash. "I see what you're driving at, Blake. Challoner may have recognised, in a so-called pillar of respectability round here, one of his guests at Bleakmoor, and, terrified of exposure, the man killed him?"

"Precisely," said Sexton Blake. "Now the second factor is the so-called Ghostmobile. I can speak with personal authority on that count. I myself saw it to-night, and I'm not usually given to hallucinations."

"And I saw it, too, guv'nor," broke in Tinker, "It was the weirdest thing, and I could have sworn I saw a skeleton driving it."

Blake put the tips of his fingers together.

"I searched the roadway pretty thoroughly after the shooting, and of one thing I am convinced. However uncanny in appearance the Ghostmobile may be, it leaves a perfectly ordinary track on the road.

"Now, inspector, if you will read over the statements made to you by the man, Mockser, Mr. Carrington Lang, and Mr. Flaxman Skinner—whom I shrewdly suspect is Ruff Hanson's friend Spieler MacBride—you will find that they are all unanimous on two points. One, the complete and awe-inspiring silence of the vehicle, and secondly, that though it loomed largely above them and gave the impression of bulk, its outline was hazy and indefinite. I had the same impression this evening," he added.

"To-morrow, when it is light, inspector, I advise you

to take a few more photographs of the spot. There may, of course, be a connection between the murders and the Ghostmobile, or there may not.

"I think we may safely rule out, for the moment at least, the complicity of the Haggarty woman, who is quite demented and should, I think, be certified for her own good, poor soul."

Inspector Graves cleared his throat. "It's very helpful, having your opinion, Mr. Blake, and I'm obliged to you."

Blake yawned.

"Thanks. But I'm afraid there is little more to do this evening, inspector," he remarked. "If you will kindly arrange with Dr. Wells for the carrying out of the plan I suggested I would be very grateful. I'm afraid," he added, "that an important case will necessitate my presence in town to-morrow, but Mr. Hanson and Mr. Page here will, I am sure, keep me posted regarding the latest developments."

Inspector Graves rose to his feet.

"I'll see that that is done at once, Mr. Blake. I shall get Dr. Wells and Dr. Novak to—"

"Emphatically not Dr. Novak," said Sexton Blake quietly.

Tinker glanced curiously at his guv'nor. He sensed that Blake was holding back something, and saw the subdued gleam of excitement in the shrewd grey eyes.

"Have you met Novak?" inquired Blake, turning suddenly to Splash Page.

"He's the fashionable psychoanalyst, isn't he?" asked Splash. "No, I can't say I've met him, Blake."

"Ah!" said the detective, with a cryptic smile. "It's a pity. A most interesting fellow. He is the foremost modern authority on witchcraft and diabolism. You ought to interview him."

"By Jove, I will!" said Splash, as Inspector Graves announced his departure.

"Tell me," said Blake unexpectedly, when Graves had wished them goodnight and was turning to leave, "when does the Megantic sail for New York?"

"Er—I can't say off-hand," replied the official, in a surprised tone. "The eighteenth, I think."

"And to-day is the sixteenth," said Sexton Blake. "Ah, well, it is immaterial! We shall see what we shall see."

"You ain't thinkin' that Spieler and Gat Masters are goin' back by her, are you, Blake?" asked Ruff Hanson.

"I should think," responded the criminologist blandly, "that it is the most unlikely thing in the world. I shall be very astonished if those two gentlemen ever see America again."

THE EIGHTH CHAPTER

The Limping Man.

THE TOWERS, THE residence of Colonel Hannibal Smith, was shuttered and dark. The wind moaned eerily in the leafless trees that surrounded the pseudo Tudor residence which Mr. Carrington Lang had designed for his employer.

A little to the right of the house was a cylindrical tower, surmounted by a semi-spherical dome. It was Colonel Hannibal Smith's observatory. The moon had long since retired from the struggle with the grey, watery clouds overhead. A solitary constable marched on his lonely beat between the ill-omened Hangman's Corner and Mandeville in the Vale.

Police-constable Pierce was a stolid, unimaginative individual, but the events of the past few days had shaken even his stolidity. He clumped slowly down the narrow country lane and shivered a little.

"What a job!" he grumbled, glancing at his wrist-watch and flashing on the rays of his electric lamp, more for comfort than for anything else.

He was ahead of time. He had nearly half an hour to spare before he was due to meet the sergeant at the other end of his lonely beat.

Constable Pierce sat down on a moist, grassy knoll.

"What a job!" he repeated. "An' if this 'ere ghost lorry comes, wot can I do with it? It ain't even got a blinkin' number I can take."

Like most lonely men, he had a habit of soliloquising aloud. He proceeded to fill a battered clay pipe, and lit a match. It was one of the darkest nights he had known for some time, and there was a miasmic mist on the moors.

He sucked reflectively at the cutty and cogitated on the problems of life as it affected a country constable along whose beat charged phantom motor-lorries.

"Queer thing—a rare queer thing!" he mused. "An' this 'ere shootin' to-night. Jem Chance 'as gone to 'is Maker, pore feller, an' it ain't exactly pleasant to think that 'is murderer's running loose."

Suddenly the constable's senses became alert. A sound reached his ears. A stumbling, shuffling sound of a belated wayfarer that came on the road with a peculiar, halting gait.

"Sounds as if there's someone limpin'," said P.-c. Pierce. "Somebody with a game leg."

Even as he spoke the words, the footsteps sounded nearer.

Pat, pat, pit, pat, pat, pit.

There was something stealthy about the footsteps. Whoever it was, he was walking with a distinct limp.

"Now I wonder 'oo that can be?" said P.-c. Pierce. "There's only one man round 'ere 'oo's got a game leg an' 'e's—'e's—"

The words died away on his lips. Only a couple of hours before, he had seen all that was left of Jem Chance borne away on a stretcher to the local mortuary.

The constable shivered involuntarily and reached for his truncheon. Though he possessed very little imagination, a primitive streak of superstition suddenly rose uppermost in P.-c. Pierce. There was something strange, queer, ghost-like about those furtive footsteps and the swish of one leg being dragged slowly and painfully after the other.

His nerves tingled and his flesh crawled on his scalp.

Suddenly the footsteps stopped.

Wild panic seized the constable. He felt that he was up against something uncanny, something unutterably evil.

"Who—who's that?" he demanded. His throat was dry. His spine felt as if someone had run an icy finger down it.

No reply.

P.-c. Pierce switched on his torch, then gave an involuntary ejaculation. Out of the darkness there sprang at him a hideous yellow face with narrow, glittering eyes, a broken nose, and a mouth that was twisted in an animal snarl.

For a second or two P.-c. Pierce stood chilled to the marrow by fear. Then, swift as the dart of a striking cobra, he felt a terrific nerve-shattering blow on the side of the temple. His brain reeled, and a red mist shot with fire flashed before his eyes. Then he swayed groggily to his knees.

The last sound he heard was the stealthy *pat, pat, pit, pat, pat, pit*, of the limping man.

Colonel Hannibal Smith's passion for astronomy was no pose, but it seemed to be carrying his hobby to extremes to spend—in his excited state—the three hours following Sexton Blake's arrival at the golf club in his observatory. Perhaps, however, a contemplation of the untroubled stars soothed him.

He had a quite good stellar telescope, and the observatory chamber itself in the top of the cylindrical tower comprised—in addition to several astronomical instruments, a very elaborately equipped laboratory with dazzling white enamel walls and two topped work-benches, on which reposed a variety of electrical instruments.

Not a glimmer of light shone from the domed chamber at the top of the tower on to the surrounding countryside. The colonel had returned from the club long before ten, and was now moodily pacing up and down the circular chamber, his forehead corrugated into a deep frown. Apparently the soothing influence of the stars had failed him.

The turret was connected with the east wing of the manor house by a covered passageway, which enabled him to devote as much time as he cared to his researches without disturbing the rest of his strange house-hold.

His nearest neighbour on the right side of the Towers was Dr. Ivan Novak, and Maltravers occupied the pretentious house farther down the lane.

The colonel completed his fiftieth turn about the room,

and his visitor swore softly.

"For Heaven's sake, man, sit down and take a grip of yourself," said Dr. Ivan Novak. "What the devil are you worrying about? Even if this man Blake is on the spot he'll never guess in a million years what we're up to with the Ghostmobile, as that fool of a reporter calls it. It's my opinion that Blake is not half as clever as he is cracked up to be. His reputation is all publicity.

"To-night—or, rather, this morning"—he glanced at the chronometer on the wall of the laboratory—"is the seventeenth. I've managed to overcome Mullin's remaining scruples, and you will be able to recoup your losses on the Wall Street smash with one bold, single stroke. After that—well, South America, my friend, sounds infinitely more alluring than this stucco garden village of yours. There are times, my dear colonel, when your habits become positive imbecilities," he added.

The colonel scowled.

"Take care, Novak—don't drive me too far!" he warned. "Remember you're in this as much as I, and if it comes to paying the penalty for Challoner's—"

Dr. Novak waved a slim white hand.

"Why drag in sordid details?" he said. "Let's go over the plan of campaign again!"

He pressed a switch suddenly, and a huge map mounted on glass set into the wall was brilliantly illuminated. It was a large-scale chart, covering a ten-mile radius, and showing clearly every road and byway in that area. He pressed another switch and a ruby light moved steadily across Wriklin Lane.

Beneath the illuminated map was a complicated instrument, mounted on an ebonite-topped bench. It looked rather like a wireless transmitting-set. A crackle of blue flame sprang between a pair of spark plugs as Novak gently fingered two shining dials.

"It works perfectly," he said. "Why in the name of sense have you got the breeze up because some low thug sent you a double-six domino as a melodramatic warning? Use your brains, man—you've grown soft with high living! Can't you get a little of your old confidence back, or must the name Rainy Day Freece stick to you for ever?"

"Shut up, curse you!" snarled Colonel Hannibal Smith, alias Rainy Day Freece. "Gat Masters is a killer, I tell you. When he and I were of the Double Six in Chicago we had an oath that—"

He broke off suddenly as an electric bulb above the doorway glowed crimson.

"Hallo, what's that?" he ejaculated. "Danger!"

Ivan Novak cursed softly below his breath and lifted a slide in the wall of the observatory. It was an ingenious periscope, or, rather, a camera obscura. In it, greatly reduced, he saw the blue-helmeted figure of a policeman at the front door of the Towers.

He bit his lip.

"Blister it, what the devil does he want?" he ejaculated. "You'd better phone up Peters to answer the door. I know the type; he'll pound it until he gets an answer."

The colonel licked his dry lips nervously and crossed over to the phone which communicated with Peters', his butler's, room. He barked a few instructions over the

190

wire, and then, grumbling, turned to Novak.

"We'd better go down and see what the fool wants!" he rasped.

Peters, professionally known as "Soapy Peters," cursed luridly as he replaced the receiver by the side of his bed. Few people would have suspected that the suave, ecclesiastical manservant was—or had been in his time—a notorious trickster. He donned his dressing-gown and hurried to answer the door.

"I will call my master," he said, in reply to the muttered query as to whether the colonel was at home.

Meanwhile, Ivan Novak and the colonel had hurried from their observatory into the library of the manor through the covered passageway.

Peters knocked at the door.

"Constable wants to see you on important business, sir. Sorry to trouble you," he announced, "but as—"

The door of the library opened suddenly with a splintering shock, and a burly figure in a policeman's uniform stood on the threshold. In his hand he gripped a blue-snouted automatic. In his pale blue eyes was implacable hatred.

It was Gat Masters, the Killer.

"I've got yer, Freece!"

That was all he said.

The pseudo colonel's face went a dirty grey colour. Fear galvanised him into action. He read death in the hate-filled eyes of the killer, and with a howl he leapt full at Gat Masters' throat.

Two shots cracked out as Gat staggered backwards

under the impetus of Freece's tigerish spring. Novak came to the rescue, yanking a gun out of his hip pocket. Gat Masters gave a yelp of pain as the butt caught him a crashing blow on the side of the temple.

Pandemonium.

"Quick, Peters, you fool, get him!" snarled Freece.

Kicking and clawing and struggling like a maniac, Gat lashed out savagely with arms like flails. His game leg suddenly crumpled up under him and he crashed floorward, mouthing incoherent obscenities. The odds were too great. Ruff Hanson's bullet earlier had shattered his thigh, and with a gasp that tore at his lungs Gat Masters collapsed into an inert heap on the floor.

Half a mile away, P.-c. Pierce shivered and found himself dressed in nothing but singlet and drawers. There was a bump on his temple the size of an egg.

THE NINTH CHAPTER

Gold, Gold, Gold!

"AND NOW WHAT?" queried Ruff Hanson.

The sun was shining brightly through the windows of the Wheatsheaf Inn. It was nearly lunch-time, and they had had a busy morning. Blake, true to his announcement the previous night, had taken the Grey Panther and left certain instructions with Tinker and his American colleague before proceeding on some mysterious errand of his own.

Splash Page looked up from the blotting pad on which he had been scribbling. He found that it clarified his thoughts to tentatively jot down the headlines of any case on which he was engaged, and he glanced with approval at his effort that morning.

"ANOTHER MURDER.
REIGN OF TERROR IN BUCKS.
THE GHOSTMOBILE AGAIN."

"That ought to please that old corpse-snatcher, Julius," grunted Splash. "And on top of that there's a touch of piquancy in P.-c. Pierce's predicament. I think that deserves a headline all to itself. Which d'you think is better, Ruff:

POLICEMAN IN PANTS,
or
CONSTABLE IN COMBINATIONS?"

"Cha!" said Ruff Hanson. "Give me action! I'd like to get that guy that plugged us last night, that's what.

"What made Blake go snoopin' up to town, Tinker?" he added. "It isn't like him to clear off when a case is half finished."

"You trust the guv'nor!" said Tinker loyally. "He knows what he's doing!"

The three friends would have been considerably astonished had they seen Sexton Blake at that moment. He had motored up to town very early in the morning, and had called at the Treasury Office, in Whitehall. From thence he had gone to a brief but illuminating interview with the Governor of the Bank of England, and that unobtrusive but immensely powerful personage, the Master of the Mint.

Judging by the expression in Blake's face, after a hurried lunch in a fashionable Strand Restaurant, both interviews had been eminently satisfactory. The half formulated suspicions in his mind had been crystallised into certainties, and the problem of the Ghostmobile was no longer without some sort of answer.

Meanwhile, Mandeville Magna seethed with excitement. The Wheatsheaf was full of alert-eyed, inquisitive young men, with a prodigious thirst both for beer and information. Amos, the landlord, when he had time to reflect, mused that the demise of Jem Chance had done far more for the village than his actual life.

Inspector Graves had spent a busy morning, too. Photographs were taken of every yard of the roadway in the vicinity of Hangman's Corner. There had been no sign of Gat Masters, but an American, corresponding to the description of Spieler MacBride, had been arrested at an obscure lodging-house in Southampton.

The Press made the most of the sensation, and Mandeville Magna found itself famous—or infamous. It depended on the point of view, as Carrington Lang said bitterly to his cronies at the club that afternoon.

"Where's the colonel?" asked young Maltravers. "This business seems to have upset the old boy pretty badly. I don't know whether you noticed it, Lang, but he's been looking positively ghastly the last few days."

Lang nodded.

"Yes, poor chap; I heard a rumour that he'd been pretty hard hit when Wall Street slumped. He invested a lot of money in the States, so he told me."

Maltravers shrugged.

"Queer bird, the colonel," he remarked. "Nobody quite seems to know where he made his money, or exactly why he built this hole down here. Has it ever struck you, Lang, that we're a queer lot altogether? Nobody seems to know much about anybody else—socially, I mean.

That chap Novak, for instance. I've heard some rum yarns about him and his queer psycho-analysis practice. Old Man Nesbit, too; he's a reserved sort of bloke. Then there's that chap Ferris, who acts as a sort of agent for the colonel. It's often struck me that there's a jolly old mystery about the whole bunch, and, to be frank with you, I wouldn't live here a day longer if it wasn't for the old man. I've got to keep in with him to see which side my bread's buttered."

"Quite, quite!" said Carrington Lang.

He himself had been getting uneasy of late. Many strange things had happened which he did not quite understand, and the shocking toll of the haunted highway was no advertisement to the ideal village he had created.

The day wore on. On the authority of the Chief Constable, Graves had called in Scotland Yard, and Coutts, burly, thick-set, and aggressive as ever, arrived just before night fell, and strutted briskly into the Wheatsheaf.

He was greeted joyously by the trio as he entered the bar, his hard felt hat cocked truculently over one eye, and one of his unspeakable cheroots jutting from the corner of his mouth.

Ruff Hanson pounded him gleefully on the back.

"Howdy, old timer, what are yeh goin' to have?"

The Yard man gruffly ordered a whisky, and then, formalities over, demanded a little brusquely:

"Where's Blake?"

Tinker shook his head.

"He's been in town all day, Coutts. He told me to let him know if anything new cropped up, but, apart from all

196

sorts of wild rumours, nothing's happened except that P.-c. Pierce had his trousers pinched by some tramp or other."

Coutts glowered aggressively at Splash.

"What's this silly rot you've been putting over about phantom lorries, my boy?" he said. "As soon as it gets dark I'm going to take a Thermos bottle and sandwiches with me to Hangman's Hill, and I'm going to sit there until I've solved this mystery."

"Good old Coutts!" grinned Tinker joyously. "And I hope it keeps fine for you."

He was not the only one to express that devout hope for a fine night.

In the turret-room in the Towers, locked and secluded from the rest of the world, Novak and the colonel—otherwise "Rainy Day" Freece—perfected their final plans. They pored over maps and timetables, and marked out with geometrical exactitude a certain portion of the arterial road by Watford which led to the Great North Road.

Freece had been drinking heavily. His twitching hands and lips betrayed that fact. Novak glanced with contempt at his accomplice.

"You fool!" he said. "Can't you see the whole thing will go off without a hitch? The road dips down in the bend just here under the bridge. Peters and Ferris have fixed the cylinders, and the bullion lorry is scheduled to pass under at about quarter-to-one this morning. Mullins tells me that there are only two armed guards beside the driver. There'll be absolutely no chance of a hitch. As soon as the lorry passes under the bridge on the north side, the gas will be released, and by the time they emerge on the other side, they'll be—"

He paused, and the pause was more eloquent than words.

"Pull yourself together, man! This isn't the first time you've been on a robbery, and this is a million pounds Sterling in gold, not a million dollars, Mr. Rainy Day Freece. Whatever happens, you and I are safe."

Freece mopped his forehead and tugged at his clammy collar.

"For Heaven's sake, let's go out and take a walk somewhere!" he said. "I'm feeling stifled! I know everything's all right, but cooped up here all day with the thought that Gat Masters is—is—"

He glanced fearfully over his shoulder.

"I should have thought you'd be relieved that the egregious Gat would trouble us no more," said Novak. "Take another snifter of brandy, and we'll walk over to the golf club. It'll look suspicious if we keep away."

"I wonder if that overrated sleuth-hound, Sexton Blake, is still hanging around?" said Freece.

Novak shrugged.

"What does it matter?" he said.

Together they descended the spiral iron stairway and emerged into the garden. The fresh air seemed to revive Freece a little. Night had fallen, and the two crooks struck out for the golf club on the other side of the common. They spoke low and earnestly of the project which they had so carefully planned during the last six months.

"I tell you, man, it's foolproof—absolutely foolproof!"

Novak insisted. "Even the meticulous Mullins admits that we've overlooked nothing. Once we get hold of the bullion, then, my friend, we can leave this accursed valley for ever."

"We don't want any more accidents like Challoner's turning up at unexpected moments. By Jove, it was a narrow shave!"

Freece shivered.

"We would certainly have been in the soup if he'd blabbed anything out at the club," he said. "By the way, I suppose it was Gat that shot at Sexton Blake's car last night?"

"Undoubtedly," said Novak. "There's only one other Rolls-Royce in the vicinity, and that's yours. He thought that it was you returning from the City. As far as I know, Gat had nothing on Sexton Blake."

"I wish the rat had shot him, anyway!" said Freece viciously. He shivered again and coughed as the dank ground mist caught his throat.

Suddenly a gaunt figure emerged like a grey phantom from behind a gorse-bush and flung back its head in a peal of horrible, maniacal mirth.

"Oh!" gasped Freece. He was trembling violently. "It's that hag again! She gives me the creeps, Novak!"

The other laughed.

"Don't be a fool! She's useful, for all her craziness. The Ghostmobile wouldn't be half as convincing without her."

"Death! Death! I am the hand-maiden of the Lord!" howled the crone, holding aloft skinny, claw-like hands, and her wild, matted grey hair flying about her gaunt head in the breeze. "Beware, O ye sons of evil, for Death comes with swift wings to those who plan evil!"

"Silence, woman!" hissed Freece.

Ivan Novak laughed cynically. His lean, muscular arm shot out and grabbed hold of the hag.

"Hearken, Mother Haggarty!" he said sibilantly. "You smell death. Tell me. Does death walk abroad to-night?"

"Ay, death and disaster!" mumbled the crone; and she capered about maniacally.

Novak's eyes narrowed.

"See here, Mother Haggarty," he said, taking out a pound note and flourishing it before her eyes. "Here is money for you to wail the dirge at the cross-roads this night. Think of it, mother. Again you shall see your son driving speedily and silently through the night. Stand there and give him greeting."

The crone's talons closed avariciously over the money, and she mumbled in her toothless gums:

"I will see my son, eh? See him again?"

"You will!" chuckled Novak. "And to-night many more brave drivers will race your son on the road of death."

The crone flung back her head and cackled derisively. Freece tugged at the other's sleeve, "Come on, don't waste time with the fool!" he snarled. "You might think it humorous to bait the poor devil, but—"

"Humorous be hanged!" said Novak. "Don't you see how effective it will be? That cackling hag in conjunction with the Ghostmobile is enough to break any driver's nerve. Artistry, my boy—artistry! The insane cannot bear witness against you. Cheer up! To-morrow, my friend, you and I will be worth a million in gold!"

"Gold, gold, gold!" howled the hag after them.

THE TENTH CHAPTER

Zero Hour.

RAIN CAME ON early in the evening, a heavy shower, but it had cleared by nine o'clock, and by the time Splash Page had phoned his story through to the offices the moon had risen, after battling successfully with a sullen bank of retreating clouds.

"And now what?" said Ruff Hanson. "I wish to heck Blake hadn't cleared off to town to-day. What is he driving at?"

Splash Page shrugged his shoulders.

"You know what Blake is," he remarked. "Unless he's absolutely sure of his facts, he seldom divulges them until he's got the whole thing complete."

Together the two friends strolled back together to the Wheatsheaf from the post office. There they found Tinker. The youngster's eyes gleamed with suppressed excitement.

"I've just got some instructions from the guv'nor," he announced. "The three of us have got to meet him at

Stavely Green, just where the Watford by-pass and the Great North Road join."

"But what for?" demanded Splash.

Tinker shook his head.

"He didn't say on the phone. All he said was that we were to pile into Splash Page's bus and reach there before midnight. At a quarter to twelve, to be exact. We've got to park the car in a disused gravel-pit close to the railway embankment, keeping our eyes skinned for the Ghostmobile."

"H'm!" said Ruff Hansom, thoughtfully patting his hip pocket. "That listens good to me, kiddo. Action is what I craves."

Splash pored over his A.A. map and found the spot with little difficulty. He wondered what Blake's object was. Inspector Graves, he discovered, was not at the police station, and when the Wheatsheaf had closed and they had partaken of a hearty supper the three friends set out in the Red Peril with Splash at the wheel.

The shortest cut to Stavely Bridge was by way of Hangman's Hill. Tinker shivered as he passed that ill-omened spot. They encountered nothing untoward, however, and proceeded on their way. Five minutes before the scheduled time Splash Page pointed to a bend in the road that led to the newly-erected concrete bridge.

Round the curve on two wheels the Red Peril swerved.

"This looks like the place," said Tinker, pointing to an irregular gap to the side of the roadway and railway embankment.

It was half hidden from the road by a group of stunted

trees, and, with a jolting of springs and protesting gears. Splash Page urged the car over the soft track into the shadow of the gravel-pit.

The three were clad in grey fleecy overcoats. They alighted from the car with an eager light of anticipation in their eyes.

"I wish old Blake had been more explicit," said Splash, in a whisper. "What exactly are we waiting for?"

Tinker smiled.

"He told us to wait and see."

The three friends crouched in the shadow of the hedge, watchful and alert. Ruff Hanson had drawn out his beloved Willy and Wally in readiness. The minutes seemed to pass by on leaden feet. A solitary Buick chugged under the bridge, and with a roar an electric train glided like a vast illuminated serpent on the embankment overhead.

Suddenly Tinker listened as he heard the rumble of a heavy vehicle. He glanced at his watch. It was five minutes to twelve. Cautiously he peered forward and nudged Splash Page.

Two black shadows showed for an instant above the concrete parapet of the bridge.

The three froze into immobility. Intuition told Splash that something was about to happen to the lumbering truck which was coming along at a steady fifteen m.p.h.

One of the heads disappeared. He heard a short triumphant laugh as the lorry approached. A cloud scurried across the face of the moon at that inopportune moment. There appeared, seemingly from nowhere in the centre of the roadway, an enormous lorry, whose outlines seemed to waver nebulously for a second before they became hard in the fitful rays of the moon. It came full head on from the far side of the bridge to meet the oncoming truck.

The three friends drew in their breath sharply.

"The Ghostmobile!" ejaculated Splash. "Look! The skeleton at the wheel!"

He pointed. Tinker's scalp tingled as he saw a fleshless face with eyeless sockets and a grinning mouth rendered incongruously horrible beneath a chauffeur's peaked cap.

The oncoming truck driver must have seen it simultaneously. A startled shout, and the vehicle swerved drunkenly to the wrong side of the road.

Suddenly a harsh voice barked out: "Now!" and a moment later three dark figures came racing down the steep side of the embankment towards lorry number one.

What happened next Tinker had no clear recollection. Ruff Hanson, impetuous as usual, leapt over the hedge-row, his two six-guns flourished in his hands.

"Stick 'em up!" he snapped.

Ghostmobile or no Ghostmobile, Ruff Hanson craved for action.

The Buick drew up with a harsh shriek of brakes, its front wheels just under the arch of the bridge. The Ghostmobile advanced with a swift uncanny silence. There came the shrill pheep of police whistles punctuated by the staccato crack-crack of guns.

The three figures who had been on the bridge scattered in all directions.

A vicious spurt of flame spat from Ruff Hanson's gun as

he took deliberate aim at the grinning skeleton at the wheel of the Ghostmobile. The phantom car did not slacken speed, but came onward with the same uncanny silence.

"Quick, Gibbon, head those fellows off!" roared a voice. Splash smiled grimly as he recognised the burly blue-uniformed figure of Inspector Graves.

He collided with someone in the semi-gloom, and, gritting his teeth, he swung a vicious left hook upward. There was a stab of flame, the crash of a deafening report, and a hot, acrid wind burnt his cheek.

Splash yelled aloud as a cloud of sulphurous smoke stung his smarting eyes. He had no very clear idea what was happening. He heard the laboured breath of his assailant, another pistol shot rang through the night.

"Go it, Splash!" shouted Tinker. "Let 'em have it."

The heavy thuds of Ruff Hanson's six-guns were unmistakable. Tinker dropped to cover behind some bushes and stared in wonderment at the phantom lorry. It had passed under the bridge, as silently and as uncannily as a shadow. Nothing seemed to stop it.

Then the countryside was suddenly illuminated by a dazzling white flash that threw the whole fantastic scene into stark relief with its brilliant electric radiance. One instant Tinker saw the Ghostmobile, and a second later it seemed to bulge outward and with a thunderous roar that seemed to burst his very eardrums, the phantom lorry exploded.

He flung himself face downward on the ground. There were hoarse shouts, a man's cry in mortal agony. Then a great pillar of red flame shot skyward.

"What's happened?" gasped Splash Page shakily.

The wide-eyed, dishevelled figure of Inspector Graves loomed towards them, gun in hand.

"Hands up!" he snapped. Then, recognising Tinker, gave a startled exclamation. "Oh, it's you, is it? Mr. Blake said that you'd be on hand."

"Holy Henry Heinz, give me something to shoot at!" boomed Ruff Hanson, appearing out of the darkness.

"There's no need," said Inspector Graves dryly. "Thanks to Mr. Blake, we've saved the Bank of England a million pounds in bullion, and solved the mystery of the Ghostmobile."

"What's that?" ejaculated Splash Page. "Here, hold hard, inspector, I don't get this at all."

"You will, Mr. Page," chuckled Graves. "I've got the three men responsible for the hold-up, anyway."

Splash glanced at three sullen hand-cuffed figures, each in the grip of a policeman. One was young Maltravers. The second was Ferris, Colonel Hannibal Smith's agent, and the third a burly looking ruffian, Splash had not seen before.

"But where the deuce is Sexton Blake?" demanded the journalist.

Inspector Graves shrugged his shoulders.

"I don't know, Mr. Page," he confessed. "All I know is that he promised to meet me at Mandeville Magna police station by one o'clock."

"Well—I'll—be—hornswoggled!" was Ruff Hanson's comment.

*   *   *

IN THE TURRET-ROOM of the observatory Dr. Ivan Novak and "Colonel Hannibal Smith" both sat, with tense gaze, watching the glass-mounted illuminated map on the wall of the observatory. It was ten minutes to midnight.

Beads of perspiration prickled through and shone on Freece's forehead. Novak's slim, capable hands played with half a dozen dials on the complicated instrument affixed to the ebonite-topped bench.

Both of them watched a moving red glow of light traced on the map which marked the by-pass to the Great North Road. The strain was telling on Freece.

"Supposing there's a hitch?" he said.

"Don't be a fool!" snapped Novak. "Haven't we tested the thing dozens of times on Hangman's Hill? We can control the car as perfectly as if we were at the wheel ourselves, and with a great deal more safety. Maltravers and Ferris are at their posts, and in half an hour the whole thing will be over."

He gazed intently at the spark gap of the intricate wireless mechanism which controlled that strange vehicle which Splash had named the Ghostmobile.

He and Freece between them had perfected a radio controlled entirely from the transmitter in the turret-room of the observatory. It was a clever bit of electrical engineering, but nothing really extraordinary, considering that aeroplanes and even battleships are controlled in like manner.

Novak, during the War, had successfully experimented with wireless-controlled torpedoes, and, by adapting the system of wireless control for aeroplanes in vogue in the

R.A.F., had applied it to the phantom lorry. The curves and contours of the road were all known and allowed for, but the only thing he could not control was the movement of other vehicles on the read. The lorry, with its awesome dummy driver, went on unheeding—hence the many accidents.

"Zero hour!" he said in a crisp, metallic voice. "It's perfectly timed, Freece."

He pressed an ivory-handled switch, and a crackle of green-blue flame leaped and wavered across the spark gap.

Suddenly Freece felt his blood run cold. A cackle of shrill laughter sounded in the room. With an oath, he leapt to his feet, and his mouth gaped, in the doorway was the gaunt figure of the ragged crone, with matted hair flowing over her shoulders and talonous left hand upraised.

"Novak—Novak, how did this mad woman get here?" he gasped.

The scientist swung round, with a cry.

The figure of the crone straightened suddenly, so that it seemed to loom large, enormous, and menacing in that strange room.

"Yes, gentlemen," said a cool, incisive voice. "It's zero hour, I think."

Freece clutched at the bench. The figure was that of mad Mother Haggarty; the voice was that of Sexton Blake.

"Stick up your hands!" snapped the detective.

His finger trembled suggestively on the trigger of an automatic, which now came into view in his right hand.

The door opened silently behind him, and the burly figure of Detective-Inspector Coutts, followed by half a dozen men, entered the room.

"Your prisoners, I think, Coutts?" said Blake.

There was a hiss of sparks, and for a moment or two the room was illumined in a ghastly, blue-white radiance. The ruby light on the map exploded with a sharp report.

Fifteen miles away, the Ghostmobile was shattered into nothingness.

"No," said Sexton Blake, "I don't believe in ghosts; I only believe in their inherent possibility."

It was two days later. The sun was shining brightly through the windows of the Baker Street consulting-room. Tinker made a wry grimace as he straightened his back and lifted his fingers from the typewriter keys.

Page and Ruff Hanson were sitting on opposite sides of the fireplace. The detective himself was lounging in his favourite dressing-gown and well-worn slippers.

Tinker yawned lustily. He had been typing steadily for over an hour, and he now clipped the sheets together ready for the famous index, under the heading of "The Ghostmobile."

"It's been the finest story of mine the 'Radio' has ever printed," said Splash Page. "By gosh, Blake, the old rag would be as dead as a parish magazine if it weren't for the stuff I get from you now and again! It went down great, and even old Julius Jones was bucked about it, though I didn't have space to give the full explanations."

"I think there's little more to clear up," said Sexton Blake. "If Novak had only used his brains legitimately he might have made a fortune out of his radio-controlled car. As it was, he gambled on gaining a million quickly.

He was aided and abetted by Freece, who had previously conceived the fantastic notion of establishing a colony of crooks in the Chilterns. With Novak's invention he hoped to become the first radio highwayman."

"By gosh, it certainly looked uncanny, guv'nor!" said Tinker. "And it was a touch of genius to put a dummy skeleton at the wheel!"

Blake smiled.

"Novak's bizarre Russian temperament came uppermost there," said he.

"And gave me some darned good headlines!" chuckled Splash Page. "The man Mullins has confessed. I suppose you know that?" he added.

Blake nodded, and filled his briar.

"Yes. Mullins was in charge of the bullion consignment to America. The special van from the Bank of England leaves once a month under armed escort for Liverpool, via the Great North Road. The Southampton route is too well guarded. Novak knew that. As for the Ghostmobile, as Splash calls it, there is nothing really new in the principal of the thing. But it was essential for them to try it out and have it working perfectly without undue interference. The fact that they ran over or killed various people didn't seem to worry them a bit.

"We already have wireless-controlled battleships and aeroplanes. Similar control of ordinary engines is quite a common thing."

"But this wasn't an ordinary engine," put in Tinker.

"No, it wasn't," agreed Blake. "Novak could probably have made a second fortune out of that, if he hadn't been so eager for easy money. The silent engine he built into that lorry has certainly been an eye-opener to the internal combustion engineers who have seen it. It's a marvellous piece of work, but it's going to become public property now, for he never even took out a patent. Oh, by the way, it wasn't only the engine that made that lorry so ghost-like. He cut out the remaining noise by using low-pressure balloon tyres."

"Ah, but how about the way it suddenly appeared and disappeared?" demanded Tinker. "I remember it seemed to—"

"Oh, didn't I tell you about that?" rejoined Blake. "Didn't I tell you about that spark gap on the bench in the colonel's observatory?"

"You did not!" accused Tinker.

"Well, I'm afraid it's a bit scientific for your immature brain," responded the detective, with a smile, "but I don't mind telling you if you can stand it. I knew the readers of Splash's infant-class 'Radio' couldn't, so I didn't give it to him."

"O.K., Blake," put in Splash, grinning. "I wouldn't have printed it, anyway. They're only interested in the ghost stuff, and the hor-ri-ble skeleton."

"Aw, can it, you newshound!" growled Ruff Hanson. "Let the professor get on with his stuff."

"Briefly," remarked Blake, "and without going into technical details, the disappearance trick was worked by means of invisible rays—another commonplace of science these days. You've heard of ultra-violet rays and infra-red rays? That simply means the rays of light which are invisible to human eyes, which can only see light—in the form of colours—in the spectrum, or rainbow, if you like. These invisible light rays occur at either end of the spectrum; it's a matter of wavelength or frequency. Light vibrations.

"Each colour has its own wavelength. A short wavelength gives us the sensation of seeing red; a longer one green, and so on."

Blake paused, and sucked thoughtfully at his pipe.

"It is a great pity that Novak managed to destroy that instrument board," he went on. "I feel convinced that he had discovered another great scientific secret, and that the disappearance trick was controlled by means of the spark gap. I have a shrewd suspicion that he used an adaptation of Mr. J. L. Baird's Noctovisor[6] in order to make the lorry appear and reappear. You remember that, when it first became visible, it seemed to look hazy for a second or two, and then came into sharp focus. I think—"

"But a noctovisor?" Tinker asked. "Isn't it something to do with television?"

"You'll have to look up the reference books if you want to know the ins and outs of that," countered Blake; "but it has to do with these invisible light rays I've been talking about, and it allows the human eye—by means of the camera—to see in darkness or fog. I think that Novak had somehow achieved the result of being able to blot out his wireless-controlled lorry at a distance by means of this infra-red ray. There must have been an area into which it plunged at certain points, just like a motor-car driving into a pond. But in this case the pond as well as the car was invisible, and the car was doubtless made so by some specially tuned-in electrical apparatus the lorry carried.

"But it is quite probable that, if we had had a camera, we should have been able to still get a picture of it, for a sensitised plate can still detect the invisible rays, although the eye cannot."

"Well, well, I'll say you're the gnat's eyebrows when it comes to doing the professor stuff!" boomed Ruff Hanson.

"Sounds feasible, though," put in Splash. "I bet if I cared to interview any of these scientific blokes, they would confirm your view."

"During the day," continued Blake, "the Ghostmobile was carefully hidden in a garage belonging to Maltravers, who as you know, was working under Novak. It could be driven in the ordinary way, when wanted."

"Yes. But what about the human angle? Eh, Blake? What about this gink Masters?" interrupted Ruff Hanson.

"His intrusion into the affair was accidental—irrelevant, so far as the crooks' plot was concerned, which was merely to loot the Bank of England lorry. Jem Chance also complicated things in the same way. He was an intrusion, too."

"Anyway, it's been a peach of a story," said Splash Page. "I suppose Maltravers & Co. intended to turn on the gas just before the bullion lorry reached the bridge, and then, when the guard was asphyxiated, transfer the gold into the Ghostmobile?"

Blake nodded.

"That was the plan according to Novak's diary. By assuming poor Mother Haggarty's character I was enabled to tramp around after P.-c. Pierce's adventure without exciting much comment." Blake chuckled. "Poor soul, she is now being well looked after in the county asylum. Which reminds me—"

He dived his hand into his waistcoat pocket and withdrew a crumpled Treasury note.

"The late Dr. Novak's gift to me—or, rather, Mother Haggarty. See that you forward it on, Tinker."

Ruff Hanson snorted.

"But what about my prisoners?" he said, in a grieved voice. "I've travelled three thousand miles to get Gat—"

"You've got Willy and Wally, you hard-boiled egg!" said Splash Page. "What're you worrying about? You ought to be thankful old Coutts didn't pull you in for not having a licence."

Ruff Hanson's snort was eloquent as he helped himself to a whisky-and-soda.

THE END

Notes

3. "Italian Larry" here replaces an ethnic slur.

4. "Lèse-majesté" means to detract from or offend the dignity of a person.

5. Ramon Navarro was a handsome film star of the period.

6. John Logie Baird was at this point in history (1931) demonstrating the technology that would soon become television. In 1926, he had filed a patent for "Noctovision," which was a technique through which images could be formed from reflected radio waves, similar to radar but without the capability of determining distance.

THE MYSTERY OF WALLA-WALLA

SEXTON BLAKE CLOSED the paper and sighed.

"Poor old Hanson."

"Poor old—why, what happened to him?" I asked.

"You live by the gun, you die by the gun."

"He was killed?"

"Shot in the back on Christmas Day, 1933."

"I'm sorry," I said. "I didn't know. I don't—" I paused to reorganise my words. "The ultimate fate of your friends and enemies was seldom disclosed."

Blake had finished his cigar but continued to toy with the stub of it, rolling it between his fingers. He murmured, "Many losses."

A silence enveloped us.

He broke it. "You mentioned you would return to the subject of Mademoiselle Yvonne. I suppose, then, that the next account features her?"

"It does," I said, and stopped, unsure how to proceed.

I made a decision and plunged straight in:

"Might I suggest that, in the same way Irene Adler was, for Sherlock Holmes, the woman, so Yvonne was to you a—"

"No!" he snapped.

"No?"

"No, you may not. I'll not have any tiresome comparisons to Doyle's creations, thank you very much."

"All right. But surely you won't deny that the author of the Yvonne tales, G. H. Teed, repeatedly alluded to a romantic undercurrent in your rel—"

Again, Blake cut me off, stabbing at the air with his cigar stub. "I've already told you that my cases were invariably simplified for publication. Simplified, but also romanticised. My 'relationship'—as you were about to classify it—with Yvonne Cartier was an exceedingly complex one. Do not overlook the fact that she was, when I first encountered her, a criminal."

"But her criminal actions," I protested, "were in revenge. She and her family had been cheated out of their prosperous ranch in Australia. She went after the men responsible."

He gave a curt nod.

This talk of Yvonne was prompting none of the emotion I had earlier detected at mention of her name. Blake had clamped down; become icy cold.

"That is true," he allowed. "But the ruthlessness with which she pursued her vengeance; the meticulous planning of it; the utter ruination to which she condemned those who had swindled her ..."

He turned his head slightly and gazed into the fire; flicked the stub into it. "A dangerous woman," I murmured.

"Yes." He turned his eyes to mine and raised an eyebrow. "Better to have her with me than against me, do you see?"

I did see, and indicated so, while asking myself: if Blake had purposely manipulated Yvonne's emotions in order to turn her into an ally, then which of them was the more ruthless?

I held up the binder to display the cover of the Union Jack I'd selected for the next story.

"In this," I said, "she regains the ranch."

He made a sound of approval. "That period was the turning point. Her retribution was complete. Her taste for adventure could now be directed toward more positive ends."

"With encouragement from you?"

"Quite so. Had I not made her a friend, and become, I suppose, something of a mentor to her, she may well have ended up as one of my most dangerous criminal opponents."

"A calculated relationship, then. Not a hint of romance?" I said, unable to keep the scepticism from my tone.

"Precisely that."

I didn't believe him at all.

THE MYSTERY OF WALLA-WALLA

by G. H. Teed
UNION JACK issue 528 (1913)

THE FIRST CHAPTER

In the Grip of Drought—Despair—Yvonne
Arrives at Her Old Home.

AUSTRALIA LAY PARCHED and gasping in the grip of drought. Thousands of square miles of what had been rich grazing country were now vast stretches of white, shrivelled grass, broken here and there by big patches of stiff red loam or hard packed "cement," from which the starved shoots had long ago disappeared. Over all hung the coating of sand which had been stirred up in the Mallee country, and had come whipping across the land on the hot wings of the enervating north wind. The branches of the big blue-gum and box shade trees rustled monotonously with a slow, listless sweep.

Still whiter than the dead blue grass and salt weed, were the snowy corpses of heavily-woolled sheep, which had been beaten down in their battle against thirst, and had died where they lay, too weak to prolong the struggle. Here and there a little lamb bleated helplessly, gazing in surprised distress at the silent ewe, which for the first time had failed it.

Even the green shoots in the bottoms of the creeks and the binabongs had given out.

The whole of the vast expanse presented a picture of panting, dying Nature.

For weeks had the drought continued. Day after day, long train-loads of stock had been hurried southwards, where, on the well-watered and green stretches of Gippsland they could exist until the drought broke, and the blessed rain came. But even then unnumbered thousands were left, and men, red-eyed from weeks of strained anxiety, gazed at the hot leaden sky with its brazen disc, and prayed or cursed as was their nature.

Not even the crops assisted in stemming the white flame of the drought. Great paddocks of wheat and oats, lucerne and ambercane had been scorched and shrivelled to hungry, weedy stalks. The grain lay in sickly tumbled heaps of whitened straw, the lucerne was burnt to brown, and the sap had long ago departed from the once-juicy stems of the sorghum.

On the plains, where the vast networks of irrigation channels assume the appearance of a giant spider's web, men fared better for a time. Then the channels had stopped their flow. Water was held back, and only dribbled out at ever-lengthening periods for stock purposes. The Murray and the Loddon had not been so low for years. The once-bursting Lannecoorie Weir, with its enormous boasted capacity, was a tiny pond, with hardly enough to float a small rowboat.

Men, who had risked their all, were forced to spend days

and nights in the saddle, helpless to assuage the suffering, and forced to watch their stock dying in thousands, but still fighting, still hoping. Others, in desperation, dug countless pits in search of water.

Owing to the configuration of the country, the water table was not far down, and many cries of joy went up when, into the pits rushed that for which they sought. But what a cruel prank had Nature reserved for them. The water was brackish—unfit for man or beast, no matter how deadly was his need.

And throughout all this period of burning death, there were men who sought to benefit from the helplessness of their fellows; men who fought and cursed and drank; men who hung, ever watching, ever ready to snatch from the weaker grasp that which they coveted.

Binabong Station, once the richest stretch of land in the district, was not immune from the general blast of the drought. Since it had been the home of Mademoiselle Yvonne Cartier, the luxuriant and rich flats had fallen on evil times. Often had it changed hands since its prosperous days under the Cartier regime, and each time had something disappeared from its well-stocked equipment.

No more the great traction engine puff-puffed up and down the great paddocks, towing after it the little procession of disk ploughs and harrows; no more waved great stretches of wheat and oats; no more could be seen the rolling paddocks of rich tallow, and no more could be heard the cheery shouts of the stockmen and boundary riders, the jackeroo and roustabouts, or the sharp, excited bark of the shaggy sheep dogs as they careered madly around big mobs of sheep to the resonant crack of the stock-whip.

Almost all its former bustle and life had disappeared. Only a few listless men remained, wrapped in the general air of desolation which overhung the place, and modelling their days after those of the owner.

NIGHT WAS JUST giving way to the golden hue of dawn. The sun's disc rose like a ball of crimson, presaging still another day of hot, rainless horror. Up in the once beautifully furnished Binabong Station homestead sat the young owner, little heeding the coming of another day.

In the slow creeping dawn-light his face looked drawn and haggard. Though barely thirty, he looked fifty. His eyes were puffed and swollen with the look one sees in those of a man who has caroused long and slept little.

The now-useless flame of the lamp which still burned, accentuated the drawn appearance of the man's face, and lent to the whole room a look of shame at being caught, as it were, by the pure brilliance of open day.

And well it might. If the man's appearance was dishevelled, that of the room itself was worse. On the table, at his elbow, stood two empty decanters, a half-filled syphon, and several glasses. The cloth was littered with cold butts of cigars, cigarettes and ashes. A few scattered cards lay about in the general disorder, while on the floor, where they had been carelessly thrown, were heaps upon heaps, presenting the appearance of a miniature snowfall.

Over all hung the heavy, stale odour of smoke and

whisky. In the centre of this hideous array sat the man, his whole attitude that of complete despondency, of absolute and utter despair.

That was only one of many dawns during the drought which John Treherne had seen under similar surroundings. For six months he had fought the creeping scourge of drought, and fought gamely. Then the madness of it all had seized him. Like even stronger men than he, he had succumbed, and cursed blindly at the implacable decree of Nature. Unlike they, however, he had not given reign to his madness in a blind whirl of revelry, from which they had emerged with shaking hands and lack lustre eyes, but still purged, and ready again to continue the fight.

Better were it for John Treherne had he done so. Instead, he had fallen into toils as sinuous and as unyielding as those of the Evil One himself.

Two months before, his neighbour, the owner of the adjoining station of Walla-Walla, had come to him with offers of assistance—assistance for which John Treherne was duly grateful. This man, Edward Jameson, had then seemed like a helping hand sent by Providence itself. At first it had been the offer of a well-grassed paddock for some of Treherne's ewes which were lambing. Then had come the offer of another paddock for a mob of weaners. This, too, Treherne had accepted.

Why it was that Jameson was carrying no stock over all his great stretch of country he did not stop to ask himself. If only then he could have read the subtle cunning and diabolical cleverness of his "generous" neighbour.

Born in the country, bred in the bush, inured to the life

of the back blocks, son of a shrewd, scheming father, who had risen from being a drover to the ownership of Walla-Walla, Jameson had cast a jealous eye at the rich acres of Binabong.

Long ago had his experienced eye seen the coming of the drought. Long ago had his fertile brain weaved its plans for clearing off his stock. This would achieve two ends at one stroke.

One was his own immunity from the effects of the drought, and the other was the reserve he needed in case Nature threw the winning cards into his hands. And with that almost uncanny encouragement which she seems to hand out to evil-doers, Nature had done just what he wished.

Patiently had he watched, while his neighbours, Treherne among them, had hurried off their stock to Gippsland. From all over the country others were doing the same. Finally the word came that no more could be received. Gippsland was full. Even that rain-blessed region had its limits. Then did men tear the very thatching from their huts in a futile effort to save their stock. Then did John Treherne begin his long fight which had ended in ruin; and then did Edward Jameson play his first card.

In the guise of sympathetic friend had he ridden over to Binabong. Treherne was duly grateful for his offer, and seized on it with avidity. Two years only had he been out from England, and his life there had given him little opportunity of probing the depths and purposes of human nature.

Even the removal of the ewes and weaners had not

availed—as Jameson, who had seen the full effect of a drought, knew it wouldn't. Then Treherne's stock had been paddocked near Jameson's boundaries. Jameson's well-stocked water tanks had been placed at his disposal. Only the huge overshot dam in Treherne's home paddock now served for Binabong's needs. The Binabong was empty; the creeks were dry.

Still the spectre of ruin stalked John Treherne, and then his wool company, who had been financing him until shearing should arrive, made demands. They must have money. He had none to give. Must he sell his sheep in order to realise? He had paid big prices for them in a booming market. Must he sacrifice them for the two and three shillings a head, which was all they would fetch in the glutted market of the present?

It seemed so, and yet, wait! There was one chance. Jameson had been more than neighbourly. He had been a godsend. He was wealthy, and, unlike most of the others, free from care. Perhaps he would help.

Acting on this thought, Treherne had ridden post-haste to Walla-Walla, and had besought Jameson's assistance.

How well he could remember his renewed hope as he rode back home with Jameson's promise of the amount he needed. How easy it had been. One word and his generous neighbour had said "yes"—with Treherne's stock as security.

In that mysterious way in which creditors seem endowed with a clairvoyant faculty, when a man is on his last legs, did others begin to press Treherne.

Nothing but money would do, and money they must

have. They might as well have tried to squeeze blood from a stone, but still they persisted, and in his new extremity, Treherne turned once more to his neighbour; nor did he know that the same hand which helped him had been the same hand which had pressed him with his creditors.

After that he lived on grimly, hopefully. The drought must break. His sheep were carrying heavy fleeces. His wool was clean, and would command good prices. Even through the drought had its "yoke" been apparent, a quality which had suffered in the fleeces of his neighbours' stock. His lambs would soon pick up, and their very pedigree would make them sought after by the "freezers."

But still that great brazen disc rose mockingly each day, and still the pit of ruin yawned. Every head of stock he owned was now pledged as security to Jameson. Yet he must have more money. To get it he must yield his last stronghold, the station itself, and that he had done.

His neighbour had come to his assistance, and though Treherne was the nominal owner of Binabong, Jameson was the practical owner. Still, if rain came, Treherne had a good fighting chance, and none knew it better than Edward Jameson.

It was then that his true cunning exhibited itself—a cunning which hastened its purpose when his experienced eyes read signs of a change in the leaden dome overhead.

With Machiavellian duplicity, he himself grew despondent and gay cheery by turns. One moment he would assert confidently that a change must come, and the next, with well-simulated gloom, he would sigh and shake his head dolefully at the inscrutable heavens.

By degrees the nerve-racked Treherne reflected his neighbour's moods, and when, with every nerve jagged from suspense, every fibre of his being shrieking aloud for some break in the awful monotony of waiting for the rain which never came, Jameson suggested a turn at the cards, Treherne agreed, grateful for the prospect of forgetfulness.

Night after night they played. At first it had been for small stakes, which Treherne always won. Then for larger, when Jameson's luck turned, and for a time they were about even. Then the nightly meetings became a regular habit. Certain hours were set apart. The stakes were again raised.

For days the north wind had been blowing with a heated ferocity which seemed to strain, with a terrible menace, at its bonds. It was not possible that such atmospheric conditions could continue without something snapping.

Treherne, now steeped in the fever of gambling, saw it not. Jameson watched its approach with a careful eye— and again the stakes were raised. For a week the play continued each night from dusk to dawn.

At the end of that time—the morning on which we see John Treherne sitting amidst the wreck of all his hopes— Jameson owned not only every head of stock which had belonged to Treherne, but he owned every solitary acre which went to make up that once magnificent estate, the pride of old John Cartier's heart, and the home of the incomparable Yvonne—Binabong.

Before, he had controlled them in that they were pledged to him. The coming break in the weather, however, had told him they might even then be snatched from his grasp.

The partial feeling of ownership had been too sweet for Jameson to relinquish easily, and so over the cards he had offered to play John Treherne for the debt on the sheep. If Treherne won he could take back every head without repaying a penny of the loan.

The younger man had jumped at the offer. They played, and Treherne lost. With seeming magnanimity, Jameson offered to repeat the offer, this time with the station itself as the stake. In his new despondency, Treherne took the bait.

Again they played. Again he lost.

Now Binabong and all its stock would pass to Edward Jameson in a transfer more binding than all the mortgages or deeds in existence, the transfer of honour.

And when, Edward Jameson rode homewards, just before dawn that morning, he had a look of satisfied greed in his eyes, and an evil smile on his lips, which only passed away when the first faint streak appeared in the east.

He had played a long game, a patient game, a cunning game, and in his pocket he held the tiny slip of paper which gave to him all that which he had coveted, and beggared the man who had blindly trusted him of all his worldly possessions.

And yet on the hot wings of the parched dawn was coming to Edward Jameson a just and sweeping vengeance. Even as he cantered homewards through the spreading light, and even as John Treherne sat in huddled despair, reviewing his shattered past and his hopeless future, did the golden sun appear.

Barely had it risen like a great crimson globe, floating in a sea of pink and gold, when against its brazen face were silhouetted two figures.

The early rising boundary-riders saw them far away over the rolling paddocks, and shrugged. Probably only two more creditors hastening to snatch what they could, as many others had done during the past few weeks, they thought.

As the galloping figures drew nearer, however, they could make out that one was a woman. Her wide hat and regularly flapping divided skirt proclaimed her sex.

The other was a man. Truly a strange pair to arrive at Binabong so early in the morning.

Nearer and nearer they drew. Another strange thing. The woman took the lead, and rode confidently on, taking advantage of a short cut here, instinctively finding the best place to jump a creek there, riding, in fact, with an exhibition of knowledge regarding the best trail through the paddocks, which rivalled that of the oldest stockman.

His curiosity aroused, one of the younger jackeroos hailed old Gene, the head stockman, who had been on Binabong in its palmy days as well as through all its vicissitudes, and who had not yet appeared. In answer to the hail, however, he poked his grizzled head out of the bunk-house door, and demanded to know, in innocent profanity, what was wrong.

"I say, Gene, do come here and have a squint," called young Roberts, the jackeroo who had hailed.

The old stockman strode through the doorway, and leaping the drafting yard fence instead of going round it, cast his keen old eyes over the paddocks.

"What do you make of them?" queried Roberts. "There, you could see them quite plainly when they topped that rise. A man and a woman. Did you see how she led the way over that crab-hole stretch? Dash it all I've been on here over a year, and I never found that path myself until a week ago. Now they are coming to the creek. There, Gene, did you see that? Not a man on the place could have gone straighter for that narrow jump than she did. And by jingo, she's young, too. You can see her face now. They're strangers, that's a dead cert."

He broke off in his excited comments, and glanced at the old stockman, surprised that he had not been interrupted ere this by a profane command to shut up. His surprise changed to wonder as he looked, for old Gene was gazing over the paddocks with the alert expression of an old war-horse. His face seemed more weather-beaten than ever; his keen old eyes seemed suddenly filmed, and his gnarled hands were clenched tightly. He seemed oblivious to the presence of the other, as indeed he was. Then, suddenly his lips parted, and he spoke more to himself than to anyone else.

"There never weren't no female what knew those short cuts but the little missie," he said slowly. "I ain't never seen no one but the little missie put a horse along like that, and who should know better than me what taught her to ride."

"What on earth are you talking about?" asked the amazed jackeroo.

But old Gene was deaf to his question; and kept his eyes

riveted on the rapidly approaching figures. Then he gave one great leap backwards, and tore at top speed for the bunk-house.

"Joe, Pete, Smith, Harris, Curly, Monty!" he yelled excitedly, dashing into the bunk-house. "Up, you hounds, up quick! The little missie is coming."

Six pairs of booted feet struck the floor at the same moment, and six faces as grizzled as old Gene's peered in unbelief at the head stockman.

"Don't stand there like a lot of dummies!" he roared. "Would you have the little missie come back without a welcome? She'll be here in a few moments."

"Are you crazy from the heat or is that on the level?" drawled Monty, though his twitching hands belied the calm of his manner.

Gene's subsequent profanity in lieu of an answer convinced Monty that it was "on the level," and then those six old veterans moved with alacrity. Six gnarled hands followed Gene's in dragging out heavy revolvers. With the smooth despatch born of long experience they filled every chamber. Then, with the head stockman in front, they contemptuously put aside the younger men who thought they had all suddenly gone mad, and, with old Gene leading, dashed out and across the drafting yards.

One long look did they take; one simultaneous gasp of surprised joy did they give as they saw the slim grace of the leading figure; then seven revolvers went up, and seven fingers emptied chamber after chamber on the morning air just as their "little missie" rode into the circle and sprang, half laughing, half sobbing with joy, into the welcoming embrace of those old veterans who had adored her from the cradle.

Many an old eye grew moist, and many a seamed face blushed with pleasure as her fresh young lips touched their weather-beaten cheeks each in turn, and then what a wild, whole-souled cheer rent the air in joyous welcome to the "little missie."

"Oh, Gene, Monty, Smith, Harris, Joe, Pete, Curly," she cried, through her tears of happiness, "how good it is to see you all again! But what have you done to the dear old place? I could barely believe I was on Binabong. But first, I want you to meet my uncle, Mr. Graves. Uncle"—and she turned to the smiling Graves—"come and shake hands with my dear old friends."

And then all tried to tell at once of the many girlish escapades of Yvonne when she had ridden through the great paddocks in joyous abandon, a stock whip in her hand and a shaggy sheep dog beside her. Once more she turned to old Gene and repeated her question.

"Well you might ask that, little missie," answered the stockman slowly. "Binabong ain't never been the same since you left. Me and the others would have left long ago only we ain't as young as we used to be, and changing goes hard. It has gone from bad to worse. First one thing and then another. When Mr. Treherne, the present owner, took it over we hoped for better things. He seemed to try and make something of it, missie, but I guess the drought and something else has about finished him."

"Something else, Gene?" said Yvonne quickly. "What

do you mean?"

"I means Jameson, missie."

"Ah, has he fallen into his hands?"

The old stockman nodded.

"I think so. Jameson has been here every day and every night for weeks. All the Binabong stock is on Walla-Walla, and if I know anything it is likely to stay there. I never did see Jameson or his father let go anything they ever got their fingers on."

Yvonne nodded slowly.

"I know, Gene. He had his eye on Binabong after father died, only Ike Vineburg and his crew ruined us first and got it. I'm afraid uncle and I have come at a bad time, but I had such a longing to see the old place, Gene, I couldn't resist the desire."

"God bless you, little missie," exclaimed Gene, "me and the boys can't tell you how glad we are to see you again! We're only sorry the place don't look like it used to. Will you stay long?"

"Well," laughed Yvonne, "we intended staying for a week or so, and were hoping to find agreeable people on the place. But if the present owner is in trouble he won't be very anxious to have strange guests about. Still, I think we will ride on to the house and see him. Perhaps you had better come, Gene, and tell him who we are. I'll see the rest of you later in the day," she added, turning to the other six. "Then we'll have one of our old gallops through the paddocks, though now there aren't any sheep to mob up," she finished, with a little catch in her throat.

"By heavens, missie, we'll get a mob of sheep for you

to muster up if we have to take them at the point of the gun," drawled Monty, and his companions echoed his sentiments in no uncertain tones.

In the meantime Gene had saddled up a horse, and, waving her hand, Yvonne led the way to the house in a sweeping gallop.

Sitting in the room which formed the tomb of his dead hopes, John Treherne heard the sound of flying hoofs as they swept over the sun-baked ground towards the house. "Good heavens!" he muttered bitterly. "Has Jameson brought his men to take possession already, or is it more of the carrion hanging about the corpse?"

He savagely kicked aside a fallen chair, and, getting stiffly to his feet, stumbled along the passage and out on to the verandah. There he stood blinking in the morning sun, his mind gradually coming from the abyss of his troubles to the fact that a delightfully charming-looking girl and a middle-aged man in immaculate riding clothes were descending before him.

As his blood-shot eyes took in the vision of fresh beauty a slow, dull flush mounted over Treherne's features, and he half turned as though to seek the shelter of the house where the signs of his dissipation would be less visible.

Graves, man of the world as he was, sized up the situation in a glance. He had seen that heavy eye and that shaky hand too often not to be able to read their meaning. With a low word to Yvonne he went ahead with Gene, and held out his hand as the latter introduced him.

Talking casually he moved towards the door, and Treherne mechanically followed. Once out of sight of the girl Treherne recovered his composure and remembered his duties as host. Turning to Graves he said wearily:

"I'm very pleased, indeed, to meet you, Mr. Graves, but, to be perfectly frank, you come at a rather unfortunate time. To put it plainly, I am no longer the owner of Binabong. The ownership passed last night to my neighbour Jameson, and I am practically only here on sufferance myself."

"Oh, that's all right!" drawled Graves cheerfully. "My niece used to own Binabong, and, as she was seized by a sudden desire to see it again, we came out from home with that intention. I'm sorry to hear that you are in trouble, and assure you we have no desire to intrude. However, you slip along and take a cold plunge. Then we'll breakfast together, and who knows, perhaps, we may be able to find some way out of your troubles."

"That's impossible," answered Treherne gloomily, "but I'll act on your suggestion. Please make my apologies to your niece and tell her I shall receive her properly in half an hour. In the meantime, please make yourself at home. Your niece will know her way about as well as I."

"Right!" rejoined Graves.

As Treherne nodded and hastened away he turned to Gene.

"On the whole, I don't know but what our arrival was rather fortunate," he said, in low tones. "I've only seen that sort of a look in a man's eyes a few times, and each time it was when he had a sudden desire to gaze into the business end of a revolver with his finger on the trigger."

"You are not far wrong," answered Gene, gazing with

239

new respect at Graves. "That look has been growing in his eyes for days. How Jameson has landed him I don't know, but I'll bet it wasn't on the square."

"Mr. Jameson evidently doesn't hold a very high place in your estimation," remarked Graves.

"You bet he doesn't," grunted the stockman. "Shall I bring in the little missie, sir?"

"Yes, you might."

Graves strolled along while Gene went to fetch Yvonne. By chance he stopped at the half-open door of the room where Treherne and Jameson had been gaming. With a grunt of disgust he strode across and threw open the window. Just as he had done so Yvonne entered, and stood looking in amazement at the scattered cards.

"So that is why our host wears such a look at sunrise," she murmured softly.

"And, if you ask me, that's how our host lost his station," replied Graves.

Yvonne's eyes clouded as she gazed at the scene of general disorder, and in her absorption she unconsciously bent and picked up several of the cards from the floor. These she absent-mindedly shuffled in her hands, her eyes looking at them unseeingly. Then as her thoughts came back to the present she glanced carelessly at their backs, taking in, as was her wont, the general details of the conventional design which adorned them.

Suddenly her hands stopped shuffling and her gaze grew steady. Puckering her face she bent lower, and for minutes studied the design with some care. Graves, who had turned and was looking out of the window, did not see her stoop and quickly pick up several more from the floor. Once more she studied the designs and then she spoke. "What is it I have always said you and your club cronies excel at more than anything else, uncle?" she asked, with apparent irrelevance.

Graves swung round quickly as he heard the curiously strained note in her voice.

"Cards," he answered laconically. "Why?"

"Because you profess to know all about cards that there is to be known, and I wish your opinion on something."

"If it's worth anything you are welcome to it. What is it?"

"Will you examine the backs of these cards and tell me if you notice anything peculiar in the design?"

With surprise depicted on his countenance Graves strode across and took the cards which she held out. Then he took them closer to the window and began to examine them. For five minutes dead silence reigned. At the end of that time he tuned slowly and their eyes met.

"By heavens, Yvonne," he breathed, "they are marked, every blessed one of them. It's cleverly done, too. None but the initiated could ever detect it."

Yvonne nodded.

"Yes, it was the curve of the scroll in the design which caught my attention. Mr. Blake explained it to me one time."

"Oh, indeed!" grinned Graves, as Yvonne blushed. "But Yvonne, this is serious," he added, more gravely. "If these are the cards with which Treherne and Jameson have been playing one of them has been playing a crooked game."

"And from visible signs I would think it was not our host," remarked Yvonne. "At any rate, put some in your pocket, uncle. We may need them."

Graves had just managed to thrust those he held in his pocket when a footfall sounded in the passage outside and Treherne entered.

His face was still drawn and haggard-looking, and his eyes heavy, but he wore a much more presentable appearance and seemed more himself. He welcomed Yvonne courteously, and in a few moments they moved towards the breakfast-room.

Whether it was Graves's languid air of understanding or Yvonne's delicately-expressed sympathy it is hard to say, but, owing to one or both, before the repast was half over Treherne's story was falling in a torrent from his lips. Not a single detail did he miss.

From the time he had bought Binabong until he had, in his madness, risked its fertile acres over the cards he told his tale, and never did his hearers listen to a more heartbreaking story of struggle and setbacks, madness and despair, unless it were the story of Yvonne's own loss of the same station.

"I hope you won't think I am flinching from the result, mademoiselle," he said. "It is only now that I realise the whirl of madness in which I lived, and the realisation loses nothing of its bitterness that it comes too late."

"Certainly I don't think so," she replied. "By the way, Mr. Treherne, I'd like to ask you something about your gaming."

"I will answer whatever you wish to ask."

"Did you or your guest supply the cards with which you played?"

"Why—er—let me see. If I remember rightly, I did at first until mine ran out. Then Jameson brought some with him when he came. In fact, now you mention it, I remember that he supplied all we used lately."

"So I thought, Mr. Treherne," said Yvonne. "Since that is the case, I am going to show you something after breakfast which will startle you considerably, if I am not mistaken."

"What is it?" he asked, with a puzzled look.

"Let us not spoil this delicious breakfast by unpleasant details," laughed Yvonne.

But after breakfast she led the way back to the card-room, and there the stupefied John Treherne gazed in spell-bound amazement while Graves gave him his first lesson in marked cards. When Graves had finished, they adjourned to the cool sitting-room, where Yvonne had had a memorable interview with two of the men who had brought financial ruin to herself and her mother. There she waved her companions to a seat, and, lighting a dainty cigarette, began to speak.

Slowly, and with soft emphasis, she explained to John Treherne exactly who Edward Jameson was, and what he was. Then she dwelt on her own loss of Binabong, and her great desire to return. From that she went to the subject of Treherne's troubles, and for another half hour spoke earnestly. At the end of that time Graves was smiling in languid enjoyment, and Treherne was gazing at her in undisguised admiration.

Silence reigned for some minutes after she had finished.

It was broken by Treherne, who rose and held out his hand to Yvonne.

"Mademoiselle," he said slowly, "I feel that your advice is good. I place myself entirely in your hands."

"Then that is settled, Mr. Treherne," smiled Yvonne. "We will start this very day to arrange our little surprise for Mr. Edward Jameson, of Walla-Walla, and when we get through, well, we shall see what we shall see."

THE SECOND CHAPTER

Blake Goes to Australia—Jameson's Story—Blake Has a Desire to Read.

SOME MEN ARE born to adventure, some men seek adventure, and some have adventure hurled at them from every point of the compass. In the latter category might be classed Sexton Blake, for, if any man ever lived in a continual round of danger and adventure, surely he is that man.

When he finally made up his mind to shelve professional duties and make a long-promised trip to Australia, where he had not been for some time, he made a vow that nothing would induce him to touch a case until his return. For a wonder Tinker heartily agreed with his master, and no more idle-looking pair could have been seen around Melbourne than Sexton Blake and his assistant, with their inseparable companion Pedro.

They were not known in Melbourne under those names, however. Blake rejoiced in the all-embracing name of Smith—without the "y" and the "e"—while Tinker posed fairly successfully as his younger brother.

Thus the "Smiths" came to Melbourne, bent on a quiet holiday, with perhaps a few races to liven up things, and thus did the Smiths get drawn into a strange whirl of adventure through no fault of their own.

The actual instrument which Fate chose to upset the detective's carefully formed plans came in the person of one Captain Brien O'Brien, late of His Majesty's Army, and one time study mate at 'varsity with Sexton Blake.

It was in the quietly elegant smoking-room at Menzie's Hotel that they met, and only a vigorous jab in the delighted captain's ribs kept that gentleman from blurting out Blake's name for all the world to hear. After he had decided to desist from using Blake's arm as a pump-handle, his incoherent exclamations gradually descended to intelligible English as approved by His Majesty's Government and from the bombardment of questions Blake managed to grasp that his old pal "would be dashed if he didn't think this was the best thing that had happened since Adam was a yearling; yes, by gad!"

After that, Blake gathered that the captain desired to know "What he had been doing with himself, old dear? What had brought him to Australia? Was he married, and was this his son? (meaning Tinker). Why was he incog?" and a dozen other whys, wheres, hows, and whos.

When the cyclone had somewhat subsided, Blake introduced Tinker, and, together, the three of them moved to a quiet corner of the smoking-room which looked out on Bourke Street.

While Blake and his old friend exchanged experiences of the years which had passed since they had come down from 'varsity, Tinker cast a contemptuous glance at Melbourne's prehistoric trams, which seemed to cling to that rising city like an "old man of the sea."

After some minutes a chance phrase caught his ear, and as it seemed to promise a change of some sort, he gave his attention to the conversation.

"But you must, Blake," the captain was saying. "Campbell is no end of a good sport, and he's got a topping place up country. Over a hundred thousand acres, all together, and, bad as the drought has been, he hasn't lost a sheep. All due to his artesian well, so he says. Anyway, I'm going up for a week or ten days. Tommy Morrison was coming with me, but he's off on aide duty to the governor, and cried off at the last minute. Campbell's younger brother is there, and you'll make a fourth for bridge. Now don't say no, old chap. Bring the lad along; you will be just as well off up there as here, and we'll have no end of a high old time."

"Campbell," remarked Blake musingly. "It wouldn't be old Dumpy Campbell, of Magdalen, would it?"

"Good heavens! yes," cried the captain, in delight. "I'd forgotten you and Dumpy used to be pals. Now I remember the twenty-round go you and he had down behind the pub on Derby night. Scott! that seems an age ago!"

"Er—yes, Campbell and I used to be—er—good friends," put in Blake hastily, with a sidelong look at Tinker's grin as that sharp-witted young man gleefully drank in the reference to one of Blake's youthful escapades, a bit of information he would casually let drop some time in the future when Blake was wigging him for getting into a similar situation.

"Well, old man, what do you say?" persisted the captain. "Shall I wire Campbell that I am bringing you? Gad! He'll kill the fatted calf when he hears you are coming."

"All right," laughed Blake. "When do we start?"

"To-morrow morning. We will take the six-thirty-five from Spencer Street, and go by way of Kerang. Campbell will have horses to meet us at Barham."

"That will suit me all right," answered Blake. "Mind, though, it's only for a week."

"Wait until we get you up there, old son," chuckled the delighted captain as he hastened away to send the wire.

TWO EVENINGS LATER, a party of joyous spirits sat down to dinner at the Campbell homestead. There was Campbell himself, a big, bluff, fair man, who had been fully as delighted at Blake's surprise visit as Captain O'Brien had prophesied; his younger brother, a miniature edition of the elder, who was swotting for the Indian Civil Service; Captain O'Brien, V.C., D.S.O., to give that high-spirited Irishman his full title; Sexton Blake, most entertaining and popular of companions; Tinker, who was still dazed at this new phase of his master, and lastly, Pedro, who had signalised his arrival by dealing out severe punishment to three sheep dogs, two greyhounds, and a German boarhound, thus winning his spurs in Australia, and at the same time the right to occupy the said boarhound's place in the dining-room, while that astonished canine sulked in the stables and nursed a jagged ear.

Just as they were sitting down, a loud clatter of hoofs sounded outside, and a moment later, a big, black-bearded man was ushered in by the Chinese house-boy.

Campbell greeted him courteously, but without warmth, and introduced him to the general company as Mr. Edward Jameson, a neighbour and owner of Walla-Walla Station, which adjoined his on the south side.

In deference to a request made by Blake on his arrival, Campbell introduced both him and Tinker under the name of Smith.

Then, in conformance with the law of bush hospitality, Jameson was invited to join the party, though, truth to tell, Blake, O'Brien, and their host would have preferred otherwise.

Any outsider, no matter how genial, was an intruder that evening, for the three old friends had many experiences to swop, and Tinker and the younger Campbell seemed to be hitting it off together in regular "fifty-fifty" style. However, there was nothing to do but accept the situation gracefully, and certainly, Jameson endeavoured to make himself agreeable enough.

As far as Campbell was concerned he neither liked nor disliked his neighbour. He himself was one of those men who make few friends in later life, preferring rather to stick to those of his youth. Of a cold, reserved manner to strangers, he was warm enough to his old school friends. Although he was neighbourly enough with Jameson, it had never entered his head to become intimate with the man. In thought, in tastes, in everything they were as far apart as the poles, and at that Campbell had dismissed the matter from his mind.

Those who knew Jameson, and knew his nature, dealt with him accordingly. In a land where sharp practice upon the new chum is looked upon as good business (as indeed it is in most new countries), Jameson was by no means considered the heavy villain of melodrama. He was reputed one of the shrewdest stockmen and sharpest business men in the state, and if he ever did do anything flagrantly over the odds, no one knew it but Edward Jameson.

There were old drovers who remembered when his father had "humped a swag" (tramped) through the bush before a stroke of luck and a colossal nerve had started him on the road to success, or, at least, to what the world calls success.

Edward Jameson was a worthy product of his sire, and this was the man whom, for the first time, Sexton Blake met that night. How little did it occur to any one of them that ere long they were to be mixed up in a seething cauldron of intrigue, where every passion of the bush was to be let loose.

For the first half hour the sole topic of conversation was the drought which had seared the country with its scorching breath, and which had not yet broken.

From that the talk veered to the Yellow Peril, and thence to the old days of the gold rush and the bushranger—the latter probably as fascinating a subject for conversation and conjecture as it is possible to find. Many and weird were the tales which went the rounds at that table, until, when the coffee was brought in and the servant withdrew, the bushranger reminiscences held first place.

And well they might, for in that very district had the famous Captain Starlight[7] and his gang spread terror and death.

"I was reading in an old book the other day all about this district during the reign of the bushrangers," remarked Campbell, during a lull in the conversation. "It is a little known fact that when Starlight transferred his energies in the direction of Oodnadatta he left behind a lieutenant, who kept up the game here. In that article I came across a most interesting thing."

"What was it?" asked O'Brien.

"I'll tell you. It seems that this lieutenant, his name was Jackson, did things on a greater scale even than his old chief, Captain Starlight. Where the captain had confined himself to robbing the gold transporters and taking a few horses now and then, Jackson went in for wholesale sheep and cattle rustling.

"This district, in those days, was held by just one or two men, who had enormous mobs of stock grazing over it. After branding, they sometimes didn't see those same cattle for a couple of years. For a man of Jackson's daring this formed a tempting opportunity, which he evidently couldn't see pass. At any rate, he and his gang began rustling off big mobs of sheep and cattle from the outside edge of the run.

"The stockmen knew this was being done, and they felt pretty certain Jackson was the one who was doing it. Time after time they set out to catch him, but always failed. More than once they kept their eye on a special mob, and waited for their man to turn up. He invariably did so, and from under their very noses took the mob.

"Now, you all know, a man can pick up a coin or a ring and stand a pretty fair chance of getting away with it. But when it comes to making a clean bolt over several hundred miles of bush country with two or three-hundred head of cattle, well, it seems ridiculous. Evidently the stockmen of those days thought so, for they lost no time in getting after Jackson. A few hundred head of cattle leave a trail behind that a blind man could follow, and yet, do you know, that not once were they able to follow Jackson. They kept track of him easily enough for a certain number of miles, and then they lost him absolutely. It was as though he and the cattle had completely vanished into the air, and yet they knew he hadn't, for about six months later they would hear that some cattle had been sold in Adelaide, whose brands looked mightily as though they had been changed.

"Where they had disappeared to, and how they had reached Adelaide was a mystery, nor has it ever been found out to this day. Now, you brainy gentlemen, there is the riddle, how did Jackson manage to practically evaporate with two or three hundred head of stock, not once but dozens of times?"

As he finished speaking Campbell re-lit his cigar and leaned back. If he had expected to interest his guests he had certainly managed to do so. Each one showed his interest in his own way. Captain O'Brien's eyes sparkled with a tactician's appreciation of cleverness; Blake's eyes rested thoughtfully on the table; Tinker still gazed in at the narrator; the younger Campbell had something of the same look; but Jameson wore the oddest expression of all.

He was leaning forward with one elbow on the table, and one great fist pressing into his bushy black beard. He was gazing at Campbell, and his eyes held a strange, tense look in them. Before anyone else broke the silence, his clenched fist dropped heavily to the table and he spoke.

"I heard that same yarn about Jackson from my father," he said, in full, deep tones. "I guess it's true enough too, but by heavens! I can tell you a stronger tale than that, and it didn't happen fifty years ago neither. It happened just this past week, and for all I know may even be happening at this very moment."

They all glanced at him in surprise. His tones were not those of the dinner table, and his manner held a hint of deadly calm, strangely at variance with the festive array.

"What on earth is it?" blurted out the captain. "By gad, Mr. Jameson, you have aroused my curiosity."

"Let us have it," said Campbell quietly. "If it can beat that tale of Jackson it must be worth hearing."

"I'll tell it," replied Jameson, "and let me say before I begin, that it is so true, there is a standing offer of one thousand pounds to the man who can explain it. It has to do with stock, and it has to do with their disappearance. Moreover, those are not the only points on which it runs parallel to the Jackson yarn.

"Two weeks ago, my stockmen split up all the sheep on my place into mobs, and spread them over the paddocks in order to equalise the food."

"Why, I thought you cleared off all your stock before the drought came," interrupted Campbell in surprise.

The silent "Mr. Smith" was the only one who saw a lightning look flash in and out of Jameson's eyes as he answered:

"So I did, but I took over Treherne's stock a short time ago."

"Oh! I beg pardon," rejoined Campbell. "Go ahead!"

"As I was saying," went on Jameson. "I gave orders to split up the stock. This was done, and owing to the continuance of the drought every mob, even those in the far paddocks, was inspected daily. Just a week ago, I was sitting down to breakfast when one of the stockmen rode up and informed me that a small mob of about four hundred cross-bred ewes could not be located. Cross-breds are the very deuce as you know for going through fences, and, thinking this had occurred, I sent him back with instructions to muster up all the sheep in the near-by paddocks, and see if they had got mixed up. It wouldn't have been hard to tell, for the cross-bred ewes were a separate lot and every one had blue raddle mark on the back.

"Later in the day, the head stockman himself turned up, and reported that they had searched high and low, but could find not the slightest trace of the ewes. Naturally, I cursed him out for a chuckle-headed idiot, but he still persisted in saying he had had the paddocks scoured, so I arranged to look into the matter myself on the following morning. Well, after breakfast I was just about to start out when one of the men rode up and said that some three hundred wethers[8], which had been in a small paddock by themselves, had disappeared overnight.

"Things began to look serious, but several hundred sheep couldn't get far without someone seeing them, and as far as I knew they hadn't acquired wings. I thought they must have worked through the fences, and made back to Treherne's station. When another clean sweep of my own paddocks gave no sign of them I felt certain this must be the case. Consequently my stockman and I rode over and investigated.

"Treherne, who has visitors, told me I was welcome to search, which I did. All his men turned out too, and it didn't take me long to discover that there wasn't single head of livestock, bar the horses, on his place. It was impossible for them to get over to your place, Campbell, for the river would prevent that."

Campbell nodded.

"Certainly," he said briefly.

"That was five days ago," resumed Jameson. "The morning after that one of the men reported that another four hundred ewes had disappeared. Things began to look serious with a vengeance, I can tell you. Hot on top of that information I sent nearly every man on the place riding across the country to spread the news.

"They went in every direction, and notified everybody. If they had been rustled off the place there was only one way for the thieves to get them away, and that was by the old stock road which cuts through this district, and runs clear on to Queensland. My men traversed that for sixty miles each way, and nary a sign of sheep or drover did they see.

"That night I sent the few men who remained on the

place to ride the paddocks and keep watch. They did so, and yet, when morning came, they found not only another five hundred wethers missing, but one of my men had disappeared as well. Taking that as a definite start we worked in every direction. Giving the thieves the very limit, they hadn't many hours' start, and as you know sheep travel slow, particularly in this kind of weather. It seemed a moral certainty that we would overtake them in a couple of hours.

"Just as we started out we met the others returning with the news of their unsuccessful journey and they joined us. We all knew every foot of the country, and yet, will you believe it, we scanned every mile of it within a radius of forty miles, and not the barest sign did we see of the missing sheep."

"Gad!" muttered the Captain. "This beats old Jackson, the bushranger, to a frazzle."

"I thought perhaps the missing man had gone after them," went on Jameson, not heeding the interruption, "but when we got back he and his horse were still missing. Tired as we all were we kept a close watch that night. Nothing happened, so leaving the men to do day duty in watches we got some rest.

"That afternoon in broad daylight two hundred weaners disappeared from a far paddock, and the search began again.

"Once more we covered every foot of Treherne's place. I could not get it out of my head that they had worked through the boundary fence, and had spread out over his scrub land. It was useless, however. Still we heard no news of the missing man, but that night—that was the night before last—his horse trotted home alone.

"Where he had been or where he had just come from, we couldn't imagine. He was as fresh as could be, and neither hungry nor thirsty. Nothing more happened until last night.

"As usual we were keeping a close watch, but from the only place where the guard was slack another hundred disappeared. You know one man on a good horse can patrol a big stretch of country by day, but when it is dark, it would take five times the number of men I have to keep a proper watch over my place.

"All day to-day we have been scouring the country high and low, without any success. It seems a strange coincidence that you should tell that Jackson yarn, Campbell, for it was to seek assistance that I really rode over to-night. That, gentlemen, is the yarn, and I think you will agree with me that it caps the bushranger's tale."

Then suddenly, before Campbell had a chance to reply, the quiet voice of "Mr. Smith" broke in.

"I make it some nineteen hundred sheep have apparently vanished from your paddocks into thin air," he said.

"Roughly that," answered Jameson.

"Mr. Smith" relapsed again into silence, and Campbell took up the conversation.

"Well, I certainly must acknowledge that your story is one of the most remarkable that I ever heard," he said. "It seems utterly inconceivable that nearly two thousand sheep and an able-bodied man could vanish in such manner. As you say, there is only one way by which they could be driven out of this district, and that is by the old stock road."

"And I'll wager a hundred to one they did not go that way," broke in Jameson. "My men searched it too carefully."

"Of course," remarked Campbell, "They couldn't get them half a mile along there without some boundary rider spotting them."

"I don't know of a single thing we haven't already investigated," said Jameson gloomily, "Every surrounding station has been searched or interviewed; boundary riders questioned; drovers cross-examined; every track and trail investigated by the boys. I tell you, say what you will, there is something mighty queer and uncanny in the way those sheep have vanished. If it were wet weather we would stand a better chance of following them, but even without that, it is hard to see where they have gone.

"Why, even supposing the rustlers managed to get the first lot or two safely away before we began our search, it would be physically impossible for them to get the other lots beyond the radius of our investigations.

"By all the laws it seems out of the question that the sheep can be far away, and yet every mile of country has been gone over. At any rate, I want the loan of a few of your men, Campbell, if you can spare them, and whoever solves the riddle gets a thousand in hard cash."

"I imagine they will jump at the chance," answered Campbell. "Of course, you are quite welcome to their assistance. I'll arrange with the head stockman to take half of them, and go over to-night. In the morning they can return, and the other half under the assistant stockman can then go over."

"I say, Campbell," broke in the irrepressible captain. "It seems to me Mr. Jameson's mysterious loss offers a topping chance for excitement. What's the matter with us taking a hand in the search? I'm sure it would appeal to Smith. That is, if Mr. Jameson has no objection."

Campbell glanced inquiringly at Blake.

"What do you say, Smith?" he smiled. "Would it appeal to you?"

The quiet "Mr. Smith" disregarded a blatant look from Tinker as he knocked the ash from his cigar.

"Well, I don't know, old man," he replied. "If the situation is as Mr. Jameson outlines, it seems to me that it should be a very fascinating riddle to solve."

"I'm sure I should appreciate your assistance immensely, gentlemen," said Jameson, rising. Then, turning to his host, he added:

"If you will excuse me now, I shall be getting along. I suppose it will be all right if I tell your head stockman you wish to see him?"

"Oh, yes, indeed, but I'll come along with you and arrange matters at once."

When Campbell and Jameson had disappeared in the direction of the front door, the others launched out into an animated discussion of Jameson's strange tale. Even though the old bushranger story was adorned with all the trappings of romance which fifty years had added to it, they one and all confessed that Jameson's tale had it beaten to a frazzle, to use the captain's expression.

It seemed endowed with all the spirit of adventure of an adventurous bush; it had the real tang of buccaneers, and they of no mean order, judging from their activities during the past week; and its very incongruity with known conditions lent to it a fascination which made even Blake's hardened pulses quicken a trifle.

As for Tinker, he was already forming half a dozen theories which might explain the remarkable disappearance of the sheep. And be sure the mystery lost none of its attraction in the contemplation of Jameson's remark, that, even while he sat there telling them of it, another mob might be going the way of the others.

The fact that one of his men had also disappeared stamped the affair with deep purpose, which could not be denied, and the inexplicable return of his horse, riderless and still fresh, endowed that particular incident with sinister meaning.

Where were the sheep? Where was the missing man? What could possibly have become of them? And above all, why—why—why? Why was Jameson made the sole recipient of the mysterious stock-rustlers? What did it presage, and behind all his outward frankness had he any real notion of the motive, and any suspicion of the perpetrators?

Though some of these questions were openly voiced, they were all being turned over and over in the analytical mind of Sexton Blake. He was still pondering over the many points which were naturally presented, when the captain, who had been talking enthusiastically with the younger Campbell and Tinker, turned to him and remarked:

"By jingo, old man, I don't know how this thing strikes you, but it has gripped me harder than anything since I read 'Treasure Island.'"

Blake smiled. The captain's enthusiasm took him back to his younger days, to that door which "once you leave its portals you can ne'er return again"—his schooldays.

"I must confess it does attract me," he said; "But perhaps Mr. Jameson is painting the thing too luridly. If it were as he says, we would be in the position of trying to believe some two thousand sheep and an able-bodied man had vanished into thin air, not to mention the horse, which evidently returned to earth unharmed after its experiment in aviation. I imagine we shall find the whole thing capable of a very simple explanation, and Jameson will see his sheep trotting home bringing all their tails behind them."

"But, guv'nor," broke in Tinker eagerly, "there's one thing which makes it seem pretty real."

"What's that, my lad?" drawled Blake.

"Why, the fact that the drought is on and feed is scarce. They can't live without grass, and surely two thousand sheep couldn't wander about at a time when every acre is precious, without someone seeing them!"

"True, my lad," laughed Blake. "That is exactly why I maintain that the thing is capable of a very simple explanation."

And only then did Tinker see that Blake had made his remark, not necessarily because he himself believed it, but because he wished to spur the others into advancing theories from which his keen mind might pick a germ of wisdom.

Just as he finished speaking their host returned, and they all noticed that he wore a serious look. He resumed his seat in silence, and after lighting a fresh cigar, turned to Blake.

"This ought to be somewhat in your line," he remarked slowly.

"Just what I said!" chuckled the captain.

"Well," went on Campbell, after a tolerant smile at the irrepressible one, "Jameson told me a few details outside which he didn't care to go into here, but gave me permission to tell you if I wished."

"Ah!" remarked Blake. "That is what I was hoping for."

"It seems," continued his host, "that for some reason or other he suspects his neighbour Treherne of having a hand in the business. Why, I don't know. It seems that all through the drought he has financed Treherne, and has saved him from ruin. The sheep which are on Walla-Walla were partial security for the money advanced, and he held a mortgage on Binabong Station itself for the balance."

"I beg your pardon," interrupted Blake quickly. "What is the name of Treherne's property?"

"Binabong," answered Campbell. "Why?"

"Did it used to belong to one Cartier—John Cartier?"

"Yes; but that was some years ago."

"I know. Go on, please."

"A week ago," resumed Campbell, "Treherne was absolutely and completely broke—or so Jameson says. In fact, Jameson went over one night, and from what he said I gathered that Treherne practically made a complete assignment of the property to him. Then, the very next day, he turned up with sufficient money to redeem the mortgage on the place.

"This Jameson refused to accept, on the grounds that he holds Treherne's written assignment of the property. Treherne has visitors there, and Jameson's theory is that they must have advanced the money. At any rate, that left a deadlock between them. Jameson claims the station as his property, and Treherne refuses to give up possession."

"The law would soon settle the question of ownership," remarked the younger Campbell.

"For some reason, Jameson wishes to avoid litigation," rejoined his brother. "Anyway, it was on the very day after his interview with Treherne that the first mob disappeared. I have met Treherne several times, and though I know he has been drinking a bit lately, owing to worry, I always thought him a very decent sort, and I can't conceive that he would do anything crooked.

"However, that is not all. When Jameson told me as much as he did, I thought it permissible to take a liberty. I hope you won't mind, Blake, but I told him your real name. He at once asked me to use my influence with you to try to persuade you to bring your powers to bear on the matter, and I told him I would. Personally—and I think the rest of you are the same—the thing attracts me marvellously. He is prepared to pay well for your services."

"I don't mind looking into it," answered Blake, after a short pause. "Of course, reimbursement is quite out of the question. I am out here for rest and pleasure, nothing else. At the same time, if we join in and help Jameson, it will give us some excuse for keeping in the saddle, if nothing else, and I think that will not do us any harm. Therefore, Campbell, on the distinct understanding that my identity does not go past Jameson, I am willing to give my assistance for what it is worth."

"Hooroo! Hooray!" cried the captain. "And now, what is the general opinion on starting this very night?"

"I say yes," replied the younger Campbell, Tinker, Captain O'Brien, all in one breath. "What do you say, Blake?"

"Well," smiled the latter, "it might be as well if some of us rode over with your men and took a hand. Since this blood-thirsty trio seem so keen on it, suppose they go? Then the captain could take proper charge of your men. As for you and myself—I suggest that we remain at home and play a hundred up at billiards."

"All right."

Barely had Campbell said the word when the captain, Tinker, and Campbell's brother rose and prepared for their departure.

Campbell rang and sent the Chinese boy with orders to have horses saddled up. Blake remained seated at the table, puffing thoughtfully at his cigar, and absently drumming on the arm of his chair with his long, sensitive fingers. Ten minutes later the three horsemen departed, to the accompaniment of a clatter of hoofs; and Campbell, who had been seeing them off, returned to the dining-room and sat down again.

"Well, old man," he finally remarked, "don't you think this affair peculiar?"

Blake nodded.

"Yes," he said slowly. "To tell you the truth, Dumpy, I intend taking it on, and endeavouring to ferret out the mystery; but not for five minutes would I pledge my unreserved services to Jameson without knowing more of the details. If he suspects his neighbour Treherne, he must have stronger grounds for doing so than he told you; for, unless Treherne were an arrant fool, he would never risk stealing a few hundred head of sheep over a land dispute of such magnitude. If he did it would ruin his case before any judge."

"By Jove, I believe you're right, Blake! But let us forget it for tonight. How about that game of billiards?"

"I've changed my mind," smiled Blake. "If you don't mind, I think I shall retire early, but before doing so I'd like to have that book about Jackson, the bushranger. I have a consuming curiosity to read it."

And as his host went to get it, he never for one moment dreamed that Blake's request had even the remotest connection with the mysterious disappearance of Jameson's sheep.

THE THIRD CHAPTER

The Sheep Stealers—Tinker Captured—His Escape.

"S-H!"

The low, sibilant sound floated gently through the night. So faint was it that it seemed to blend with the soft rustling of the leaves in the surrounding trees.

The hot Australian night was but a black replica of the day just gone. Overhead the stars glittered strangely bright in their sea of indigo. The purple dome appeared to be pressing down with implacable force upon gasping Nature. From far away came the low neighing of a horse; somewhere in the distance could be heard the plaintive bleat of a thirst-maddened sheep; nearer at hand came the unmistakable odour of cattle; while over all hung the dusty, pungent, alluring smell of the stock-route and paddocks.

It was a true bush night, one of those nights when men beyond the outposts of the empire lay on their backs with memories of home and friends blending with the hot smell of the paddocks.

"S-h!"

Again the sibilant sound floated out on the night breeze, and this time it was followed almost at once by the soft crashing of bushes, as first one mounted figure, then another and another, rode quietly out from a dark patch of scrub, and drew up their horses beneath a big gum tree.

There were ten in all, and when the last horse had been drawn up in the shadow, the first figure which had ridden forth detached itself from the group and rode out a short distance. There it stopped, and for five minutes horse and rider were motionless as a statue. At the end of that time it turned and rode back to the group.

Could a light have been cast on the mysterious party which seemed so intent on keeping their movements quiet, it could have been seen that the figure which appeared to take the leadership was that of a woman, and that her features were those of the charming girl who was visiting Binabong. Nor would one have been mistaken, for it was none other than Mademoiselle Yvonne.

Edward Jameson was not far wrong when he suspected the mysterious disappearance of his sheep as emanating from Binabong; and yet, though he felt vaguely that this was so, his several sweeping searches over that station had yielded not the faintest item whereby he might pin his suspicions to solid fact. A thing which is not surprising, for Mademoiselle Yvonne's bronze-crowned head had cooked up a most baffling plot against Edward Jameson, and under her slim hands the baking was being done to perfection.

It was true that from Treherne's visitors had come the money which he had offered to redeem the mortgage on Binabong. Had the owner of Walla-Walla been as cautious as his reputation proclaimed, he would have accepted this money, wondered as he might, and set it down to an unexplained failure. But old Gene, the head stockman on Binabong, had not been far wrong when he said once the Jamesons got their hands on a thing they found it hard to let go. It was exactly this, the sweet feeling of possession, which had blinded Jameson's clear judgment of details.

Never for a moment did he connect Treherne's repudiation of his assignment over the gambling to aught but a refusal to meet his obligations of honour. The fact that the marked cards might have been spotted did not enter his head. He felt quite confident that long ere this they had been swept up by the servant and burned.

Had he only possessed the faintest inkling of the identity of Treherne's guests he would have found therein some considerable shock to his hardened nerves. He did not know this, however, and consequently he railed in futile anger at the baffling and mysterious disappearance of mob after mob of sheep.

To those who have no intimate knowledge of the bush, it might seem that large lots of sheep could not be spirited away without leaving a broad trail behind them. That is quite true—and had there not been several months of drought, Yvonne's plans would have been impossible to carry out.

The months of burning rainless conditions, however, had packed the ground as hard as cement. And this ground still retained the crossing and re-crossing tracks of mobs of sheep over a long period of time.

Consequently, when Jameson's mobs were spirited away, they were sent over this criss-crossed land into a maze of tracks which the cleverest stockman found impossible to decipher.

But that did not explain where they now were, nor would that riddle be read for some time. That was Yvonne's secret and well had she guarded it for many years.

The nine figures which she approached lounged easily in their saddles awaiting her orders. Old Gene was at one end of the line and Graves at the other. Between them were Treherne, Monty, Pete, Joe, and the rest of the old veterans who had met Yvonne with such a whirlwind greeting on her return to Binabong.

Nine grim, determined, hardened horsemen, seven of whom, at least, were as much at home in the bush at night as the average Londoner in Piccadilly. Nine armed, mounted men, each and all of whom answered in perfect accord to the orders of the slim girl who sat her horse with such perfect ease.

Presently she spoke.

"Gene!" she hardly breathed.

"Yes, missie?" whispered back the stockman.

"You take Monty and Pete with you. Circle around until you come to the far gate in the lower paddock. Joe and Smith will come with me. We will circle in the opposite direction. You, uncle, with Mr. Treherne, and the others, ride straight for the gate. Whoever gets there first do nothing but wait for the others. In that way we can get an idea as to where Jameson's guards are to-night. We shall make an attempt to get that small mob of wethers in the lower paddock. Now, ready—ride!"

Silently, nine figures swung and sought their respective places. Then, at a further command, they broke off into three parties, and stole off like silent shadows through the night, the muffled hoofs of the horses making no sound on the hard ground.

As they parted and rode forward each one loosened the heavy revolver in his belt, and took a firmer grip of the long, snake-like stock-whip which was coiled about his free arm. Jackson, the bushranger, and his companions never conceived a more daring raid, nor did they ever carry it out with more practised stealth than did Yvonne and her companions that night.

Well she knew that Jameson was not the man to take his losses lying down, and well she knew every man he could command would be on guard that night. Gene and his grizzled companions had brought in news regularly of how the owner of Walla-Walla and his men were scouring the ranges for miles in an endeavour to locate the missing sheep. With many chuckles of delight did the old stockman tell of the futile search over Binabong and the repeated questioning of boundary riders and owners.

In order to ensure secrecy and guard against betrayal, Treherne, at Yvonne's suggestion, had let go all his men, with the exception of Gene and his companions. Owing to the fact that Binabong was denuded of stock, and everybody expected to hear of Treherne's ruin any day, this had been accomplished without arousing any suspicion in the minds of the men concerned. Then Yvonne had called around her the loyal old fellows who had fared so well when the Cartiers owned Binabong, and to them had propounded her plan.

Not since he had ridden the ranges down by the Rio Grande and had lived in the cattle atmosphere of old Texas and Arizona had Gene been so delighted.

With Joe and Smith riding silently on either side of her, Yvonne began circling around towards the rendezvous, with all the caution of a born scout. Through great stretches of treeless paddocks she rode, over dried-up streams, and into black patches of scrub where the swish, swish of the branches against the horses' flanks gave the only indication that the shadows concealed moving life. Then along through a gaunt-looking expanse of ring-barked country until she reached the boundary fences dividing Binabong from Walla-Walla.

Even as the trio of riders reached this did Joe's keen ears detect the pad, pad, pad of a horse with unmuffled hoofs, and with one accord Yvonne and her companions rode silently into the shadow of a big gum tree.

Barely had they gained the safety of this retreat, when the sound they had heard increased, and silhouetted against the studded heavens they made out the figures of two horsemen cantering by on Jameson's side of the boundary fence.

"Our friend is risking nothing to-night," breathed Yvonne, when the riders had disappeared into a patch of scrub. "But come, we will need all our caution."

At her word they moved on again, keeping close to the fence.

For a full half-hour they rode on in dead silence, until they reached a cluster of gum trees, from which came the soft hoot of an owl. This, the prearranged signal, meant both the other parties had arrived. Gene and his companions had seen three of Jameson's men riding past; but Graves and Treherne, who had come direct through the Binabong paddocks, had seen or heard nothing.

"Even if he suspects that the sheep are disappearing in the direction of Binabong he is bound to have guards all round his boundaries," whispered Yvonne. "At the same time, he may have on an extra force, so move cautiously, and keep your ears and eyes open. Slip on ahead and open the gate, Gene."

The stockman rode on ahead, followed by the others. He stopped in the corner formed by the boundary fence and a sub-divisional fence, and after a few moments' manipulation at the high, skeleton-looking cyclone gate swung it back on its hinges, and the party rode through.

"Where did you see the sheep at sundown?" whispered Yvonne.

"Up here to the left, missie," answered Gene. "They were mobbing up for the night right near the boundary fence."

"Then lead the way, Gene, and we will follow. One of Jameson's men is bound to be not very far away from them, so move quietly."

Following Gene, they rode on silently through Jameson's paddock, keeping close to the fence. Then suddenly Gene drew up, and as the others approached they could see against the ground a large number of shadowy white blotches like so many kneeling Arabs at prayer.

There was no need for instructions then. Each man knew what he had to do. Spreading out as only experienced stockmen can, they circled the mob of sheep, which lay in a bunch, as is their habit, and when they had gained the far side brought into play the stock-whips which all this time they had carried.

With a good sheep dog to spur on a mob of sheep it is a comparatively easy matter for one man to drive a large number when he has the light of day to guide him and has not the need to work in silence; but at night, when a voice must not be raised, when a dog must not be used, and when a stock-whip must be flicked about their legs, but not "cracked," it is no easy matter, even though the number of the sheep be small and those who are driving them numerous and experienced. However, Yvonne and her companions had done it before, and they intended doing it again.

While half of them dismounted and, with bridle-reins trailing over their arms, went in amongst the startled sheep to rouse them, the other half went to work at the rear, flicking gently but persistently with their stock-whips, until the recumbent animals rose and crowded on against those in front.

Then the men amongst the sheep made their way out. Mounting, they spread out along the flank on the far side from the boundary fence. Gene and his half kept working in the rear; the boundary fence itself formed a barrier on the other flank.

The silent, persistent, irritating flick at their legs kept the sheep on the move, and perforce they moved in the only direction which was possible—ahead.

On they went in this fashion until the leaders, who had been rubbing against the fence, felt a sudden end to this barricade, while in front appeared a new obstacle in the form of the sub-divisional fence. Forced on by those behind, they took, as always, the line of least resistance, and poured through the gate into the paddock belonging to Binabong—the same gate through which they had gone to Walla-Walla when Treherne had first fallen into Jameson's web.

The last one through, Yvonne and her companions closed up and followed. Gene was behind, and just about to close the gate, when a soft pad, pad sounded, and the dark silhouette of a flying horseman appeared. Without pausing, he rode on recklessly to within a few feet of the silent party, and even in the starlight could be seen the steely glint of his revolver as he threw it up and cried out:

"Hands up—quick!"

"What for, mister?" drawled Gene, riding forward, and followed at a short distance by Yvonne.

"For sheep stealing," came the steady voice from behind the gun. "Put them up, I say, and keep them away from your belt."

Old Gene obediently raised his hands, but pressing with his knees still guided his horse onwards until its flank and that of the newcomer's horse were pressing against one another.

"What will I do now, mister?" asked old Gene softly;

while from Yvonne came a soft laugh.

"Do you expect to shoot us all?" she asked.

"No; I can see you are too many for one," came the quick retort. "But I can get help and overtake you before you get far with those sheep."

With that, the speaker lowered his revolver and jerked at his rein, intending to turn and ride for help. He counted without one thing, however, and that was the presence at his side of one of the most experienced and canniest stockmen who had ever ridden the ranges.

Even before he had pulled his horse's head round old Gene had leant over and grasped the bridle-rein with one hand, while with the other he wrapped the rider round in a grip of iron. As though at a prearranged signal, Pete and Monty dashed forward, and before he had time to barely gather what had happened the lone horseman found himself held in a pair of brawny arms, which closed about his throat and prevented him from calling, while two more pairs of hands deftly bound and gagged him.

Then, after he had been strapped to the saddle, Monty took the bridle rein of the horse, and in this fashion Yvonne's little party moved back through the gate, their captive being helplessly led behind.

Old Gene closed the gate; and once more they spread out around the sheep, starting them on again across the Binabong paddocks to as strange a place of concealment as Nature in her most perverse mood ever provided.

Before Ike Vineburg and his crew had broken up the happiness of Yvonne's old home, and when she, in all her girlish light-heartedness, rode the paddocks which she loved, many and long were the journeys of exploration which she took into the stretches of mysterious and fascinating scrub and gullies which lay in the very centre of the estate, and which were marked on the estate plan as "unknown rocky gullies and canyons—no grass, no water, no soil; inaccessible and barren; unexplored."

She made no mention of her lone journeys into the unknown heart of the estate, for the simple reason that such mention would have brought down her father's ban at once. Unsurveyed and unknown, this spot, which lay in the heart of Binabong like a stretch of wilderness in the midst of plenty, was the bugbear of every stockman and boundary rider in the district.

Once, when Binabong had great mobs of cattle roaming over it, there had been a stampede one night, and many hundred of cattle had disappeared over the mysterious edge of the wilderness—never to return. Mysterious, because the stockmen had followed their tracks to the edge of a cliff which seemed to drop into an eternity of rock and scrub, and which revealed no bottom.

After this it was given a wide berth, and went always by the appropriate name of Death Valley.

About the same time a copy of the book which Campbell had read, and which Blake was reading that very evening, fell into Yvonne's hands. It didn't take her long to connect the mysterious spot on Binabong with the very place which Jackson, the bushranger, had used, the location of which had been forgotten after his death.

"If he and his companions knew of a way into the seemingly impenetrable fastness then, that way must still exist," argued Yvonne.

Forthwith she set out to explore still further, and how well her efforts succeeded will be seen as this story of her return to Binabong proceeds.

She and her companions paid little attention to the silent captive who was being led along in the rear. All their attention was given up to the sheep, for, as on previous nights, Yvonne wished to make the hiding-place by daybreak. Where it was a possibility to guide the sheep through the well-known paddocks by night, and to keep them in travelled stretches in order that their trail might be lost in the general maze of tracks of former mobs, it was another thing to get them into the hiding-place. For this daylight was essential, and yet if must not be too long after sun-up, for boundary riders have keen eyes, and they might be seen by one who happened to be crossing Binabong in order to cut off several miles of a journey.

On through paddock after paddock they went, Gene and the other stockmen working incessantly to keep the sheep on the move.

Finally, the friendly shadow of the big gum and box trees was left behind, and just as the first faint streak appeared in the east they broke out on stony ground. Then did Yvonne take the lead.

In the cold dawn-light the country before them appeared to be a wilderness of scrubby, stony, rolling gullies and cliffs through which no man could possibly desire to pass. Riding along a rocky valley between two breasting hills, Yvonne kept on to the far end, where the land suddenly dropped into a sheer cliff, whose base was hidden from view. Opposite this another bulging cliff crossed at an angle, hiding from view the land beyond.

Yvonne paused on the very brink, and for a moment her eyes swept the barren, forbidding stretch of gullies. Then she turned her horse's head abruptly to the left, and disappeared over the brow of a hill into the midst of a stretch of open scrub. Behind her came the sheep being driven by the stockmen. At the bottom she turned along the bed of a dead water-course, and for twenty minutes rode in silence. At the end of that time another sheer cliff appeared, and the tenderfoot would have sworn her horse was standing on the very spot it had stood on before.

It was not, however, but was only one of those baffling likenesses which befool men, and send them wandering for days until they know not where they are.

Once again Yvonne turned abruptly to the left, and for the second time rode through a patch of open scrub to the bottom of a gully. There she again followed the bed of a dead stream, this time for about ten minutes longer than before. These ten minutes were almost the sole proof that her course was a different one, and had an important bearing on the secret way, for it meant that all the time she was travelling in a vast circle, and the ever-increasing depths of the gullies indicated that she was ever getting lower.

Time after time she turned, until at last the bald edge of the gigantic cliffs could be seen piercing the morning sky, their points and jagged corners stabbing the pink and gold like a multitude of minarets and domes. Lower and lower went Yvonne, her big roan picking his way with the sure-footedness born of knowledge, for, indeed, he and the girl who swayed so easily to his every move had travelled that long descent many times.

At last she drew up and turned her head. Behind her came the dusty mob of sheep, with Gene and his companions, now the need for caution gone, shouting and hi-hi-ing the while they cracked and double-cracked their long stock-whips. Further in the rear rode the captive between Treherne and Graves, the latter puffing nonchalantly at his eternal cigarette.

With a sudden delicious laugh and a wave of her hand, Yvonne turned back, and spurred in through a short, shallow gully, until, on turning the bend, she came out suddenly upon as fair a view as Nature ever fashioned.

All around her, like a great wall, losing itself in the distance, stretched the giant cliffs, their sides sheer and impassable. Before her was a vast expanse of riotous green dotted here and there by wide-spreading trees. From low down at one side a silver stream gushed out merrily, winding onwards through the dense green meadow like a white ribbon. Far away, near the centre, it trickled softly into a small lake, around the banks of which Yvonne knew Jameson's missing sheep would be clustered in lazy enjoyment of the early morning sun.

Although the extent of the place could not be seen from any position, Yvonne knew, from many journeys around it, that it comprised some three thousand acres of rich grazing land, always green and always watered. Immune from the most severe drought, hidden away from the outside world, guarded by a tortuous path which, until

Yvonne had discovered it, had lain disused and unknown ever since Jackson, the bushranger, had died, it was truly a haven of solitude, an Arcadia for man or beast, an impregnable stronghold against an army.

Evidently the sheep thought so, at any rate, for as they entered the short gully which was the last stage of their journey, they scented the smell of the fresh green ahead. First the leaders lifted their heads and sniffed, then those behind got the scent. Forgetting their tired limbs and parched throats, the whole mob broke into a hopping run, and rushed pell-mell into the beautiful green stretch which unfolded itself before them.

Yvonne laughed softly at their silly antics as they gambolled away over the green, seeking the silver stream. Well she knew they needed no guard now. The trouble would be in persuading them to leave such an attractive spot. Gene and the others rode through the gully more slowly. Yvonne waited until they drew near, then signed to Graves to bring on the captive.

She gazed in puzzlement at the odd expression on her uncle's face as he rode forward, leading the captive's horse. She could not see the features of the prisoner himself, for the broad-brimmed soft felt hat he wore was pulled down over his eyes.

As Graves drew close he raised one hand and swept the prisoner's hat from his head, and Yvonne found herself gazing into a pair of boyish eyes which she knew only too well.

"You!" she gasped in stupefaction.

"At your service, Mademoiselle Yvonne," came Tinker's

voice, as he bowed stiffly.

For once in her life Yvonne was completely swamped for a reply. Evidently Graves was not above appreciating the situation, for he was smiling broadly at Yvonne's confusion.

"You! You!" she repeated feebly, as she sought to discover if she were dreaming.

"Again at your service," grinned the lad— "though I'd find it more comfortable if you would release my hands," he added.

"What are you doing here?" demanded Yvonne, regaining her self-possession.

"I really don't know," answered Tinker, "since I was brought here against my will."

"I don't mean that. What were you doing in Edward Jameson's paddock?"

"Trying to discover where his sheep were disappearing to, and I guess from the look of things I have found out."

Yvonne nodded her head thoughtfully. "I suppose it is safe to assume that your master is also in Australia?" she said slowly.

Tinker smiled, but made no attempt to reply.

Yvonne turned and beckoned to Gene. When this old stockman came up, she bent her head and whispered:

"Gene, yonder lad is the assistant of a man who has at times been an enemy and at times a friend. This time he happens to be on the side of the enemy, and for that reason that lad must not escape. He knows a thousand and one tricks for getting loose, so watch him carefully, Gene. When I tell you his master is the only man who can seriously menace our plans, you will understand how necessary it is that this lad be held."

"You leave it to me, missìe," replied the stockman, dropping a caressing hand to the butt of his revolver. "If a youngster like that can best old Gene—well, then it is time I lost myself."

"All right, Gene; I leave him in your hands. Take him along to the bushrangers' huts, but keep him separated from our other prisoner."

She smiled mockingly at Tinker as Gene led him away, but the lad gave no sign.

Truth to tell, Tinker had been as dumbfounded at discovering Yvonne to be the cause of the mystery as she had been at seeing him in Australia. When he had ridden away from Campbell's station with the party which had been detailed to lend their assistance to Jameson, the present denouement had been most remote from his thoughts. He and Captain O'Brien had been amongst those who patrolled the boundary fence between Binabong and Walla-Walla.

For several hours they had kept together, sitting motionless in the shadow near the very mob of wethers which was to be Yvonne's objective that night. Then the impatient captain had ridden away in the hopes of running into the rustlers, leaving Tinker alone to guard the wethers.

The lad had shared the captain's opinion that, if the night were to see an attempt, it would be at another spot. He still stuck to his post, however, and the captain had been gone less than half an hour, when the soft click of the gate had warned him that someone was approaching.

Keyed up to the last pitch, he bent forward silently, the while he worked his revolver loose and held it ready. Then low voices broke on his ears, and his pulses raced as he realised that he and he alone was to be the only witness of another attempt.

For a moment he weighed the advisability of firing into the air in order to attract attention from others of the watchers who might be within hearing; but, he realised that this would only alarm the rustlers, who would have every chance of getting away.

He resolved to sit tight and do nothing. Then, when they had departed with the sheep, he would creep after them, and track them to their destination. It was at that moment that pure accident precipitated his advance, and caused all his careful plans to collapse into ignominious capture.

When the party of rustlers circled the mob, they passed very close to Tinker, and it was because he felt positive one of them had seen him that he boldly rode forward and attempted to bluff. He blamed himself afterwards for not firing to give the alarm, and running his chances of escaping, but it was one of those cases when all the forethoughts came as afterthoughts, and, really, circumstances were to blame, not the lad.

And now, here he was in possession of startling information which, unless he could escape, was useless. Even as old Gene led him away, however, his mind was busy with plans for escape. They had not blindfolded him on the way in, and Tinker felt that if he could once reach the gully, he could find his way out.

He and Graves had recognised each other when daylight had made their features distinguishable; but Yvonne's uncle, beyond a smile, had given no sign, and Tinker said nothing. All he wanted then, and all he wanted now, was to escape too close attention.

He had a very cogent reason for wishing this, and it came from the fact that, all the way from the scene of his capture, he had been working surreptitiously at the cord which bound his wrists. The gag had been removed, but he knew he might as well shout for help in the middle of the Pacific Ocean as to expect to be heard from the depths of that fastness.

Evidently the stockman thought his bonds needed no examination, for he led the lad's horse along the base of the cliffs until he reached a tumbledown shanty which stood amongst others in a little grove of trees. There he lifted Tinker from the saddle, and carried him bodily into the hut. Tossing him into the corner with about as much ceremony as he would have bestowed upon a sack of flour, he calmly bit off a chew of tobacco and turned to leave.

At the door he paused.

"Now, young feller," he said, punctuating his words by tapping on the butt of his revolver, "here you be, and here you stay! Understand?"

Tinker vouchsafed no reply.

"And if you try to escape—well, my son, I kin cut a rope with this little rib-tickler at some few paces, an' I warn you good and plenty that I ain't standin' no foolin'! Do you get me?"

"I get you, Steve," answered Tinker cheekily; and with an appreciative grin at the lad's spirit, old Gene withdrew.

But Tinker know that, regardless of the smile, the stockman meant business, and would keep his word about shooting. Nevertheless, such knowledge did not deter him from his purpose, and he gave a grunt of satisfaction when he found his hands were not to be inspected.

"If I can get an hour without being interrupted," he muttered, "I can manage to get those things off, and then old grizzly will find two can play at the shooting game."

Barely had the rickety door closed behind Gene, when Tinker was once more at work. To saw at them was useless, for they were of tough cowhide, and the old hut contained nothing having a cutting edge which would go through that. Consequently, all he could do was to work patiently away, taking all the advantage he could from the careless knot.

As he felt the outer wrappings loosening he redoubled his energies. Slowly, by dint of twisting and turning his wrists, he managed to loosen the next layer then the next and the next, until finally he got one hand free, and the job was done. Exultant over his success, he was just about to creep over to the door to inspect the outside, when, without the slightest warning, it flew open to a heavy kick, and Gene thrust his grizzled head in.

Tinker drew his hands behind his back, and lay still, returning glance for glance as coolly as he could, though all the time his heart was beating madly as he wondered if the stockman suspected.

He breathed more easily when the door again closed.

"If he doesn't suspect now, the chances are he won't look in again for a little while," muttered the lad, "and if I am going to get away, I'd better make a move."

With infinite caution, he crept across to the rickety door which had lain so long in disuse. Owing to this, the action of the elements had provided it with numerous cracks, where the rotting boards had fallen apart. Through one of these Tinker peeped, and seeing no signs of movement outside, stealthily pushed open the door a few inches, and thrust out his head.

Everything was as still as the grave. The sun, now high in the heavens, beat down warmly on the little Arcadia, and the green glade in which the huts were nestled seemed already drowsy with the warmth. A few birds twittered in the trees overhead, but of human beings there were no signs.

After a moment's inspection Tinker opened the door still wider and slipped through. He paused only long enough to close it; then, taking cover in the trees, he sped softly through the glade until he came to an open patch. Beyond, in a bed of green, he could see the little stream, while still further along he could make out the figures of three horsemen. He did not know it then, but Yvonne, with Treherne, Graves, and three of the stockmen had already started for Binabong homestead, leaving Gene and three of his companions to guard the prisoners and the sheep.

Even as the lad surveyed the three horsemen who were on their way to the lake, was Gene in another hut attending to the other prisoner.

Tinker, seeing the coast comparatively clear, wasted no time, and risked a dash across the open space until he reached the cover of another clump of trees. In this way he made his way in alternate dashes and reconnoitrings until he had left the huts a good half-mile behind. Then the mouth of the gully came into view, and he risked all on one mad rush.

He had hoped to be able to find the horses on his way, but saw no signs of them, and dared not risk a delay. He reached the mouth of the gully panting, and paused to look back.

At that moment the sound of a shot from a heavy calibred revolver floated across the still air. He saw the three distant horsemen wheel and gaze back. It didn't need much to make him realise that the shot had come from Gene's gun, and, turning sharply, he sped swiftly along the gully.

Again a shot rang out, then three others more distant sounded in answer.

The horsemen had heard the alarm. Tinker's escape had been discovered. In five minutes they would be in pursuit.

And Tinker, running with a regular lope, fought down his inclination to increase his pace, for he realised it was a long stiff trail out of that spot, and he would need every ounce of strength he possessed if he were to reach the top before his mounted pursuers.

THE FOURTH CHAPTER

Blake Gets on Tinker's Track—And Meets Yvonne.

THOUGH SEXTON BLAKE spent far into the night poring over the old book which dealt with the doings of Jackson, the bushranger, there were still no signs of the party when he put out his light and retired.

His host had gone to his room early, in order to be in good trim for the morrow.

Even when Blake rose the next morning Captain O'Brien, Tinker, and the younger Campbell had not retired. He joined Captain Campbell, and together they made a run for the big cement swimming-tank, which was fed from the artesian bore.

They were splashing about in the cold, bracing water when the captain and the younger Campbell entered, looking tired from their night in the saddle, and covered from head to foot in the dust of the paddocks.

"Well, did you catch the rustlers?" called Blake from where he stood poised on the springboard ready to dive.

The usually cheerful captain looked strangely serious.

"No," he replied, shaking his head; "but they got away with a mob of sheep just the same."

"You fellows deserve a medal," jeered Campbell. "It's a wonder they didn't get away with one of you as well."

"They did," answered the captain shortly.

"Who?" demanded Campbell incredulously.

"Where is Tinker?" broke in Blake suddenly.

The captain lifted his hands helplessly.

"That is what we have been trying to find out ever since two o'clock last night."

"Do you mean to say they got him?" asked Blake sharply, as he reached for a towel.

The captain nodded.

"Yes, and in a way I blame myself for it. But get dressed, you chaps, and I'll tell you everything when we get to the house."

Blake was already getting into his bath-robe, and Campbell lost no time in following suit. Then the quartet made their way to the house, where Blake signed to the captain to proceed with his story.

"I'm awfully sorry, old man," he said soberly. "I know how you must feel, and I'll be as brief as possible."

Blake made a gesture, and the captain continued.

"When we reached Walla-Walla we placed ourselves at Jameson's disposal. He divided us into pairs, and spread us clear round the boundary fences. Tinker and I happened to get paired, and went on guard in one of the far paddocks which adjoins Binabong. We had a distance of four miles to patrol, and on my advice we took up our position in about the middle of our beat.

"My idea was to put in some time there; then I would ride two miles in one direction, and on my return Tinker would ride the other two miles. The only sheep near our beat were mobbed up for the night right near the middle, and this influenced my plan, for you can see one of us would have them under observation continually.

"Well, I suppose I was beginning to get impatient. At any rate, as we hadn't heard a sound I thought I would do my two miles, and ride along the next beat to see if the other party had heard anything. This I did, leaving Tinker to watch the sheep. I was gone about three hours altogether, and when I returned gave the whistle on which we had arranged.

"I got no reply, and, on riding nearer to where Tinker had been left, I saw that not a single sheep was on the spot where the mob had been when I departed. I whistled again, and still heard nothing.

"Then, feeling that something must be wrong, I rode as fast as I could back the way I had just come, until I picked up two of the Walla-Walla stockmen who were on the next beat. I told them what had happened, and one of them came back with me while the other went to spread the alarm.

"In half an hour we had about thirty men on the scene with lights.

"For the first time since the Jameson's sheep have been disappearing there seemed a definite clue. Right near where the wethers were there is a big cyclone gate set in. By their lights the stockmen followed the tracks of the sheep through this gate and into the adjoining Binabong paddock. At the very most, supposing the sheep had been driven off immediately after my departure, they couldn't be very far away.

"We spread out in a great circle, and rode straight across Binabong in a way which we felt must pick up the sheep. Daylight came then, and helped us considerably; but, will you believe it, those sheep might have vanished into the air for all the sign we saw of them?"

"How about the tracks from the gate?" asked Campbell quickly.

"The stockmen went back there, but it did no good. We followed them to the gate all right, and can swear they passed through, but there the trail ends. The whole place is covered with a maze of sheep-tracks made during several months. In places the top layer of ground has pulverised and broken into dust, but generally the place still retains the tracks. There seemed to be a general tendency of the freshly trampled ground to run in one direction. This we followed, and finally decided that it must be the trail of the sheep. It ended abruptly on stony ground, however, and from that we lost it.

"They are still searching, and may run up against something at any moment. We have hunted high and low for Tinker but he seems to have vanished as utterly as have the sheep. We thought the best thing to do was to ride on here at once and tell you, for we knew Blake would wish to know."

When the captain had finished Blake looked thoughtful.

Campbell appeared to be turning over in his mind the question of the trail.

Finally Blake spoke. "You say that what you took for tracks ended in stony ground?" he said slowly.

The captain nodded.

"Yes."

"Is this ground you speak of very extensive?"

"Yes, it stretches away until it develops into a big expanse of country, which lies in the middle of Binabong. It is called Death Valley, and certainly looks the part. It is nothing but a wilderness of stone and scrub, breaking into gullies and cliffs, quite impassable, and absolutely barren."

"I see," responded Blake. Then, turning to his host, he said, "Have you a surveyor's map of the district?"

"Oh, yes! There is one in my office which was made out about ten years ago. Of course, this district has never been surveyed in detail, but it gives a fair idea of the country and the boundaries are pretty correct."

"I will go along to the office with you and have a look at it," answered Blake.

"What do you want us to do?" asked the captain. "Shall we go back and join in the search for Tinker, or would you rather we waited for you?"

Blake stood in thought for a few moments.

"There seems no doubt but that the lad has gone the way of the sheep," he said slowly; "but, in my opinion, neither they nor he will be rescued by force. The only thing which will meet the case will be strategy. Numbers will spoil that, so I would suggest you get some rest. I have no definite theory yet, but I may have after I have seen the plan. In any case, I shall start out soon to search for him, and will work alone. On the whole, I think you had better retire."

"Gad! I can't do that!" exclaimed the captain. "I feel half responsible for his disappearance, so if I can't be of any assistance to you I will return and help the others."

"All right," said Blake. "Suit yourself."

The younger Campbell evidently felt as the captain did, for he accompanied the latter outside, and shortly after the clatter of the horses' hoofs could be heard as they galloped away.

Campbell wore a puzzled look as he led the way to his office. He had read much of the doings of his old school friend, and, in common with everyone else felt that Blake was well-nigh infallible.

On the present occasion, however, he considered that the subject in hand was more in the line of the stockmen than in that of the brilliant detective, even though the latter had spent a good part of his time with stock. He failed utterly to understand why Blake wanted to see the surveyor's map, but as host it was not up to him to question his guest's strange fancy.

The map itself was a faded blue print, which certainly looked its age. When Campbell had unfolded it and handed it to him Blake spread it out on the desk and studied it closely.

For half an hour he gave no sign; then he turned, and said briefly:

"I hear the sound of horse's hoofs, Dumpy. Would you mind seeing who it is? I think you will find it is someone bringing word that Tinker's horse has returned riderless."

Campbell glanced at him in surprise, but said nothing as he hurried out.

Less than a minute later he was back, looking more surprised than ever.

"Well, I'm dashed if I can see how you knew it," he blurted out, "but you are right."

"Exactly," smiled Blake. "Horse returned in fresh condition—not hungry, nor thirsty. Am I right?"

Campbell nodded.

"Yes. By heavens! Right in every particular!"

"That is what I was waiting for," said Blake, rising. "And now, if you will order a horse for me I shall start out."

"Hadn't I better come along with you?"

Blake shook his head while he slipped a fresh clip in his automatic.

"No, I'd rather go alone, if you don't mind. I shall take Pedro along with me. To tell you the truth, I have a certain theory. If I am right, it will need great caution. On the other hand, I may be wrong, so I shall go off on my own and investigate. In the meantime, the others can be keeping up their search."

"All right," laughed Campbell ruefully. "I'm hanged if I follow your line of reasoning, but you seem to have a clue which I haven't."

"My dear chap, you yourself gave me the only clue I have," smiled Blake.

"I!" echoed the other.

"Yes. If it turns out to be worth anything I shall tell you all about it later."

With that Campbell had to be content. Five minutes later Blake was in the saddle. He had fashioned a long leash for Pedro, who was to accompany him. Hanging from the saddle was a water-bottle and in his pocket a large packet of sandwiches. Evidently Blake expected his search to consume a fair amount of time.

Waving his hand to his host he took a hitch in Pedro's leash. Then he dug his heels in his horse, and went galloping away in the direction of Walla-Walla.

Though the lay mind might have made some connection between the story of Jackson the bushranger and Jameson's remarkable tale, it would also dismiss the connection as coincidence.

To begin with, the bushranger had lived half a century before, and in that time the tales of many of his doings had been so exaggerated by constant repetition that, in a way, it was difficult to say what was fact and what was fiction.

On the head of this, hundreds of experienced stockmen had at different times searched for the place where he was supposed to have concealed the cattle he had stolen; and the very fact that no such place had ever been discovered seemed to stamp that story as being pure romance.

Death Valley had, amongst other places, been considered, but the oldest man in the district would tell you that it was nothing but an impassable stretch of rocky scrub and cliffs which no man had ever crossed, and no man would, and if any man tried he would be a fool.

Consequently, it had never entered the heads of the searchers after Jameson's sheep that Death Valley might, after all, contain grass in the midst of its rocky ravines, and, even if it had, they would have scouted the idea as preposterous. At first blush Blake had been inclined to share this opinion, but while the others had been excitedly discussing the affair, his mind had seized upon one item and around it he had built.

That item was the disappearance of one of Jameson's stockman, and the subsequent return of his horse in a fresh condition.

"In the first place," he mused, "all highly coloured theories must be abandoned. Here we have the regular disappearance of good-sized mobs of sheep. Jameson and his men have scoured the district in the most thorough manner. That means, no matter how impossible it may seem, they are not far away. Secondly, the disappearance of his stockman and the return of his horse lends colour to this theory.

"Then, is there any stretch of land in this district which is untravelled, and which is extensive enough to provide feed for such a number of sheep? If so, why hasn't it been searched?

"Item two: What is the possibility of any connection between the old bushranger tale and this mystery?

"Item three: The very mystery of the affair proclaims the possibility of a simple solution.

"Query: Why is Jameson the sole victim, and what motive can there be?

"On Jameson's own showing he is at loggerheads with his neighbour Treherne, and even goes so far as to say he suspects the latter. Why? If their relations are as Jameson says, Treherne would not be fool enough to do anything so serious for the sake of petty revenge.

"Item: Look up story in the book which deals with the bushranger and examine a survey map of the district."

Thus far had Blake's mind worked on the night before. Following up these suggestions, he had, as will be remembered, spent some time reading the book. Then he had searched the survey map. One place, and one place only, was marked on the old blue print as being unknown. It was Death Valley, and on the map was classified "Unknown barren stretch. Rocky and scrubby gullies and cliffs. No feed. No water. Dangerous for stock. Unexplored."

Before the captain and the younger Campbell returned, Blake had formed a tentative theory based on those arguments.

True, the disappearance of Jameson's stockman may have been an isolated event; but if the same thing happened again—well, it would strengthen his theory that both sheep and men were near at hand. It had happened again, and its effect had come closer to Blake than to anyone else, for Tinker had been the second victim.

Something of the same line of thought was in his mind as he cantered through the paddocks and turned through the gate leading to Walla-Walla. He did not stop at the homestead to see Jameson, but kept on to the scene of the disappearance.

There he found everything just as the captain had said.

The ground, hard though it was, presented a scuffled appearance where the wethers had been. It was easy enough to follow their tracks through the gateway, and from where he stood Blake thought he could make out the darker coloured line which, in the opinion of the stockmen, marked the course taken by the sheep.

Instead of following this up until he came to the spot where the tracks were lost on strong ground, Blake slipped out of the saddle, and tied his horse to the fence.

"There is one thing certain," he muttered thoughtfully, as he surveyed the ground. "In driving off those sheep during the night they had to be mighty quiet, and, unless I am mistaken, it was done by stock-whips, and on foot. Anyway, that is a bare chance."

He tied Pedro's leash to the fence, and, drawing out his powerful pocket glass, he dropped to his knees in the midst of the tracks and went to work. Jameson's stockmen had already been over the spot both on foot and mounted, and Blake realised he had his work cut out to find that for which he sought. He knew it would be a mere waste of time to search in the main body of the tracks, for there, if anywhere, would he get confused.

Consequently, he knelt close to the boundary fence where his only chance of success lay. Lying flat, he held the glass close to the ground, and in this fashion crept slowly along, stopping at intervals, until he reached the cyclone gate. Each time he had stopped he had uttered a grunt of satisfaction, but, beyond this, it was impossible to tell how he was making out. Opening the gate, he again dropped to the ground, and in this manner crept through into the adjoining Binabong paddock.

It seemed an utter impossibility for any man to find

anything distinctive in the trampled ground which met Blake there. What with the passage of thousands of sheep during the dry months and the tracks left by stockmen, the place left little for even Blake's keen eyes to seize upon. He persevered, however, and after twenty minutes' solid work, he rose, dusty, but triumphant.

He had found little, it is true. Only the partial impression of a heavy heel with three little holes along the edge, showing where the nails had protruded a trifle. But this same impression was that which he had followed on the other side of the fence, and, from its very proximity to the boundary, he knew it was a good gamble that it belonged to one of the rustlers.

Stepping back through the gateway, he untied Pedro, and led him along to the first impression he had examined. There he gave the bloodhound time to get the scent well before he mounted. It was only a chance, and Blake knew it, but if Pedro couldn't trace the rustlers after their visible tracks had become obliterated on the stony ground, then nobody could. The scent he intended following might turn out to be one of Jameson's stockmen, and then it would be only so much time wasted. That was a chance which must be risked.

Pedro was already straining at the leash, and, stopping only long enough to close the gate, Blake started his horse. Away they went across the Binabong paddocks, Pedro travelling strongly and Blake keeping pace. As yet he had seen no signs of any of the other searchers. He judged, and rightly, that they had again drawn a blank.

In one thing he saw the stockmen had been correct. The

slightly discoloured streak of soil was undoubtedly the trail of the sheep, for Pedro stuck to it closely. Until he reached the stony ground, however, Blake could not tell for certain whether he had struck the trail of one of the rustlers or that of some stockman.

He was not to be kept in ignorance long, for, as he breasted a low ridge, he saw the slope ahead dip away, the grass suddenly grow sparse, and, further on, a wide expanse of stony ground which stretched away like a chill, grey sea to break in rocky waves against a veritable wilderness in the distance.

"So that is where Death Valley lies," he muttered, pulling up. "It certainly doesn't look as though it could possibly conceal anything attractive, and I don't wonder the stockmen give it a wide berth."

He started again, and, on reaching the stony ground, smiled grimly, for Pedro kept straight on in the direction of the wilderness.

All visible tracks had disappeared. Only the rough, barren, stone remained, but that seemed to matter little to the bloodhound. On he went, drawing nearer and nearer to the uninviting desolation ahead. Suddenly he swung to the right and skirted the edge of a sickly-looking bunch of scrub. For twenty minutes he travelled thus, until the stony ridges broke into a deep gully, and down this Pedro turned.

Barely had he started along it, however, when he suddenly stopped and began worrying about. Around and around he went, seeking for the scent which he had lost. Blake dismounted, and led him about in ever-growing circles, but all Pedro's efforts were useless.

"Ah!" grunted Blake. "That should have occurred to me. The rustler probably mounted his horse here. Never mind, old chap," he added aloud. "You have shown the way, at least, and we'll follow it as well as we can."

He was just on the point of remounting when the sound of pounding hoofs broke on his ears. Springing into the saddle, he swung his horse, and, pulling on the leash, dashed into a patch of dense scrub just as four horsemen swept up the gully and pulled up not ten yards from where he was concealed.

Blake drew his revolver and leaned forward. He could see their faces plainly, and as they began to speak he listened.

"He never got this far, Gene," one of them was saying. "He must have heard us coming, and probably took into the scrub along one of the gullies."

"I'm thinking he never came up the trail at all," broke in another. "In my opinion he is still back in the bottom lying low and waiting his chance."

Blake was shrewd enough to guess that they were discussing the escape of someone, and he devoutly hoped it was Tinker. Had he known, however, of the awful experience the lad was to have, he would have devoutly wished the opposite. As the man called Gene began to speak, Blake bent forward still more in order to catch what he said.

"Either of you may be right," he said savagely. "Anyway, he was game, and we must catch him. You stay up here, Harris, and watch for him. We will ride back to the bottom and search there. He won't keep his freedom long."

Harris nodded, and dropped his bridle rein over his horse's neck the while he began to roll a cigarette. Without further words, Gene and the other two turned and clattered back down the gully. Harris's back was towards the man who was concealed in the scrub, and, as he lazily puffed at his cigarette, he did not see the steady hand which lifted a business-like looking automatic.

He heard the swish of the bushes, and the ring of the horse's hoofs as Blake rode out, however, and swung like lightning, dropping his hand to his hip.

"I wouldn't do that if I were you," drawled Blake. "Put your hands up. Quick!"

Harris wavered; then, quelled by the look in the other's eye, obeyed.

"That's better," said Blake. "Just keep them up and let me suggest that you try no games. This trigger is balanced very delicately, and a sudden movement on your part might cause trouble."

"Who the devil are you, and what do you want?" growled Harris.

"Who I am doesn't concern you," answered Blake. "As to what I want, you will find out in good time. First, I want that revolver of yours."

He rode forward as he spoke, until the shoulder of his horse was against that of Harris's horse. Then, still keeping his man covered, Blake bent quickly, and jerked the other's gun from its holster.

"Now we can talk more comfortably," he said backing his horse away. "Lower your hands."

Harris obeyed.

"Put them behind you."

Again the command was obeyed.

"Keep them there, and Heaven help you if you try any funny business."

"It seems to me you are pretty high-handed, mister," grunted Harris.

"Do you think so?" remarked Blake pleasantly, again riding forward. "Now then cross your wrists. That's it, my friend. Steady now, and we'll have you trussed up beautifully."

As he spoke, Blake was working busily at the other's hands. Using a strap from his saddle bags he tied them deftly, and when he had finished, lifted the bridle rein of Harris's horse, and threw it around his prisoner's neck.

"That will help to keep your horse from stumbling," he remarked in the same deadly pleasant voice which was beginning to make his prisoner glance at him with new respect. "Now then," went on Blake, "just prod your animal gently, my friend, and lead the way into this place."

Harris eyed Blake truculently, then he glanced at Pedro.

"I don't know who in blazes you are," he grumbled, "but if you want to go in here, come on."

With that he prodded his horse, and led the way. Blake followed, leading Pedro, and in this fashion the little procession started.

Blake knew very well that he was, so to speak, entering the jaws of the tiger. Up to now he had no idea of the organising brain behind the sheep stealing, and what he had seen so far, convinced him that it must be an ordinary case of stock rustling. Still he held his final judgment in abeyance, realising that while he was risking all on entering Death Valley, he had a gambling chance in that he possessed a hostage.

He had been in positions of a similar nature to that of his prisoner's, and he knew full well what was going on in the latter's mind. His ready acquiescence had not fooled Blake. At the top of the gully, bound and helpless, Harris had no chance, while at the bottom of the wilderness there were friends who would use their best endeavours to free him.

Besides, he must feel that he had been negligent in the pursuit of his duty, so easily had he been captured. Altogether, he stood more chance by obeying Blake's orders than in disobeying them, so having made his decision, he urged his horse to the descent.

As they travelled along the tortuous path, which Yvonne had discovered, Blake kept his eyes open, taking in all the peculiarities and landmarks of the trail. Slowly, as they went along, he was taking a mental photograph of the way which would never fade; and, did circumstances arise which made it necessary for him to make a sudden retreat, he would know his way. Turning after turning they took until Harris reached the short gully which led into Yvonne's retreat.

Blake had no idea how far down the bottom might be, but he was sharp enough to know that it could not be much farther. Unless the height of the surrounding cliffs were of no indication, then the steady descent must be bringing them near their goal.

He marvelled at the intricate trail, which in itself formed such an impregnable bulwark, and he looked forward with no little interest to seeing what might lie hidden in the heart of this rocky, forbidding wilderness.

He began closing up gradually on his prisoner, and when they turned the last bend, Blake was close behind. Then the whole beauty of the retreat lay spread before them.

Blake gave an involuntary gasp of pleasure as he saw it, but quickly turned his attention back to his prisoner, who had a suspicious look in his eye.

"Ah! Would look you?" snapped Blake, spurring forward and clapping his hand over Harris's mouth just as the latter opened it to give a yell of warning to his friends. "I guess you will do better with a gag between your teeth, my friend. I'll supply that deficiency, and then you can rusticate in the scrub whilst I investigate this Arcadia."

Suiting the action to the word, Blake gagged his prisoner and tied a handkerchief over his mouth. Then he slipped out of the saddle, and dragged Harris to the ground. Half carrying, half dragging him, he made his way into the scrub which lined the sides of the gully, and secured his prisoner to a tree. This done, he led the horses in, and tied them also. Releasing Pedro's leash, he pointed to the prisoner.

"Watch him!" he ordered, and even as Blake crept away down the gully, Pedro was sitting in front of Harris making that veteran decidedly uncomfortable by the exhibition of a set of wicked-looking teeth.

On reaching the grassy bottom, Blake reconnoitred. At first he could make out no signs of the men whom he sought. What he did see, however, was the group of huts, and towards these he began to creep. Using practically the same methods which Tinker had used in leaving the place he wormed his way along, taking advantage of every bit of cover which offered, and dashing quickly across the open spaces. He reached the first hut without being seen, and lay in the grass behind it watching for signs of life.

Barely had he gained that position, when a door in one of the other huts slammed, and old Gene came along. He was heading for the hut behind which Blake lay concealed, and the detective could see he wore a decidedly savage expression. Whether or not his companions were about Blake had no idea. If they were they were keeping mighty quiet.

As though in answer to his thought there suddenly appeared, far in the distance, two horsemen. Then Blake remembered what had been said at the top of the gully about searching the bottom for the escaping prisoner.

By this time, Gene had drawn close, and gripping his revolver Blake made a quick decision. Rising like a shadow he levelled his aim and said:

"I'll trouble you to put your hands up."

The old stockman stopped dead in his tracks, and gazed in stupefaction at the apparition which had risen from the grass.

"What the—" he began.

"Up with them, my friend," drawled Blake. "Don't hitch that way. That's better. Now turn round and stand still."

Striding forward, he jerked Gene's revolver from the holster as he had that of Harris. He was casting about for something with which to tie his prisoner when he was startled by a loud voice which came from the hut.

"I say, who is out there?"

"Who are you?" called back Blake, seeing Gene made no sign.

"A prisoner. Are you a friend?"

"Yes. Are you bound?"

"My hands are."

"Can you kick open the door, and come out?"

"I think I can manage it."

Silence reigned for a few moments. Then came a pounding noise as the man in the hut kicked at the rickety door. A moment later it flew out, and the dishevelled figure of a stockman stumbled out.

He gazed in open-mouthed astonishment at the sight which met him.

"I heard you hold up Gene," he said, "and hoped it was a friend."

Blake nodded.

"Come along here, and I will cut your bonds."

The man obeyed. Blake kept Gene covered with the revolver while he drew out his knife and severed the cords which bound the other.

"Now then, take off your belt and tie up our friend," he said when he had finished. "I imagine it will be a pleasant duty."

"You just bet it will," answered the other grimly.

"Well hurry up," rapped Blake. "There are two more in

the distance, and they are coming this way."

The released man needed no further bidding, and, though Gene looked as though he would like to fight, the steadily held automatic was a powerful argument, and he submitted. A minute later, with a gag between his teeth, he was occupying the hut in place of his late prisoner.

The two horsemen were riding along the bank of the stream drawing closer every moment. Blake surveyed them from the shelter of a clump of trees, then he turned to the man he had released.

"I suppose you are the stockman from Walla-Walla who was caught," he said.

"Yes," nodded the other.

"What is your name," asked Blake.

"Richards."

"Well, Richards, we have got to get that pair. I think the best plan is to take cover, and fire a shot. They will take that as a signal from their companion, and will ride up. As they approach we can keep them covered. It ought not to be very difficult for you to remove their weapons and tie them while I show them the business end of my automatic."

"I guess you are right," answered Richards. "You sure took old Gene neat."

"I have another up the gully," said Blake. "Now then, to cover, Richards."

They sank down behind a clump of bushes close to the path, which led between the huts. When they were settled, Blake lifted his revolver and fired a single shot.

A few minutes later, they heard the hurried clatter of

hoofs drawing near, and the two horsemen came riding at a canter along the path.

"Now," whispered Blake.

With one accord they leaped out, and covered their men. The two horsemen jerked their horses back on their haunches, and their hands flew to their hips. The steely eyes and set jaw behind that black automatic convinced them that Blake meant business, and in obedience to his sharp command, their hands went up.

"Now then, Richards, look alive," jerked Blake. "Toss out their guns and tie their hands behind them."

Nothing loth, the stockman leaped to do Blake's bidding. Remembering his own recent plight he was far from gentle in his methods, and, by the time the new arrivals fully realised what was happening, they were securely bound.

"Fetch out Gene, and mount him," commanded Blake.

Richards did so, and at Blake's further command ran up a horse for himself.

"Now, my friends," went on Blake addressing his prisoners. "We are going out of here. My companion will lead the way. You will follow, and I will bring up the rear. We make one stop in order to pick up your other companion. Beyond that, I wouldn't advise you to attempt to stop or to play any hanky-panky tricks. Now then, march!"

And they marched, or at least their horses marched.

Blake walked behind until they reached the mouth of the gully where he had left Harris and Pedro. There he got his own horse, and assisting Harris into the saddle, the procession again started. They had covered perhaps half the distance when the sound of flying hoofs reached their ears, and Blake gripped his revolver as he saw the look of hope which overspread the faces of his prisoners.

Nearer and nearer came the sound until, on rounding a bend, they caught sight of a mounted figure riding recklessly down the trail. The rider was a woman, and Blake gazed in utter bewilderment as he recognised the features of Mademoiselle Yvonne.

THE FIFTH CHAPTER

Yvonne v. Jameson—His Threat—The Attack.

WHILE BLAKE HAD been following up his theories, startling events had been taking place elsewhere—events which culminated in Yvonne's unexpected appearance at Death Valley.

To say that Edward Jameson was dumbfounded at still another disappearance of sheep was to put it mildly. Nor were his feelings salved by the additional information that one of Campbell's guests had also been spirited away. Practical to the last degree, it was difficult for one of his temperament to see aught in the series of outrages but the bold operations of an exceptionally clever band of stock rustlers. And yet the very lack of that sensitive fineness which was such an inherent part of Sexton Blake was the very thing which finally caused Jameson to experience the same indefinable feeling of rage which had already gripped the men on his place.

Put any one of them on a bucking horse, and he would

stick to it until the beast was conquered; send him into a mob of cattle to cut out a steer, and he would sweep into that ocean of horns without a second's hesitation. Those things a stockman could feel and could understand. They were living and tangible. But this uncanny spiriting away of whole mobs of sheep was unnerving, to say the least, and the bush-bred stockmen made no bones about saying so.

For all his vast acres, Jameson was of the same stock as they, and when he did begin to waver he went down with a crash. What it was, who it was, how it was, he could not fathom, but in the yielding of his practical judgment he yielded also that veneer which went with his acres.

Like a mad bull who sees red, he became consumed with a terrific infuriation, a wild impulse to grip something tangible and blindly crush it between his great hands. And as Fate would have it, his thoughts turned in that moment of rage to the man whom he felt was responsible in some mysterious manner for his troubles—John Treherne. Hot on the thought, with his rage still seething, he ordered a horse and, while his men were scouring the countryside in search of the missing sheep, Jameson himself was on his way to Binabong, intent on vengeance. He arrived shortly after the return of Yvonne and her companions from seeing the sheep safely into Death Valley.

They were by no means surprised at seeing him approach, for by Yvonne's reckoning he should have taken the bait ere this. It had been her purpose to mystify and puzzle him, in order that he might make some move whereby she could confront him with the facts. If she could lure him into doing something rash, so much the better.

As they saw him sweeping up through the home paddock, Yvonne smiled a brief smile.

"Our neighbour, Mr. Jameson, of Walla-Walla, is coming," she said. "If I am any judge of facial expression, I would say that he is in a towering rage, and its cause, I imagine, comes from the fact that he feels the disappearance of his sheep emanates from Binabong, and yet he doesn't know."

Graves smiled, and lit a cigarette. He looked forward with keen relish to the coming visit. As for Treherne, he was nervously gnawing at his under lip. Although he had witnessed visible proof of Yvonne's brilliant generalship, and though the whole-hearted worship of Gene and his companions impressed him considerably, he had yet to see her wriggle herself free from the undoubted gravity of the situation.

The fact that her bridge to success was to be his "assignment of honour" of Binabong to Edward Jameson, did not tend to lessen the unpleasant prospect which he saw ahead. However, he had bound himself to do as Yvonne said, and now that the crisis had arrived there was nothing to do but meet it.

Jameson wasted little ceremony at the door. Throwing his bridle rein over a post, he stamped heavily up on the verandah and pounded at the wire door. Without waiting for his summons to be answered, he threw it open and marched down the hall. At the door of the room where he had gambled so successfully against Treherne he paused, and his teeth bared in a half snarl as he saw the three figures within.

"Treherne," he snapped, "I have business with you—private business. You may not wish to have me speak of it before your guests."

"My guests will remain, Jameson," answered Treherne quietly. "Whatever you have to say, say it before them."

"I will do so," replied the other, tossing his hat on the table. "In the first place, I presume you will not deny that I practically saved you from ruin during this drought?"

Treherne made a gesture, but did not speak.

"And I doubt if you will deny that I loaned you money on your stock. Do you?"

"I do not."

"Nor will you deny that after that I loaned you a further sum on the property itself?"

"I do not."

"Very well. In my pocket I hold your written assignment of the place. You have seen fit to ignore that. You offered to take up the loans as though this assignment did not exist. We have had some strange types of Englishmen out here, John Treherne, but of all the types I think you are the worst. It has always been an Englishman's boast that he paid his debts of honour."

The blood rushed into Treherne's cheeks, then receded and left them white as paper as he heard Jameson's taunt. His hands clenched convulsively, and he half started up. A warning gesture from Yvonne, however, recalled him, and he sat silent.

"So that fails to move you, does it?" sneered Jameson.

"A coward as well as a defaulter, eh! Well, look here, Treherne. This is my final word. I give you two hours to vacate Binabong. At the end of that time I shall treat you as a common trespasser and evict you. I have the law on my side and, if necessary, I shall use force."

"When you speak of eviction, you are addressing the wrong person, Mr. Jameson," broke in a cool, silvery voice.

Jameson swung and contemptuously regarded the slim girl who had spoken.

"Might I ask in what way?" he demanded sarcastically.

"Certainly," answered Yvonne. "Mr. Treherne does not happen to be the owner of Binabong."

"Indeed! I am afraid I do not understand."

"No? Then I will enlighten you. Binabong was sold and legally transferred by Mr. Treherne yesterday, the purchaser assuming all his liabilities, Mr. Jameson."

"So he is a swindler as well!" snapped Jameson.

"In what way?"

"By selling that which did not belong to him."

"That is a point on which I do not agree with you."

"You seem to be pretty well informed, madam. Perhaps you will tell me next that you are the purchaser."

"Marvellous!" returned Yvonne. "How did you guess it?"

"I don't know what your game is," blazed Jameson, losing his head under her cool mockery, "but I can tell you this. Whichever of you owns this place you have my orders to vacate. At the end of two hours I will return with my men, and if you are not gone I shall deal with you in my own way."

"You will make that move by the authority of the assignment you hold from Mr. Treherne, I suppose?" drawled Graves.

"Certainly."

"Then I would suggest that several minutes of the two hours have already elapsed," broke in Yvonne. "Good morning, Mr. Jameson."

For a moment Jameson glared at her. Then, turning on his heel, he picked up his hat. At the door he paused.

"I suppose you think I don't suspect who got away with my sheep," he jerked. "Well, I do. I don't know how you did it, but, by heaven, let me tell you I mean business! Remember, two hours!"

With that he stamped out and threw himself into the saddle. As he galloped away from the house, Yvonne rose and stood before Treherne.

"Cheer up, Mr. Treherne," she said, smiling. "You did nobly to restrain yourself under his insults. But, never mind, you will have a chance yet to get your own back."

"I am in your hands," answered Treherne. "It was mighty hard to be called a defaulter over a debt of honour, though!"

"I know, but it couldn't be helped. We want Edward Jameson to make exactly the move he threatened to make, and had we shown our hand everything would have fizzled out. But he means business, all right. He had vengeance in his eye, and hasn't the faintest idea that we know the truth about the playing cards. He judges others from his own point of view, which is clumsy. Had the same thing happened to him, he would have exposed the perpetrator at once. Mr. Jameson is not the type of man who appreciates or understands subtlety in others, though in his own crude way he has a vague notion of that quality, as witness his manipulation of the marked cards.

"However, there is no time to be lost. We are prepared for a siege, and Jameson will make one. Our prisoners form a complication, for we are short handed. Gene and the other three stockmen must be brought back here. I myself will ride to Death Valley and bring them. You, uncle, see about the guns and ammunition. Mr. Treherne can ride to the bunk-house for the men who are there. Then lock up.

"I do not know that I can make the valley and return in the two hours. At any rate, if Jameson attacks before I return, don't wait for us. Barricade the doors and windows and hold the place. I have always the winning card, so if the worst comes to the worst I can play that. The main point is to have Jameson attack us. I am sorry that it means risking life, but it is the only way, now we have gone so far."

"Do you think Blake is really here?" asked Graves.

"I don't know," answered Yvonne. "It seems as though he must be, and yet if that is so, and he is working with Jameson, it is strange that we have seen nothing of him. Perhaps Tinker is out here alone. I will endeavour to find out at Death Valley. And now I must be gone. Don't forget. If Jameson shows up before I return, don't wait. Let him fire the first shot; if he goes far, then retaliate, but not until you have to."

319

"I wish you would let me ride to the valley," said Treherne. "You may run into them on your way back, and in Jameson's present mood he will not be inclined to treat you gently."

"I can take care of myself," laughed Yvonne. She turned as she spoke and slipped a small automatic into the holster at her belt. Picking up her gauntlets, she waved her hand and hurried out. Her big roan, ready saddled, was hitched to a post outside, and a moment later she was in the saddle, flying at a hard gallop for Death Valley and reinforcements.

As soon as she had gone, Treherne mounted and rode in the direction of the bunk-house, in order to get the few remaining stockmen. Graves busied himself in getting ready the guns and ammunition, and, by the time Treherne had returned with the three stockmen, he had a regular arsenal laid out on the table. Then they all began to prepare for the expected attack.

Binabong homestead had been built years before, when the Aborigines[9] still existed in that district, and, like all other homesteads of those days, had been provided with heavy wooden shutters against any attack. In the shutters were loopholes, which gave a view of the approach to the house, and on the present occasion they would serve for defensive purposes.

Yvonne, who had hoped and planned for this move on Jameson's part, had, with her usual capacity for detail, seen that the old shutters were in working order. Consequently, it did not take long for Monty and his two companions to close and bolt them. One was left open, in order that Yvonne and the reinforcements might enter, and also that speech could be had with Jameson did he wish to parley.

Then the five men sat down and smoked in silence, as men will who are expecting a hostile attack. Their preparations had taken a little over an hour, and by Monty's reckoning Yvonne ought to have reached Death Valley and be on her way back. It would be a race between her and the Walla-Walla crowd as to which reached Binabong first.

Now and then one of them would rise and inspect the rifles. Then he would return to his seat and run his hand caressingly over his revolver. Beyond that there was no indication that the nerves of each one were strung up to a high pitch.

Of all the things in a situation of that kind, waiting is the hardest even for men who have tasted fire before. With those who have never been in an engagement the suspense of a wait is unnerving until the first shot is fired. Then self is forgotten in the excitement of the moment, and the whole mind is concentrated on the joy of conflict, which is awakened by the pungent smell of powder and the shrill screaming of the shells. In that party Treherne was the only one who had not been under fire. His feelings were somewhat of the above order in consequence, though his mind was also dwelling on the apparent seriousness of his own position.

Monty was the first to descry the approach of anyone, and Graves immediately turned his field-glasses on the distant object in order to see what it was.

"A band of horsemen on the gallop," he announced quietly. "About thirty of them. Yvonne has lost. It is Jameson and his men."

"She may come across from the left," muttered Monty hopefully.

"If she does she will have her work cut out to beat them," replied Graves, still studying the approaching body of horsemen. "They are riding hard, and I can now make out Jameson. He is in the lead, and they are all armed."

"If it wasn't for the danger the missie is running I'd say let 'em come," grunted Monty, twirling the cylinder of his revolver. "I haven't seen the chance of such fun since Bendigo Joe jumped my claim way back in the seventies."

"Unless Jameson's look belies him you will have your wish," drawled Graves. "He certainly hasn't grown any sweeter-natured since we saw him two hours ago."

The oncoming party of horsemen had now reached the home paddock and were coming on with unslackened speed. In five minutes they would be within hail.

Graves laid aside his glasses and stood close to the window, one hand ready to close the shutter quickly should the necessity arise. Curly had left the room to examine the paddock through a loophole at the rear, in order to see if there were any signs of Yvonne and Gene. He returned just then and reported that she was not in sight.

"All right," answered Graves. "Get ready, boys! Jameson has halted his party and is riding on alone. He evidently intends to speechify again."

They held their weapons loosely and crowded up behind Graves just as Jameson rode to within a few yards of the window and pulled up. For a moment he and Graves eyed one another. Then Jameson spoke, and the quiver of his tones proved how hard it was for him to control himself.

"Who claims to be the owner of this place?" he demanded loudly.

Graves placed one hand over his heart and bowed ironically.

"I am authorised to treat for the owner, Mr. Jameson. What have you to say?"

"I have this to say," shouted Jameson, holding up a sheaf of papers in his hand. "I have here a copy of the mortgage which I hold over the stock previously on this station. I also hold a copy of the mortgage on the station itself, given to me for moneys advanced. In addition to these, of a later assignment date and superseding the mortgages, I hold an unqualified assignment of Binabong Station from one John Treherne to myself.

"Furthermore, I publicly charge the said John Treherne that he, together with other persons at present unknown, did conspire to steal and did steal a number of sheep from Walla-Walla. As the true owner of Binabong Station I demand that John Treherne and any others who may be on the property leave peacefully and at once. If this demand is refused I, as owner of the property, will enforce my demand against those who remain in illegal possession.

"And, further, I demand that the said John Treherne deliver himself up peacefully on the charge stated. I make the demand as the rightful owner of Binabong, and also as Justice of the Peace for this district. I give you five minutes to decide. If at the end of that time you refuse to comply with my demands I shall take what measures I deem advisable to evict you by force."

"Not bad," drawled the imperturbable Graves. "You ought to run for Parliament, Jameson."

Jameson snorted, but vouchsafed no reply, as he rode rapidly back to his men. Graves once more swept the paddocks in search of Yvonne.

"Nothing doing," he muttered slowly. "Something has delayed her, boys. Close the window. Mr. Jameson is not bluffing. See to your guns, I think we will be getting it warm in a few minutes."

Monty closed the shutter and bolted it. Then he and his two companions took up their posts in other rooms while Graves and Treherne remained to guard the front. At the end of the allotted five minutes Graves applied his eye to the loophole and peered forth. He could see Jameson speaking to his men. Then they spread out in a wide circle, and, at a sharp command, drew their weapons. A moment later the whole party started at a swinging gallop for the house.

"Here they come!" shouted Graves. "Be ready, boys, and, remember, let them fire the first shot!" At that moment the heavy pounding of hoofs broke on their ears, then came a heavy volley, followed by the heavy plunk of lead as the bullets hit the shutters.

The fight was on.

THE SIXTH CHAPTER

Tinker's Ghastly Discovery—An Unlucky Fall.

IT WILL BE remembered that, when Tinker escaped from the bottom of the wilderness, Gene and his three companions had not lost any time in giving chase. It will also be recalled that they had reached the top of the valley without overtaking him, and that while they halted there Blake had overheard their remarks.

Two theories had been advanced. One was that the lad had heard them coming up the trail, and had sought cover in the scrub which covered the gullies. The other was that he had never left the bottom, but was still lying low there, waiting for a suitable opportunity to make a safe get-away. The former of these theories was the correct one, and it is just possible that they might have caught the escaping prisoner had not Blake's successful strategy upset their plans.

When Tinker started on a steady lope up the trail he had wisely husbanded his strength. Had he only known of Blake's nearness he would have been saved much suffering, but he did not think it possible that even Blake's methods would discover the secret of Death Valley so soon.

He felt fairly certain of the way, for he had a retentive memory and had kept his eyes open on the way in. If he could once reach the top in safety he knew he had a good chance. He had covered what seemed a tremendous distance, though in reality it was only about third of the way, when the sharp ring of hoofs behind told him his pursuers were gaining. He had counted on the necessity for the horses to walk up the trail and on his own ability to keep up a swifter progress, but old Gene had taken advantage of every level bit and was setting hard pace.

As the sound grew nearer Tinker realised that he must take cover. Still loping he turned into a patch of scrub which stretched up the side of the gully in which he happened to be, and dropped down panting, just as the four horsemen swept by.

Poor Tinker, if he had only known that at that very moment Blake and Pedro were riding along the gully at the top!

As Gene and his companions passed on Tinker rose and cautiously crept still further into the scrub.

"I'll wait a few minutes," he muttered. "They are bound to go clear to the top, but I can probably manage to get on another stage before they return. When they find I haven't reached there they are sure to post a guard, but I have to run my chances of slipping past him. If I remember rightly the scrub is fairly thick there."

With this consoling thought he lay still until his wind returned. Then he rose and made his way, as he thought, back to the trail he had just left. Certainly, it was the bottom of a dead water-course into which he emerged, and, as far as he could see, it was the identical spot where he had entered the scrub.

He started along at a brisk lope, keeping his ears open for sounds of the returning horsemen. For ten minutes he travelled steadily, then, on reaching a bend, he turned round it and pulled up with a gasp of amazement, to find he had almost plunged headlong over the jagged edge of a sheer cliff.

"Crikey!" he muttered, gazing about him in puzzlement. "How does this occur? I'm hanged if I remember this in the descent!"

He turned and went back round the bend, gazing along the way he had come.

"It certainly looks like the trail," he grunted, "but there is something wrong somewhere. I'll try over to the left. Perhaps the trail goes that way instead of this."

Suiting the action to the word he made his way in the opposite direction. A small, rather well-defined gully opened up, and he breathed easier.

"I am all right now," he thought. "That cliff gave me a shock for a moment."

He again broke into a lope and travelled on quickly until he reached another bend in the gully. This he turned, and suddenly his face went very white.

For the second time he had barely saved himself from plunging over a high cliff into eternity. He slowly retreated around the bend and gazed back down the gully.

"I guess I'm off the trail," he muttered. "The only thing to do is to go back the way I came and keep on until I reach it. I must have passed the turning without noticing it."

He moved at a steady walk back along the gully until he reached the spot where he had struck the first cliff, and from there turned down to the left.

As he walked along he tried to reckon how long he had taken from the time he had started. One moment he thought it must be about ten minutes, and the next it seemed that he had been twice as long. All the time his eyes kept darting from side to side in search of the trail. He had been walking for several minutes when he saw another gully on his left, and gave grin of satisfaction.

"That's it," he said aloud. "What an ass I was to miss it, and what precious time I have wasted. I'll have to hustle if I am to make up for it."

Turning into the gully he broke into a run, and for several minutes kept a straight course. Then another bend appeared, and he turned it confidently. If he had been startled at the sight of the cliff on the two previous occasions he was doubly so now at the sight which met his eyes. For the third time he found that he had come out to the face of a cliff, but in this case there was a broad ledge between him and the edge, and on that ledge he saw a sight which made his flesh creep.

Lying in a tumbled heap were two bleached skeletons, their bony fingers still curled about the handle of a rusty knife, and the twisted attitude of the limbs told their own tale. They had died in mortal combat. When or how was a mystery. That it must have been years before was evident from the whitened condition of the bones.

Tinker gave a shudder of distaste and gazed about him. For the first time he noticed the opening of a cave which gave on to the ledge, and, for the moment forgetting his own predicament, he approached it. At first his eyes failed to pierce the gloom, for outside the sun was beating down with terrific force.

As his pupils widened, however, he made out what seemed to be a heap of boxes in one corner of the cave. He struck a match and stepped inside. By the light of the vesta he saw that his first thought was right. There were about twenty boxes piled up against the further wall. They were not large, and Tinker wondered what they could contain.

At that moment the match went out and he lit another. Holding this aloft he approached closer, and put out his free hand to drag one of the boxes around for inspection. His eyes widened in surprise when he found it refused to move, and, dropping the match, he gave both hands to the job. The light from the opening now enabled him to see fairly well. He found that by exerting considerable strength he could lift the box, and this he did. He staggered to the opening of the cave with it and dropped it on the ledge.

"Heavens, that must be full of lead!" he muttered, mopping his brow. "Anyway, I'll investigate it."

Going back into the cave, he lit another match, and began searching amongst a heap of utensils in the corner.

He gave a grunt of satisfaction on discovering an old rusty tomahawk, and with this in his hand, returned to the ledge.

Turning his back on those two awful grinning skeletons, he began hammering and prising at the lid. Whoever had nailed it on had meant it to stay, for though the heads of the nails were rusty, they held stubbornly. By dint of perseverance, however, Tinker got it started, and once that had been accomplished, the rest was easy. He tugged and pulled until he got the lid lifted high enough to insert the handle as a lever. Then, with a mighty heave, he strained upwards, and the lid went splintering.

Exactly what he expected to find Tinker couldn't have told. As a matter of fact, he had hardly considered the matter. He knew from the great weight in proportion to the size that the box must contain a very heavy substance, but little did he dream that it was packed with the most precious and almost the heaviest of all metal—pure bar gold.

He sat speechless for several minutes. Were the other boxes packed with gold, and, if so, where on earth had they come from? He was so held in stupefaction that for some time it never occurred to him to examine the other boxes, nor, in fact, to do anything but build a structure of feeble theories. Then his mind came back to earth.

Jumping up, he rushed into the cave, and began straining at the next box on the tier. It was quite as heavy as the last, and, on reaching the ledge with it, he could see it was to all intents and purposes the same as the first one. Again he brought the tomahawk into requisition. He worked feverishly now, all his own troubles forgotten in the excitement of the moment. After some ten minutes' work, he managed to prise off the lid. His expectations were realised to the full. The contents were exactly the same as those in the first box.

"Crikey!" he gasped, squatting down on his heels and lifting out a bar of the precious metal. "Gold—pure gold! There must be four or five thousand pounds' worth in each box. That means in the twenty boxes there is a fortune of eighty or ninety thousand pounds. How, in the name of all that's mysterious, did they get here?"

Mechanically he turned his attention to the two skeletons, taking in the details of those sinister positions which told their own tale. Unconsciously, he was nodding his head slowly and mentally ticking off the suggestions of the attitudes. The twisted limbs, the outstretched right arms, the crumpled up left arms, the pointing of the skeletons head to head, all proved that both had met their fate in a desperate encounter, and did the lad need further proof, there were the knives, caked with a brown rust which was not the rust of water.

Slowly Tinker advanced to the nearest of them, and gingerly drew out the knife from between the bony fingers. He glanced at it closely, and bent lower as he saw two initials cut on the handle. It was with difficulty that he made them out, so old and worn were they, but finally he deciphered the first one a "P," then the second, a "J." Dropping the knife, he stood up.

"Well, by ginger! There was only one notorious individual in this district whose name began with these initials," he muttered. "That was Jackson the bushranger—Peter Jackson. So I guess it's a safe bet that the gold in this cave was Jackson's hoard. But who was the other? Was he one of Jackson's band who wanted a share, or was he some prospector who blundered in here and discovered the hiding-place?"

Tinker was never to know. And yet, sixty years before, when the Indian Mutiny was raging, when Australia was almost totally unexplored, and when gold was still the lure of California, those two men had stood on that narrow ledge and fought their savage fight to the death.

Tinker's conjecture that it was a member of Jackson's band was correct. Thieves had fallen out, and by the mockery of Fate they had both paid the penalty. All those years had that gold lain there undiscovered and untouched. Much good all Jackson's hoarding had done him in the end.

To die by the hand of an enemy, with the curses of his dying opponent ringing in his ears, almost within touch of his treasure, to fall there in the blazing sunshine on that ledge, unwept and unmourned, the helpless victim of the birds of prey who swiftly gathered to the banquet. That had been his end, and still the gold had remained as though in glittering yellow mockery of man's futile efforts.

It was some time before Tinker's thoughts came back to his own situation. When they did he realised that the sun was past the zenith, and that he was hopelessly lost. He had had nothing to eat since the night before, and already the pangs of thirst were beginning to make themselves felt. Was this open tomb to be his own fate? He shuddered as the thought occurred.

Getting to his feet, he went back along the gully still searching for the trail he had missed. On and on he wandered, his every thought now bent on finding his way out. As the maddening thirst increased, he thought of the trickling silver stream at the bottom. The gold attracted him no more. He would gladly have given it all for the privilege of burying his face in that clear stream.

Still the sun kept dropping, and still he stumbled on. He had lost every sense of direction now. All the stories he had heard of Death Valley and its impassable gullies occurred with redoubled force. His throat was parched and dry, and his tongue beginning to swell.

Finally, a mild form of delirium seized him. Time and again he was sure he had found the trail, only to discover that it ended in a yawning chasm. Several times he tumbled and fell, but dragged himself to his feet again and stumbled on. He finally remembered his revolver. Even being a prisoner was preferable to this.

He realised that comparatively few people knew Death Valley, and those few probably had no knowledge of any part of it but the trail to the bottom. If he were to succumb it might be years before his body was found, perhaps never. The thought sobered him.

He drew his revolver, and emptied every chamber in the air. For some time he listened for a reply, but none came. With a sudden frenzy of rage he hurled the revolver from him. Once again the delirium seized him and he stumbled on.

Finally, on turning a bend, he saw before him the grinning skeletons on the ledge. He had been travelling in a great circle. He gave a dry sob and staggered forward.

As he did so, his foot caught in a small crevice. He caught wildly at the empty air in a frenzied effort to save himself. His fingers closed convulsively, and with a hoarse croak he plunged over the edge into the abyss beneath.

THE SEVENTH CHAPTER

In Time—Blake as Mediator—Jameson Fooled—The End.

IF BLAKE WAS startled at seeing Yvonne approaching down the tortuous trail which led to the bottom of Death Valley, he gave no visible sign. At the same time, had a physician placed a clinical thermometer in the hollow of Blake's arm, he would have noticed that the detective's temperature had gone up a point, due, possibly, to the arduous climb.

As for Yvonne, she drew her horse back on his haunches, the action sending a little cascade of stones rolling merrily downwards. Richards, who was leading the way, promptly covered her with his revolver, and the four prisoners growled savagely at him as their horses came to a stop. Blake signed to Richards to lower his revolver; then he stepped forward.

"Good-morning, mademoiselle," he said, smiling ironically.

"Good morning, Mr. Blake," she replied. And though

her lips were unsmiling, her eyes glinted softly, and her delicately flushed cheeks told their own tale. "For a Londoner, you seem—er—fairly well acquainted with Death Valley," she added mockingly.

"A charming spot—at the bottom," drawled Blake. "An ideal place for sheep during these dry months. It occurred to me while I was down there that it would be a splendid retreat for, say, stock rustlers."

"Indeed! I am afraid that occupation has died out, hasn't it?"

"Well," answered Blake, wrinkling his brows as though in deep thought, "until very recently I was under that same impression. It seems, however, that I was mistaken. These four gentlemen who look annoyed, strike me as being a particularly murderous lot; and I greatly fear they have been helping themselves to stock which did not belong to them. In fact, it seems odd that all the sheep I saw at the bottom of the valley bore the brand of Walla-Walla. When I was in Australia before, sheep-stealing was a serious matter. To my knowledge the law regarding it has not been changed."

Yvonne shifted impatiently under Blake's irony.

"Enough," she said, with a click of her white teeth. "Supposing I acknowledge that for the moment you hold the advantage of me. What do you propose doing?"

"My intention, mademoiselle, is to take these four worthy men to Walla-Walla, and turn them over to the law as represented by Mr. Edward Jameson, who is, I understand, a Justice of the Peace. After that I propose finding out what has become of my lad, Tinker."

Yvonne looked at him with a puzzled glance, which changed to a look of mute inquiry as she turned her gaze to the bound Gene. Gene read her look, and for the first time since he had been made a prisoner, he spoke.

"He escaped, missie," he said gruffly. "We were searching for him when we were outwitted."

"I am surprised that three experienced stockmen, all armed, should be outwitted by one man," she replied, with a hint of sarcasm in her voice.

Gene writhed, but made no reply. Then Yvonne turned back to Blake.

"May I speak with you—privately?" she asked slowly.

Blake nodded.

"Yes, providing the prisoners pass their word not to try any hanky-panky business."

"They will do that," answered Yvonne. "Come, please."

She turned and rode a short distance up the trail, followed by Blake. When a bend hid them from view of the others, Yvonne drew up and waited until Blake reached her side. Then she thrust out her small gauntleted hand.

"Won't you shake hands?" she asked naïvely.

Blake laughed, and, putting out his strong, sunburnt hand, grasped hers.

"Of course. But, mademoiselle, why have you done this? You must know how serious it is."

Yvonne looked at him with a serious expression.

"What are you doing in this affair, Mr. Blake? Are you working professionally?"

"No, not exactly. Jameson sought my assistance, and I gave it—informally."

"Are you stopping at Walla-Walla?"

"No. I am visiting at Mulwana, Campbell's place."

"Ah! It adjoins Walla-Walla. Won't you withdraw from this and let things take their course, Mr. Blake?" she asked, with pleading eyes.

"I am sorry, mademoiselle. It is impossible. Yesterday I might have done so. To-day I cannot. Besides, you yourself have made that impossible by capturing Tinker. By the way, where is he? I must insist on his release, and then, if you are wise, you will surrender peacefully. I will do what I can to persuade Jameson to take no further action."

Yvonne's silvery laugh rang out; then she grew sober, and gazed at Blake in silence for some moments.

"Do you know what is probably happening at this moment?" she finally asked.

"I must confess that I am not clairvoyant."

"In all probability Jameson and his men are besieging Binabong homestead. Jameson threatened to do so a little over an hour ago, and he certainly looked as though he meant it."

"This is serious," replied Blake gravely. "If there is bloodshed it will complicate matters considerably."

"Exactly. I was on my way here to summon help when I met you and discovered that you had arrived first. You have only heard Jameson's side of this argument, Mr. Blake. Do you feel inclined to hear my side of the story?"

"You have never found me unwilling to listen, and then weigh, have you?" he asked gruffly.

"No," she said softly; "never. It won't take long, and I will be as brief as possible."

She bent forward and laid one hand on the neck of his horse. Then she began speaking in low, rapid tones.

She began with her longing to see Binabong again, and from that went on to the arrival of her uncle and herself. Then she dealt with the haggard owner they had found, and the story of hard luck he had told. Of the assistance he had received from Jameson and the nightly games of chance in which the two men had indulged. Of the loss in this manner of all Treherne's possessions, and her discovery that the cards were marked.

Without pausing, she told him of the idea which had occurred to her, based on her knowledge of Death Valley, and how well her plans had succeeded. Then she told him of her motive, and went into detail regarding the offer to lift the mortgage, and how Treherne, at her insistence, had repudiated the gambling assignment.

Finally, she told of Jameson's call barely an hour before, and of his threats while there.

"So you see," she said, "from my point of view I am in the right, and though my methods have been irregular, it seems to me that conditions justified them."

For some time Blake made no reply. The average observer would have thought that he was reflecting deeply upon the story he had just heard. As a matter of fact, he was not. Impelled by that mental phenomena, the association of ideas, his mind had gone trailing off on an incident entirely alien to the subject in hand.

It had come about through a gesture made by Yvonne as she talked. It stirred some chord of memory, and then he recollected what it suggested. He had seen that gesture before. When or how he could not for the moment remember. His abstracted gaze rested on a single red rose which was thrust in Yvonne's belt, and then he remembered.

It was in London, at the Venetia, after the highly satisfactory ending to that now notorious case, which was popularly called "The Black Jewel-Case." He and Yvonne had lunched at the grill-room of the Venetia, and it was there that she had worn red roses. It was also there that she had used the quick, graceful gesture which she again used now. Sub-consciously his keen mind was weighing the facts she had presented, but it was not until she laid her hand on his arm that he shook himself from his reverie.

"I beg your pardon, mademoiselle," he said, flushing faintly. "I am afraid my mind was straying."

"That is not very complimentary to me," she laughed.

"On the contrary," he smiled. "I was thinking of you."

"Then I am indeed flattered," she replied, also flushing.

"Now about this other matter," went on Blake, breaking what threatened to degenerate into an awkward silence. "As I told you, my interest in the affair is strictly of an informal nature. At the same time I felt moderately certain that Jameson must be in the right, although I did not like his suppression of the details regarding his trouble with Treherne. Of course the fact that he used marked cards in order to fleece Treherne, alters the case entirely. As for me, I must say I hardly blame you for your feeling of indignation, although I by no means condone your methods. At the same time, since I am mixed up in this thing, I propose seeing it through, so it seems that once again we are to work as friends, not enemies, mademoiselle."

Yvonne's voice was trembling slightly as she thanked him, and with clasped hands they gazed at each other.

"About Tinker?" said Blake, releasing her hand slowly.

"Truly, I am as mystified regarding his whereabouts as you are, Mr. Blake. He escaped, that is certain, but he may have taken cover in the scrub, or again, he may have reached the top in safety. We can ask Gene."

They rode back together, and found the five horsemen as they had left them. Richards wore a worried look, for he could not understand his rescuer's apparent attitude of friendliness to the leader of the rustlers. He was to wear a much more worried expression, however, when a few moments later, he saw Blake lean forward and release the bonds of the four prisoners.

"I say," he stuttered. "What are you doing that for?"

"For reasons which you wouldn't understand," replied Blake calmly. "Now, Richards, my plans are changed. Toss over your gun, please."

The man looked mutinous, but one look at the steady eyes decided him. He passed over his revolver, and sat waiting for Blake to continue.

"I am not going to make you a prisoner again," went on Blake, "and you will be free to go where you will when we reach the top. I shall take your horse, however, and it will be necessary for you to return home on foot. Have you any objections to that?"

"I don't see what good it would do if I had," growled Richards.

"Not a bit," answered Blake cheerfully. "Now, Gene," he went on, turning to the head stockman, "Where is the lad you captured?"

"Tell him all you can, Gene," broke in Yvonne.

"There ain't much to tell," grunted the stockman, who still felt decidedly ill-tempered over being tricked first by Tinker and then by Blake. "All I know is he got away. I don't know exactly how much start he had, but it couldn't have been over half an hour. I called the others, and we started after him at once. We saw no signs of him on the way to the top, so we left Harris on guard. Then this man took a hand in the game, and played the winning card. If the lad went up the trail he must have managed to get clear. On the other hand, if he took cover in the bottom to watch his chance, well, then he's still there. That is all I know."

Blake nodded thoughtfully.

"H'm," he muttered. "It looks as though he had succeeded in getting clear. In that case he will be making his way on foot across the paddocks."

"I guess that is the case," remarked Gene.

"Then nothing is to be gained by remaining here," went on Blake. "If you are ready, mademoiselle, we will move on and see what developments are taking place at the homestead."

"Then you will help?" asked Yvonne eagerly.

"Of course," answered Blake quietly. "Shall I take the lead?"

"Please."

And as Yvonne's eyes followed his swaying figure up

the trail she sighed, and the little demon of hopelessness again stabbed her as she thought what it would be to have him always take the lead for her.

In this fashion the little party again started, with Gene keeping as close a watch on Richards as the latter had previously kept on the stockman. Blake's unhesitating movements showed how well he had studied the trail on the way in, and on reaching the top he signed to Gene to relieve Richards of his horse. When that had been accomplished, and the angry stockman had started on his long walk across the paddocks, Blake turned to Yvonne—

"Are we ready?"

"Yes."

"Then follow me."

He dug his heels into his horse's side and followed by the others, swept away over the stony approach to Death Valley, at a hard gallop. For twenty minutes they rode steadily without drawing rein. At the end of that time, just as they were emerging from a patch of scrub, Gene gave a loud hail, and Blake drew up.

"What is it?" he asked sharply.

"Body of horsemen to the left," grunted Gene laconically. "Might be some of Jameson's men."

Blake looked in the direction indicated, and for some moments studied them in silence.

"I make eleven," he said.

"That is what I make, too," said Yvonne, "I wonder what Jameson's men are doing out there?"

"I don't think they are his men," rejoined Blake, shading his eyes with his hand. "Unless I am mistaken that is my host, Campbell. I can recognise him by the white horse he is riding."

"By Jingo! that is right," broke in Gene. "Mr. Campbell always rides a white horse, and I don't know of anyone else in the district who does."

"Then we will ride to meet them," said Blake. "If Jameson has kept his word, their assistance will be of value."

As he spoke, he started off, and in a moment the whole party were riding in the direction of the others. They, in their turn, had evidently been seen, for Blake saw the white horse come to a stop, and the others follow suit. As he drew nearer he could distinguish the features of his host, who wore a look of surprise.

"What's up?" he called, as Blake got within earshot.

Blake made no reply until he pulled up beside the other. Then in few brief words he told Campbell enough to show him how matters stood.

"The point is, old man," he said, when he had finished, "will you come along and help?"

"If the situation is as you say it is, of course I will," answered Campbell. "Though it is a ticklish business mixing up in these bush feuds, and I want to be dead certain where I stand."

"You have my good word for it that the situation is as I have stated it to be," rejoined Blake quietly.

"That's good enough for me, old man. Lead on. We follow."

Blake turned his horse and galloped off, with his augmented party following. Yvonne was riding neck and neck with him, and from time to time she gazed across at the stern profile which rose and fell so easily to the motion of the horse. Ten minutes' hard riding brought them to a dry creek, and as they gained the further bank, the sound of intermittent firing broke on their ears.

"He has kept his word," called Yvonne. "That sound comes from the direction of the house."

Blake nodded, but did not reply. Instead, he set a harder pace than ever, and as he rode, drew his revolver. The others did the same, and in this fashion they swept into the home paddock. Already could be seen white puffs of smoke issuing from the loopholes in the windows, and from the cover of a small blue-gum plantation could be seen others showing where Jameson's men lay.

Whether it was because both besiegers and defenders saw the approaching body of horsemen, or for some other reason, Blake did not know, but as they drew nearer, the firing stopped. Blake swept on until he was within a hundred yards of the plantation before he drew up. The rest of his party grouped themselves about him, and barely had they done so when Jameson himself broke cover and rode towards them.

On recognising Blake and Campbell he naturally concluded that the new party were friends.

"By thunder! I'm glad you have come," he said, pulling up and mopping his brow. "I've got thirty men, but we haven't been able to——"

He broke off as his eyes rested on Yvonne and her four stockmen.

"What are they doing here?" he asked, with darkening brow.

"They are my prisoners," replied Blake coolly. "But tell me, Mr. Jameson, why are you attacking this place?"

Jameson ponderously drew out the documents which he had read aloud before the attack, and once more read them over.

"Those are my reasons, and as a Justice of the Peace, I am entitled to take the measures I have taken. I gave them warning to vacate the place, and, in addition, demanded the surrender of the stock rustlers. They complied with none of my demands, and as individuals in wrongful possession of my property I am well within my rights by doing what I am."

"Any of your men hit?" asked Blake casually.

"Five of them winged, two seriously."

"Supposing I agree to persuade those in possession to turn the place over to you peacefully, Mr. Jameson, will you call a truce?"

Blake turned to Yvonne.

"Have I your authority to deal in the matter?"

"Whatever you do I will abide by."

"But I must have Treherne given up!" snarled Jameson.

"If, when we finish, you still insist on that, I promise you he will go without resistance," said Blake. "Now are you satisfied to have me conduct the negotiations?"

Jameson nodded.

"Yes," he said curtly.

"Then I will ask you all to wait here with the exception of mademoiselle. She will come with me."

Together the two rode towards the house, and the opening of a shutter indicated that the defenders had been watching the conference. Graves stood in the window, a revolver in one hand and a cigarette in the other. He nodded to Blake as the latter rode up.

"Glad to see you!" he drawled. "Friend or foe?"

"Friend," smiled Blake, slipping from the saddle and giving a hand to Yvonne.

They stepped across the verandah, and in through the open window, where Blake was introduced to Treherne. A glance at the haggard but honest eyes told Blake that Yvonne had not been mistaken in her judgment of the man.

"Anyone hurt?" he asked, taking a cigarette which Graves proffered.

Treherne shook his head.

"Not a scratch on one of us."

"They have been potting at us like anything for half an hour," grinned Graves. "I think we got some of them, though."

"You did," said Yvonne. "Five."

"Good enough. They opened fire first, and by thunder they aimed to kill, too. But what is the next move?"

Yvonne explained how she met Blake, and the little surprise he had prepared for Jameson.

"That suits me," said Graves, when she had finished.

"How about you, Treherne?"

"Oh, I'm agreeable," he replied gloomily. "As far as I can see, I am in for it seriously."

"You wait," remarked Blake. "Now, then, since you all agree that I conduct matters, I think it would be as well to have Jameson come along."

He moved to the window as he spoke, and beckoned to the owner of Walla-Walla. "Will you come in, Mr. Jameson?" he called, as Jameson approached. "They have all agreed to my acting for both parties."

Jameson threw the bridle-rein over his horse's head and stamped across the verandah. A moment later he stood scowling amongst them.

"Let us sit down," remarked Blake, in his suavest tones. "There are several points to discuss."

When they were all settled, Blake turned to Jameson.

"Now, Mr. Jameson," he said, "let me get all the facts before I make my suggestions. If I am right, your claims are based on the following points. If I am wrong, you will please correct me.

"To begin with, you loaned Mr. Treherne a considerable sum of money, taking his sheep as security."

"Yes."

"After that, you loaned him further sums, and took a mortgage on Binabong Station."

"Yes."

"Then you received an unconditional assignment of the property from him to you."

"Yes."

"Following this, Mr. Treherne offers to redeem the mortgage."

"Yes."

"This you claim he had no right to do."

"Certainly. He had already assigned the place, and had nothing more to do with it."

"On top of this he sold the place to this lady, and she

assumed all liabilities in connection with it.'"

"Which was illegal, and, of course, void."

"We will discuss that later. You then gave notice that possession must be given to you within a specified time?"

"Yes."

"Failing this, you would take it by force?"

"Yes."

"They refused and, using the assignment as your authority you kept your word?"

"Yes."

"In addition to this, you accuse Mr. Treherne of stealing your sheep and kidnapping your stockman?"

"Yes; and as Justice of the Peace demand his surrender."

"Exactly. Well, I can tell you, Mr. Jameson, that your sheep were taken by the people you suspect, for I have found them!"

"Where are they?" cried Jameson in amazement; while Treherne looked at Blake as one looks at a traitor. Only Yvonne was smiling.

"They are on this property," replied Blake. "You see, you have in me a good witness. Now, I would like to ask you a question, Mr. Jameson."

"Go ahead, Mr. Blake," he replied, with a self-satisfied smile, feeling that in Blake he had an ally who was worth while.

"For what consideration did Mr. Treherne give you an unconditional assignment of Binabong?"

"Is that essential?" asked Jameson, shifting uneasily.

"Certainly. Unless I know all the details I cannot referee properly."

"Well, he owed me a lot of money over cards, and I gave him his chance to get square. He accepted, and if he tells the truth, will acknowledge that I was mighty generous in the matter. I offered to release him from all his obligations if he won. If he lost, I was to take the property. You can see that he had decidedly the best of the bargain, for I had already loaned him a big sum on it."

"Your offer was undoubtedly of a very generous nature," said Blake suavely. "I must say that, on the face of it, your case is very strong, Mr. Jameson."

Once more the self-satisfied smile appeared on Jameson's face. The mention of the gambling had been the only awkward point, and he had surmounted it beautifully. Blake rose and leaned against the table with crossed arms. "Mademoiselle, will you please give me a pad of paper?" he said, turning to Yvonne.

This had been agreed upon by them at Death Valley as Blake's signal to her to smuggle him a few of the marked cards. Yvonne rose at once and left the room. Silence reigned until she returned, bearing the pad of paper. She handed it to Blake, and resumed her seat.

"Now, if you are all agreeable, I am ready to deliver my judgment," said Blake.

One and all agreed silently. Then, lifting the pad in his hand, he began to speak, looking at Jameson.

"My judgment is," he said slowly, "firstly, that all the sheep on Binabong and Walla-Walla be turned over, unconditionally, to Edward Jameson. Secondly, that Binabong Station be given up to Edward Jameson, and a proper transfer duly executed. Thirdly, that John

Treherne and all others resident on Binabong surrender peacefully to Edward Jameson, to stand their trial for sheep stealing."

As each sentence fell in measured accents from Blake's lips, Jameson nodded his head in satisfaction.

Graves smoked nonchalantly, while Yvonne studied the floor. Treherne had gone white, and was shifting nervously.

"Those are the conditions to be complied with by those resident upon Binabong, providing" —and he paused on the word— "providing Edward Jameson fulfils the two following conditions: Firstly, that he withdraw his men and uses no further force——"

"Sure!" broke in Jameson, with a grin.

"And secondly, that he satisfies me regarding this."

As he spoke Blake opened the pad of paper and flicked the cards in his fingers. Jameson first looked puzzled, then a deep purple dyed his face.

"I don't understand!" he said thickly.

"These cards," went on Blake, imperturbably, "were the cards used when John Treherne lost his property. On examination they prove to be marked cards, Mr. Jameson, and Mr. Treherne says they were provided by you. What do you say?"

"I say it is a cursed lie!" snarled Jameson.

"I believe you are prepared to swear that you found them in the room shortly after the game was over, mademoiselle?"

Yvonne bent her head.

"And you, Graves?"

"I am."

Blake turned back to Jameson.

"In that case, Mr. Jameson, there is only one thing to do, and that is to take the whole thing into court. There it can be thrashed out, and the question of those marked cards proved."

If each word had been a drop of ice it could not have affected Jameson worse. He gazed at Blake in fascination, realising at last that the detective had been playing with him all the time. He had flattered himself that he had successfully pulled the wool over Blake's eyes, and the latter's whole judgment had seemed entirely in Jameson's favour until the last condition.

Jameson's face changed from purple to blotchy grey, and he glared at Blake speechless with baffled rage. He was beginning to feel the vague clutchings of fear at his heart, and the keen rapier point of deadly meaning behind Blake's calm mask.

"There is no necessity to go into court," Jameson finally managed to articulate. "I hold all that is necessary for me to take possession!"

"Exactly!" replied Blake suavely. "You see, though, as referee in the matter, I must be absolutely fair to both sides. That being so, it is essential for me to consider the question of these cards."

For a moment he held Jameson's gaze; then he went on softly:

"That marked cards were used there seems no doubt. Mr. Jameson disclaims all knowledge of them. Mr. Treherne does the same. In that case, all I can see is that the matter be taken into court. The use of such cards in any gambling transaction is a most serious matter; but when the transfer of property like Binabong rests on it, then there is nothing else to be done."

Jameson made an inarticulate sound, but Blake gave no notice. Instead, he continued more softly and more slowly than ever:

"Of course, in this affair, as in all affairs, there is an alternative. As referee in the matter, I would suggest the careful consideration of it. A lawsuit based on the question of marked cards would be a most odious affair, whichever way it went."

"What is the alternative?" asked Jameson thickly.

"The alternative is a compromise."

"In what way?"

Blake gazed at the floor, and tapped slowly on the table.

"If Mr. Treherne, or whoever is the present owner of Binabong, should offer to repay to Mr. Jameson all moneys borrowed, and if Mr. Jameson accepted this offer, it seems that all claims of justice would be satisfied. In addition, I would suggest that Mr. Treherne hand to Mr. Jameson the pack of marked cards, and in return Mr. Jameson give back to Mr. Treherne the assignment which he holds. In that way all parties are just where they stood before. No one loses by the transaction. Of course, by doing that, Mr. Jameson gives up all claim to Binabong; but perhaps he would prefer such a course to the notoriety attendant upon an unsavoury lawsuit. That, gentlemen, is my suggestion. It is up to you."

Blake drew out a cigarette as he finished speaking,

and looked down into Yvonne's smiling eyes. Graves still smoked nonchalantly, while Treherne and Jameson regarded each other cautiously. Finally, Yvonne spoke.

"What is your decision, Mr. Jameson?" she asked sweetly. "Do you feel inclined to hand back the assignment for the cards?"

For answer, Jameson stood up, and with a barely suppressed oath drew out the assignment and dashed it on the table.

"Give me the cards," he muttered chokingly.

Yvonne opened a drawer, and took out the balance of the pack. Blake added the few he held, and Jameson seized them viciously. Once they were in his possession he swung on Treherne.

"Curse you! You have schemed cleverly, haven't you?" he blazed. "I'll give you until to-morrow to take up that mortgage. If you don't do so then, you will hear from me in another way."

"You are addressing the wrong one, Mr. Jameson," broke in Yvonne. "I have already informed you that I am now the owner of Binabong. If you will hand over the documents you hold, you can have the money now. I have it ready."

As she spoke, she again pulled open the drawer, and took out a thick bundle of notes. These she tossed to Blake.

"Will you please act in this as well, Mr. Blake?"

"Certainly, mademoiselle," smiled Blake. "Is this for the loan on the land or for the stock as well?"

"For both."

"What do you say, Jameson? Are you ready?"

Jameson signified that he was, and in five minutes the matter was completed. Only when Yvonne signed her name did he turn and study her closely.

"Cartier?" he muttered absently.

"Why, yes, Mr. Jameson," smiled Yvonne. "I am surprised that you did not recognise me before."

Jameson glared and rose.

"You have beaten me," he said savagely. "But there is a future."

"Exactly," answered Yvonne—"and there are also marked cards. Good-bye, Mr. Jameson; I think your party is growing impatient."

Without a word Jameson turned, stepped through the window, and stamped heavily across the verandah. A moment later he was galloping towards his men and, as though in final mockery at the plans of man, a black cloud was already rimming the horizon, presaging the coming rain and the breaking of the drought.

The continued non-appearance of Tinker was beginning to make Blake look anxious. As though in answer to his master's thought Pedro, who had returned from Death Valley with Blake, rose from his place under the table and gazed upwards with a look of mute inquiry. Yvonne placed her hand on the big fellow's head and regarded Blake shyly.

"You have been awfully good to me, Mr. Blake," she said softly. "I won't thank you, for I know you would rather I wouldn't."

Blake shrugged.

"You are worried about Tinker, aren't you?" went on Yvonne.

"Yes, I am getting a bit worried."

"You will go in search of him?"

"Yes."

"Will you let me and my men assist you?"

"Gladly."

"What is your plan?"

"I think the best plan will be to take Pedro along, start at the hut where Tinker was a prisoner, and follow his scent from there."

"Of course. That will save time. I will have Gene muster the other men at once."

"Thanks!" said Blake. "In the meantime, I will ask Campbell to join us."

At that moment Campbell himself appeared. A few words from Blake explained how matters stood and, like Yvonne, he insisted upon joining in the hunt.

Ten minutes later every available man was mounted, and with Blake leading the way they swept off at a hard gallop in the direction of Death Valley.

Arriving at the bottom, old Gene went in front, and led the way to where Tinker had been a prisoner. There Blake put Pedro's muzzle to the scent, and the big bloodhound started off strongly. Across through the patches of trees which Tinker had used as cover he went, and on reaching the short gully turned up it and took his way along the trail to the top. Blake's face cleared somewhat as he did so, for if Tinker had reached the top, the chances were he had gone straight on to Campbell's place. His brow again wrinkled, however, when Pedro turned into the scrub.

Blake pulled up and dismounted. The others followed suit, and leaving three men in charge of the horses they followed Pedro on foot. Along the trail taken by Tinker he went. At the first precipice Blake drew in his breath sharply, but breathed more easily when Pedro turned and went along to the left. He got another shock when they came out at the edge of the second precipice, but once again Pedro turned back. Yvonne was close to Blake, and as they went along the bottom of a gully she spoke.

"He was confused," she said in low tones.

Blake nodded, but did not speak. He knew those signs only too well. Once in his younger days he had been lost in the Great Salt Desert, and knew what it was to go wandering about lost in a wild expanse where no man might be met. His eyes were clouded, and his face very grim as he went on. Behind him came the others. Gene and his companions suggested spreading out and sweeping through the scrub, but Blake signed for them not to do so.

Pedro had the scent strong, and would lead them in the right direction more quickly than a hundred men could. Twice they passed the same point, and Blake knew Tinker had begun that most awful of all experiences—travelling in a great circle.

Another hour passed, and still Pedro kept on. Finally, on turning a bend. Blake gave a sharp gasp as he saw the edge of another cliff, and on the ledge before him two whitened skeletons. Dashing forward he drew up sharply, and gazed in amazement at the two opened boxes of gold which lay before him.

"He has been here," he said steadily. Then raising his voice he shouted: "Tinker! Tinker!"

No answer. Again he shouted, and still no answer. Only the cliffs beyond caught up his voice and threw it back in mocking echoes, the whole vast amphitheatre formed by the cliffs jeering Tinker! Tinker! in an uncanny duplication of Blake's voice.

Those behind had crowded forward at sight of the gold, but Campbell and Yvonne waved them back.

"We don't know what it means," said Yvonne, "but for the present it must wait. The lad is more important."

All this time, Pedro was straining on the leash. Gene had dashed into the cave, and came out to report the presence of more boxes, but no sign of the lad. By one accord they avoided the grinning skeletons.

Pedro seemed so anxious to go ahead that Blake eased the leash. His face went strangely white as the bloodhound moved straight to the edge and did not come back. Instead, he lifted up his voice in a deep bay which sent a chill to the hearts of those who heard it. With a smothered groan, Blake dropped flat and crawled to the edge. It was a thousand foot drop to the bottom of that precipice, and if its face was as sheer as the faces of those surrounding it, then nothing of any description would protrude and serve to break the path.

Sick with the thought, Blake crept outwards and looked down. As he did so his heart gave a great leap and his pulses hammered. His hand shook in a manner strangely unlike him, though what he had seen had been sufficient to make the strongest heart quail. About thirty feet down he saw a small clump of trees which apparently grew from the sheer face of the cliff.

In the midst of their branches he had seen a sprawling figure, and that figure was Tinker's. The branches swayed dangerously with the unaccustomed weight, and it seemed as though every moment must see the lad's body go hurtling into the bleak eternity beneath.

Blake got slowly to his feet, and with tense features faced the others. He swayed like a drunken man, and spoke thickly.

"Belts, stock-whips, stirrup leathers—quick!" he ordered.

Yvonne, reading his expression, crept to the edge and peered over. She drew back, pressing her hand convulsively to her breast.

"Oh, quick!" she gasped. "He looks as though he might go at any minute!"

With that knack which is the bushman's, every man in the party had ripped off his belt, while half a dozen had followed old Gene back to where the horses had been left. Precious moments passed, but though it seemed they would never come they were in reality less than half an hour.

On their return they lost no time in twisting the pieces together into a strong rope. Then each man volunteered to descend, but Blake waved them back.

"This is my job," he said gruffly.

Slipping one end of the improvised rope under his arms, he stepped to the edge and peered over.

"Hold tight, and lower me slowly," he said. "Watch that it doesn't fray on the edge."

With that he sat down, and while the stockmen strained on the rope he slipped over the edge. Now that he was actually doing something for the lad's release, he was as calm as ever.

Yvonne had again crept to the edge, and as she saw Blake swinging in space above that awful drop all the pent-up love in her heart welled up and fought with her tears for the control of her eyes. Blake glanced up and met her look. His own eyes softened for a moment, then he looked down and signed to Campbell to lower away.

Down, down he went until his feet almost touched the top branches of the tree in which Tinker lay. Lower still he went, until he was on a level with the lad. Then ever so slowly he started swinging until each swing brought him nearer and nearer to the place where Tinker lay. His hands went out cautiously, for one false move might cause the branches to sway and precipitate the lad into the abyss beneath. Then his fingers grazed the lad's shoulder, and the next moment he had gathered all his strength into one great effort.

Yvonne watched in fascination, as he stretched out his arms and grasped the unconscious lad under the shoulders. The tree swayed ominously. The next moment Blake had swung free, gripping Tinker, who dangled beneath him, Blake's hold the only thing between him and eternity.

"Oh, pull, pull!" gasped Yvonne. "He has got him!"

The stockmen needed no second bidding. Slowly and steadily they drew up in order that no undue strain would come on the rope. Foot by foot Blake rose, until his head was on a level with the ledge. Higher he came, then one great heave and he was over. A dozen hands grasped Tinker and drew him over as well, and a mighty cheer rent the air at the success of Blake's truly magnificent rescue.

Yvonne took his hand and, regardless of the presence of the others, held it, while her whole soul gazed at him from her eyes. Then she released it and, stumbling to her feet, sank down on a box of gold.

Campbell was already busy over Tinker. A swallow of the strong spirit from Campbell's flask caused his lips to quiver and then open. He gazed about him for a moment, dazed. Another swallow sent the blood rushing through his veins, and brought back his recollection. Though still weak he was unharmed.

"I remember now," he muttered. "But how did you get me up?"

Campbell pointed to Blake. Tinker gripped Blake's hand. He was too full of gratitude to speak, but those two understood each other.

A few minutes later, when Tinker had eaten a couple of sandwiches, he began to tell them his experiences, which dealt with his finding of the gold and culminated in his sudden plunge over the edge of the cliff.

It was a very excited party which carried out the other boxes and opened them. Blake judged the quantity in each box to be less than Tinker had estimated. He put it at three thousand pounds, but, even so, that gave a total of sixty thousand. Truly a magnificent hoard to find.

When the last box had been opened and the last gaze satisfied, when the strange find had been discussed from every point, and the knives had received their due share

361

of attention, the stockmen shouldered the boxes, and the whole party made their way back to where the horses stood. Pedro kept very close to Tinker, and in some strange, canine way seemed fully aware of the terrible situation in which his young master had been.

It was at the close of a very eventful day that they reached Binabong. On the way it was decided to report the find of gold to the authorities. Yvonne insisted on Tinker taking the full percentage as the finder, but the lad stubbornly refused to do anything else but divide whatever he got with her, so at that they left it.

The cloud on the horizon was now a huge black stretch which was slowly creeping across the heavens. Treherne's eyes filled with hope as he watched it, for Yvonne had offered him the managership of Binabong on a half-share basis—an offer which he gladly accepted. Gene and Yvonne's other stockmen departed to bring back all the Binabong stock from Walla-Walla, and Campbell with his men had gone home, Tinker going with them. Graves had gone to his room, and only Blake and Yvonne remained. She followed him outside when he went to get his horse, and as he sprang into the saddle she laid her head against the horse's shoulder.

"Are you leaving soon?" she whispered.

"Yes, I will go to Melbourne to-morrow," answered Blake gently.

"Then—then I won't see you again?"

He shook his head slowly.

"Not out here."

"It is good-bye, then?"

"Yes."

She straightened up wearily, and stood for a moment with bent head. Then she lifted his hand, and for one brief moment laid it against her warm lips.

Releasing it, she turned and stumbled blindly back to the house, while Blake, with a deep sigh and misty eyes, dug his heels into his horse and, with Pedro following, rode away across the paddocks, his hand still burning from the touch of her lips, and his mind still thinking of the look in her eyes when he was dangling over the abyss.

THE END

Notes

7. Captain Starlight was a character in the 1882–83 novel *Robbery Under Arms*. Its author, Rolf Boldrewood, based Starlight, in part, on Henry Arthur "Harry" Readford (December 1841 – 12 March 1901), a notorious stockman and cattle thief who operated in Queensland, Australia.

8. A castrated ram.

9. The word "blacks" has been replaced by "Aborigines".

BAKER STREET, LONDON

"A REMARKABLE WOMAN," Blake said. "Ahead of her time, as were many others of her gender that I encountered over the years. If anything, they were toned down by their authors; made more typical for the reading public."

"I suppose equality of the sexes was something of a contentious subject, back then," I commented.

"For the story papers, certainly," Blake agreed. "But, thankfully, time marches on, and we progress."

As he handed the binder back to me, I echoed him: "We progress," then added, "But in 1933, it might have appeared otherwise for Sexton Blake enthusiasts. That's when the Union Jack was transformed into the Detective Weekly, a large-format paper with an ugly yellow-toned cover."

Blake gave a wry smile. "Indeed. A minor executive at Amalgamated Press had concluded that the title of the Union Jack was responsible for low sales in Ireland. Thus the metamorphosis." He made a throwaway gesture with his left hand. "In truth, the old paper probably couldn't have continued anyway. In its 'golden years,' it had featured master crooks but, by the 'thirties, another war was looming, and just as the first conflict had spat out that extraordinary breed of criminal, so the second swallowed them up."

"The nature of your cases changed," I observed.

"Precisely, and the longer-length Sexton Blake Library became a better vehicle for reporting them."

I slid the binder into my briefcase, aware that the interview was coming to an end. "Even so," I said, "the 'DW,' which folded after just seven years, is generally regarded as the beginning of the end as far as your popularity was—is—concerned. Did you feel, perhaps, that you were being eclipsed by the new hardboiled style of detectives, the Sam Spades?"

He raised an eyebrow. "No. Might I draw your attention to the fact that the SBL prospered right through into the nineteen-sixties?"

"It did," I conceded, and got to my feet. "So, for the next anthology, we'll turn our attention to that particular periodical, and, specifically, to your activities on the Home Front."

Sexton Blake gave a grunt of acknowledgement and gestured insouciantly toward the door.

I was in that manner dismissed. I gave Pedro a pat, and departed.

Next:
The Sexton Blake Library

ANTHOLOGY IV: SEXTON BLAKE
ON THE HOME FRONT